The Lost Element

Book One of The Pillars of Life

Ž Hatlek

ISBN 978-3-9824847-2-3

CONTENTS

To my children, Vanesa, Majk, and Tania, without whom this book might never have seen the light of day.

With concentration
at work or school,
and imagination at home,
anything and everything
is possible.

CHAPTER 1

The Homeless Boy

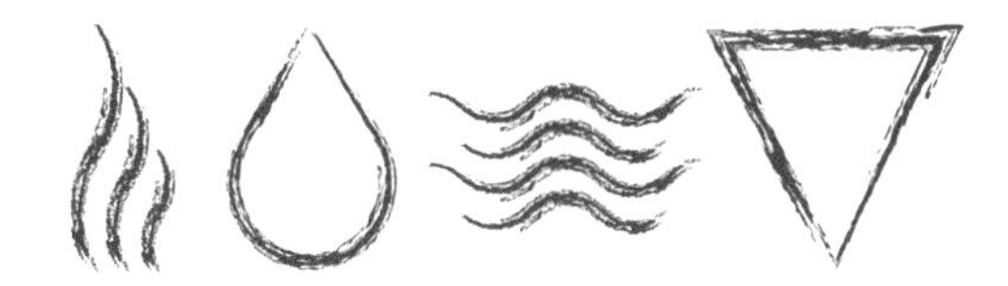

When James reached the bottom step with a suitcase in his hand, he turned toward the front door of the orphanage one last time. Through the glass, he saw the principal looking back at him with a sideways frown and a creased brow. Beside him was the deputy principal, Ms. Bulgar, or Maria as she had always insisted he call her. She appeared weighed down by the weight of her own shoulders and the deluge of tears in her eyes.

James paused, raised his hand, and whispered, "Thank you." Although he knew Maria could not hear him, James annunciated his words so she would be able to read his message off his lips, and she covered her face with her hands soon after. The principal did not give up his grim look, and James turned away. Slowly, he looked first to one side of the street and then to the other, then headed in the direction he hoped would take him to the ocean.

It was a warm September evening in the Miami suburbs, without a cloud in the sky, and while the sun would still be up for some time, the street lamps had just come on. The scent of flowers and trees from a nearby park mixed with the warm sea breeze to guide James toward the water, only occasionally to be interrupted by the sharp, harsh fumes of the passing cars. People were still outside on the streets, sitting on benches, talking, laughing, unaware that someone was walking past them for whom their whole world was falling apart.

James paused by one home, a bungalow with a paved courtyard and well-trimmed garden that was packed with people. The place was decorated with balloons, flowers, and large, paper-cut letters that spelled out Happy Birthday. The indecipherable drone of adult conversations was complemented by music, laughter, and the sound of children playing.

He didn't know how long he spent gazing at the people enjoying their evening garden party, but whether it was his imposing height and dark hair or that a sixteen-year-old stranger with a suitcase was lingering only a short distance away, the partygoers started to notice him and wince in his direction. James squirmed as he felt his cheeks warm up, mumbled an apology, more to himself than anyone else, and resumed walking.

More than an hour and several city blocks later, he decided to rest on a street bench. He still didn't really know where he was going—Maria had mentioned something about how he might have some luck finding work and board down at the docks the day before—and his old and shabby suitcase was starting to feel heavier at every street corner. James propped his feet on the suitcase, tilted his head back, and stared at the sky.

What now? he thought.

As he admired the purple and orange hues in the sky, James realized it was the first time in his memory he'd been outside the orphanage come nightfall. While he couldn't remember it, he knew from what the staff had told him that the last time he'd been off the grounds at night had been when he'd been just four months old; when his mother had left him half a block away, wrapped in a thick blanket.

This story had been told to James for so many years and from such a young age that he'd felt embarrassed by how long it had taken him to ask how the staff had known it had been James' mother to leave him and not someone else. He could still picture how flushed Deputy Principal Maria Bulgar had looked when she'd admitted there had been a letter in the folds of the blankets when they had found him. Whenever he asked to see the letter over the years was the only time the normally calm and serene Maria would become impatient with him.

"Not until you're eighteen, James. All I can tell you is that her name was Victoria and she expressed in the letter that she didn't want to give you up."

He'd never understood why he had to wait to get the letter. Although all the admitted children were provided with accommodation in the orphanage until they were eighteen, James had never read anything in the rules about not being given access to personal property, and he knew of other children who even used the cloths they had been swaddled in as security blankets throughout their early years.

In the end, James had been given the letter early, but only on account of the principal deciding it was time for him to leave the orphanage; a whole year before he'd expected to leave. As such, the letter that James had longed to read his whole life—the letter he had sworn he'd study for clues of his past more closely than any detective—remained in his suitcase, untouched and unread, while he instead continued to gaze at the slowly darkening sky, thinking about where he was going and where he had come from.

The first time James could remember being called a troublemaker was when he had been about six or seven years old. Fred had thrown James' toothbrush into the toilet. He recalled the emotions he had felt at the time—anger and sadness—then the distinct sensation of a heavy drop of water striking his shoulder. Lifting his gaze, James saw something resembling a white mist on the bathroom ceiling that only seemed to become darker and thicker until he'd felt a few more drops on his head and shoulders. Before he knew what to make of it, it was raining...indoors. Fred and the other children in the bathroom at the time were drenched in a matter of seconds and ran through the door crying, and the water that had so quickly accumulated upon the white tiles spilled into the hallway. The bathroom was on the first floor of the orphanage and water reached all the dormitories and even the ground floor.

In James' confused state, he'd exited the bathroom last, at which point he was confronted by the pounding of approaching footsteps and the deep voice of the principal. "What the hell is going on here?"

He was still dressed in his morning robe, and for some reason, James could recall a visible stain of coffee on it. Cries from the kitchen and office filled the air as the water made its way down the hall and under doorways. But by the time the principal reached James and marched him back inside the bathroom, whatever he had seen swirling against the ceiling had seemingly disappeared. With a heavy pout, the principal had run his hands along the pipes on the walls and ceilings around the bathroom, touched his dry fingers together, then stared at James. "What happened here? Where did so much water come from?"

James, not even knowing what had happened, had just shrugged while keeping his eyes fixed on the floor.

James adjusted himself on the Miami suburb bench and bit the inside of his cheek as he recalled another unusual event that had happened on his tenth birthday. In the orphanage, the staff always prepared a slightly more special party for each child's tenth birthday, and James had known there would be a show, a bigger selection of treats, and even more gifts than usual.

"As you all know, today is a special day for our James," the principal had said after everyone had finished breakfast.

"He's celebrating his tenth birthday today, so let's congratulate him."

"Happy birthday, James," they all shouted together, and James had delighted at the warm buzz in his stomach as he'd thanked everyone and led them to settle on the benches.

"Everyone, listen here," Maria Bulgar had cried above the din of young voices. "First comes the show, followed by games, cake, and gifts. You all know the rules. Don't repeat the scene from Alice and David's birthday party, please!"

And so the morning proceeded as planned, and right on cue, the kitchen staff brought the cake and presents into the hall. The cake was large—enough for every child there—with ten lit candles. All but a few children tossing a ball back and forth gathered around. James had laughed as Deputy Principal Bulgar had pointed the camera at him, giving him the OK to blow out the candles.

James inhaled and just as he was about to blow out the candles, BAM! The ball the children had been playing with flew right into the cake, exploding over James and everyone around him. Lifting his shaking eyes, James saw Fred, the same boy who had thrown his toothbrush into the toilet a few years earlier, and two other boys standing by the gift table. One of them was holding one of James' already unwrapped presents.

James felt his face turn red. He was so angry that he simply froze where he was standing. For a few moments, the sky outside darkened, a strong wind blew through the open windows, and the ground began to shake.

"Earthquake! Remember the drills. Everyone, gather around me," the principal shouted.

But no one moved out of fear. Then, when James had slowly turned his head to the windows, he'd seen apples begin to fall off the tree outside, the glass starting to shake, and rain pattering against the panes. He had a vague recollection of his friends frantically running around the hall, but he mostly just remembered how angry he had been at that moment, his hard stare firmly fixed on Fred and his two friends. It was only after everything was over that James realized the stage on which the play had taken place had started to lean onto its side as the earth underneath seemed set on swallowing it.

But while the children had run in panic, and the principal and kitchen staff had raced after them to keep them calm, only Deputy Principal Bulgar had come to James to shake him gently by the shoulders. "James! James! Stop it! Please, stop."

James blinked as if pulling himself out of some half-sleep until he could at last focus on Maria. The wind stopped howling, the ground and windows stopped shaking, and the dark clouds receded, once again allowing the warm sun beams to fall on the orphanage.

James had vaguely remembered the deputy looking at the principal, who seemed more irritated than concerned, before she had taken James by the hand and led him outside to rest a little.

From that day, James had been blamed for every broken pipe, cracked ceiling, burst tire, and power outage. The truth was, James had no idea what had happened, but the more the other children teased him and the more the principal shouted at him for somehow putting everyone in danger, the more these mysterious events had occurred over the years.

Eventually, shortly before his seventeenth birthday, the deputy's pleas for James to stay had failed at last, and the principal had decided that James had to leave for the benefit of the other children.

James snapped himself out of his daydream, stood up from the bench he had been resting on, and raised his hand to stop a taxi; he'd never make it to the docks before nightfall now.

It was 9:26 p.m. when he got out of the car and paid the driver with the handful of cash Deputy Principal Bulgar had given him. Approaching the gate, the dock appeared abandoned, but James peered into a hut to see a guard sitting in a comfortable armchair. The TV was on, but he was sleeping, and James had to knock twice before the guard flinched awake.

"What are you doing here? Who are you? Do you know what time it is?" the guard asked hurriedly.

"I'm sorry I woke you. I just wanted to ask if you're looking for workers and if there's a job for me that I could do?"

"At this time of day, you won't find any work here. Nor anywhere else as far as I know," the guard replied, pointing at the dusty clock on the wall behind him.

"I have nowhere to sleep. I was told I could get a job here and even temporary accommodation until I found something else."

"And where'd you come from?" the guard asked, now with a little pity in his voice. "Look, you're not wrong. We always need more manpower. But they're all very difficult and demanding jobs here on the docks."

"It doesn't matter," James interjected quickly. "I'm willing to do any job."

"You sure, kid? You're tall, don't get me wrong, but those scrawny arms don't look like they've done a lot of heavy lifting. I've seen stronger men than you come and go."

"I can do it!"

"All right, if you say so," the guard said. "But the boss won't be here until the morning."

"Never mind. I can sleep over there until—"

"Not a chance, lad!" The guard stepped out of the guardhouse. "Come with me. We've a room on site. It's nothing special but it has a small bed, a shower, and a TV." He led James across the dry path and around the closest corner to a small wooden shack and opened the door. "Here. This is it."

"It's perfect. Thank you," James said enthusiastically, breathing a sigh of relief that, if nothing else, he'd have somewhere dry to sleep for the night.

"Perfect? I'd love to know where you've slept before tonight," the guard murmured. "All right. You get comfortable and rest. I have to get back."

"Wait a minute, I don't even know your name. I'm James. James Tanner."

"Alan Brick."

"Nice to meet you, Alan. And thanks again."

"You're welcome. Come on, rest now. I'll wake you in the morning before my boss gets in. Good night."

"Good night."

James turned to look around the small room. In one corner was a bed that he estimated was just about big enough for him. Barely a foot away from it was a table with two rickety chairs and an old TV on it, and in the corner was a small cupboard and a tiny electric radiator. James pushed a wooden door back a few inches. It squeaked on its hinges to reveal a small bathroom with a stained shower, sink, and toilet. The space was cramped, but James just felt pleased to have a roof over his head.

Putting his suitcase by the closet, James headed for the bed. As he settled under the scratchy blankets, he looked through the window and gazed out at the few lights hanging above the water's edge: an orange street light, a handful of white lights on the sides of some of the smaller, closer boats, and their reflections danced in the rippling water. One light, in particular, caught his attention. A flash, like from a camera, only blue, flickered through a small window some fifty yards away. Seconds later, another, this time red and barely one hundred yards from the first flash.

James shrugged himself under the blanket and pulled the curtain closed as he felt the physical and emotional toil of the day force his eyes to close.

CHAPTER 2

A Message from the Past

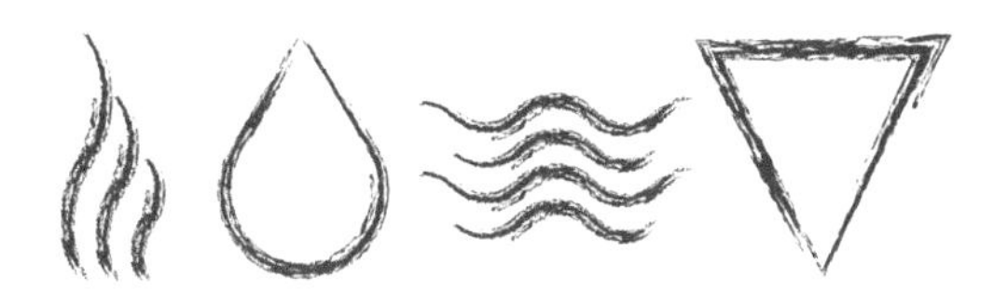

JAMES WAS AWOKEN BY a knock on the door.

"Here I am. I'm awake. Just need to get dressed."

"Let's hurry," Alan said. "The boss has arrived and is expecting you in his office."

"All right. Coming," James replied. After dressing quickly, James opened the door and headed to the office with Alan.

"Don't be nervous. He's a good man," Alan said, leading James through the docks.

"I'm OK. What can happen? He can only tell me he doesn't want to hire me."

"You're right," Alan said, tapping James on his back.

After he left him, James turned toward the office door, took a deep breath, and knocked three times.

"Yes?" a voice said from inside the office.

James opened the door and entered. Instantly, the smell of stale and damp air reached his nostrils. The office looked like it hadn't been cleaned for a long time. To James' right was a desk with an old, heavy-looking computer that was covered with dust. There was another, more modern laptop on the desk right in front of him, surrounded by messy papers. Behind it, was a younger man than James had expected, deeply immersed in his computer. As the apparent site manager, James had pictured a bent figure with gray hair and crooked bones. Instead, the man tapping away at his computer was the image of the young businessman: three small picture frames on the table; a back wall full of framed commendations; and a pile of thank-you notes addressed to someone named Stanley.

James took a few steps forward only to stumble on the edge of the old carpet, almost falling into the desk. The carpet was stained with, James assumed, all the grease and oil from the workers coming in and out of the office. He quickly straightened up, outstretched his hand, and introduced himself.

The man retaliated with the same measure. "I'm Stanley Walden, the manager here. Alan briefly explained the situation to me over the phone this morning."

" I heard that you are looking for new workers and that even on-site accommodation is available. I have nowhere else to be, so I can be on-hand to work for you whenever you need."

"You got good information, James. But I'm not sure it's a job for such a young boy. How old are you?"

"I'll be seventeen in a few days."

"I don't think this kind of work would be appropriate for a boy your age."

"I'm just looking for an opportunity," James said, clasping his hands together. "Let me prove myself. You won't regret it."

"Do you know what we do here?"

James shrugged. "I'm a quick learner and I'm willing, sir."

Stanley watched him closely, and James felt his heart race. "It can be dangerous work, James. We're primarily responsible for loading and unloading the boats and ships that dock here. That requires using lots of heaving equipment. Equipment you need to be trained to use. Equipment than can injure and maim if not used correctly."

"I'll do whatever it takes, sir. I need a job. I need a place to stay. Maybe there are some smaller, safer jobs that your more skilled staff doesn't like to do? I'll take on anything."

Stanley tongued the inside of his cheek for a moment. "Alan said that you lived in the orphanage. Do you mind if I ask what happened to your parents?" he asked, twirling a pen in his hand.

"I never met them," James replied. "My teachers told me that my mother is the one that brought me to the orphanage and left me there." James had arrived so late and tired the night before that he'd completely forgotten about his mother's letter. He made a mental note to read it as soon as he had a free moment.

Stanley rubbed his fingers over his mouth and chin, his eyes flickering between James and the pictures of people

James assumed to be Stanley's family on his desk. "I could never understand something like that, but who am I to judge?" He exhaled softly. "You say you're not even seventeen yet, and you came here yesterday evening looking for a job without any alternative? What happened at the orphanage that meant you had to leave so quickly? Seems a bit heartless to kick a kid out before he's got something else lined up, no?"

James inhaled deeply and prepared to answer, but the phone on Stanley's desk interrupted him. He released a small sigh of relief; in truth, he didn't know how to respond to that question without it sounding like he really was a troublemaker.

Stanley lifted his finger. "Excuse me, I have to take this." He picked up his phone and listened while James devised an answer to Stanley's question. The call lasted a couple of minutes before Stanley, who had mostly only listened as the voice on the other end said whatever it needed to, eventually hung up.

"All right," Stanley said, looking down at the table. "I like to give everyone a chance, even if I've come to regret it. Look, it can be very difficult here. We work long days; even nights, sometimes. The ships determine our work schedule, not the other way around. Not everyone can deal with it."

"I can, sir." James' lip quivered slightly. "I have to. I don't have a choice."

Stanley's frown was deep and sad. "All right, I'll give you a shot. I don't know why you were asked to leave the orphanage before you were ready, but I'll be damned if I'm going to toss you out, as well. You can start right away." He extended his index finger at James and his expression switched to one that was much more serious. "You'll be doing small jobs. Lifting and moving light crates, loading the smallest boats, only the most basic wood and metal work, got it? If I catch you messing around with machinery, tools, or vehicles you haven't been trained to use, it's my ass as well as yours, and you're out of here, OK?" James nodded. "Alan tells me he put you in the hut last night. It's the only on-site accommodation, so you'll stay there. Let me know if there are problems with the plumbing. And as for your salary...we'll determine that later."

"Thank you, sir—"

"Call me Stanley, James," he said with a smile. "There's no need to be so formal."

"Thank you so much, Stanley. I promise to be careful. And I'll work hard for you, you'll see."

"Let's head to the foreman's office next to dock three. Mr. Terry Jordan. He'll be responsible for setting your work assignments. You do everything he tells you, OK? More importantly, you don't do anything he doesn't tell you to do."

"Thank you, Mr. Stanley—" James paused when he saw the manager's hand rise again. "Sorry. I mean, thank you, Stanley."

Stanley laughed lightly as he stood up, then he moved one of his hands to his back. Stanley noticed James looking. "My back is killing me. I wish I could say it's because I do the heavy lifting around here, but the truth is, I was up most of the night taking care of some unfinished paperwork."

James followed Stanley down the steps and outside, where he bounced across the hot asphalt. Dark clouds hung over the harbor as they walked toward a warehouse back in the same direction as James' hut that he could now call his own, at least for the time being. James breathed in the fresh morning air, tinged with harsh diesel, and he took in the surroundings for the first time now he could see in the light of day. All around him were tall buildings and warehouses. The walls of the buildings matched the gray sky behind them. He saw shutters with big doors that guarded the entrance to each depot, while each door had a big number painted on it in white. Several people in waterproof overalls walked briskly past them, nodding at them as they went by.

As they passed a large warehouse with a giant *1* painted on its shutter door, James looked across the water and suddenly recalled the flashes of light he had seen the previous night from his window. There was nothing there that would have made such flashes as far as he could tell. No poles, ships, or any permanent fixtures.

Had there been a ship there last night that left before I woke up? he thought. I don't remember seeing—

"James, look out!" Stanley said. He reached out but was too late, and James walked straight into a traffic pole embedded in the walkway. Stanley pulled a uneasy expression as James quickly straightened up and pretended to be fine, even though he felt a sharp pain in his thigh.

"I'm fine." James tried his best to hide his new limp and to walk off the pain. He realized he'd just demonstrated a lack of concentration after promising Stanley he would be a reliable worker on a dangerous work site. He picked up his pace, hoping Stanley wouldn't say anything or change his mind about hiring him.

"We use lots of heavy machinery here, which you aren't qualified to use," Stanley said, apparently willing to forgive James' misstep. "But you can use our tools for the smaller jobs. Have you used any before, James? I'm guessing you haven't in a professional capacity, right? Considering your age and your former place of residence."

James appreciated Stanley was trying to choose his words carefully, but James had never understood why people outside the orphanage were always so reluctant to call it by its name. It was the only home he'd ever known, and despite the strange events that had happened, he had mostly been happy there.

"We learned a lot of different things at the orphanage. From gardening and cooking to computer skills and metal work. Our deputy head always told us, 'Knowledge and competence have never harmed anyone.'"

"Metal work, eh?" Stanley said. "That's very good to hear."

Arriving at dock three, James saw a skinny man in blue jeans and a black short-sleeved t-shirt standing next to a truck and explaining something to the driver. It looked like the driver had made a mistake and the skinny man was trying to turn him around. When James and Stanley were alongside the truck, the shouts died down; the driver finally admitted his mistake and the truck started beeping as he put it in reverse.

"Good morning," Stanley said.

"Morning," the skinny man replied with some frustration in his voice. "I am fed up with these drivers who think they know everything. How do they get across the country with all their cargo intact, yet struggle so much to read the dock numbers painted on the doors so big that you could see them from a plane?"

Stanley chuckled. "I would like you to meet James. James, this is Terry."

James extended his hand and they shook.

"Strong grip you have there, son," Terry said, eyeing him up.

"He's going to work for us," Stanley said. "You said you needed more manpower."

"Indeed, I do," Terry replied, still not taking his eyes off James. "Don't you worry, son, I'll show you everything you need to know. Pop into my office, just over there, and grab some overalls and boots from the closet." He pointed at a door not far from where they were standing.

Inside the office, James noticed how much cleaner and more organized it was than Stanley's office. The floor was free of oil stains and all the paperwork was neatly stacked. The windows had been left open, so fresh air filled the room. An old picture of the Titanic hung on the right-hand wall, perfectly centered. James found a pile of waterproof clothing in the cupboard, which he changed into. He couldn't find any boots in his size, so he opted for some with steel-capped toes that were one size too big. He folded his own clothes, scooped them into his arms, then returned outside.

"I see you're all dressed up," Terry said.

"Clothes fit?" Stanley asked, and James nodded.

"We should get started then," Terry said and started walking away. James thanked Stanley, who gave him a quick wave, then hurried after Terry with excitement in his step. After passing several docks, they came to a building with a painted sign outside that read *Maintenance*. Stepping inside, James entered a large, open-plan room full of tools, cranes, and old vehicle parts for trucks, ships, and even cars. The walls were covered in plastic signs that looked beaten and blackened with age, each one as intimidating as the next. One sign signified a ban on smoking. Another showed a black circle around what looked like a surgical mask. As far as James could tell, another indicated the obligatory use of protective clothing. There were some less obvious ones though; he hoped they weren't something he needed to worry about.

"This is going to be your first job. See that pile of parts?" Terry said, pointing to a large pallet in the left corner of the workshop. "They need to be cleaned and oiled so they don't rust. And then you put them back on the pallet, sorted by serial numbers."

"Yeah, no problem," James said excitedly. He lifted some heavy-duty gloves from the wall rack and headed for the pallet.

"It's a boring job, but a necessary one. We mostly do maintenance here. I'll need you here most days, at least until we get you trained up. Sorry, but without the proper training, it's just too dangerous. You'll work until four in the afternoon. You get a break at ten for fifteen minutes, and at one for your lunch," Terry said, pointing at a large clock hanging from the ceiling in the middle of the workshop.

"All right," James said.

"One more thing," Terry said as a man came out of a nearby room. "This is Ted." He pointed at the man. "You can never work alone. Understand? It's not safe."

"Hi, I'm James."

"Nice to meet you," Ted said, then turned his gaze to Terry. "I didn't know we were getting reinforcements."

"Until today, I didn't either," Terry replied with a grin.

"Come," Ted said to James, "let me show you around."

James was so engrossed in his work for the rest of the day that it seemed to fly by. After a bell sounded the end of the shift, James took off his gloves and headed for his small hut. Just before he reached it, he spotted Alan arriving for his guard shift.

"I got the job!" James said.

"I was sure you would. I've been working for Stanley for a long time. He's a good man. He's helped me a lot of times when he didn't have to. The more you give, the more you will get back from him."

"I noticed. By the way, I thought you covered night duty. Aren't you a little early? It's just after four."

"Double shift tonight," he said with a slight frown. "A friend called me to see if I could cover for him. You must be tired after your first day, James. Go and rest up, then come to the guard house tonight. You can keep me from getting bored."

"Deal," James said before he left for his hut.

After taking off his dirty work clothes and dumping them on the bathroom floor, James changed into the same shorts and sleeveless shirt he'd worn the day before. The sun had come out since the morning, and the afternoon was muggy and warm.

Now that he'd stopped working, James realized how hungry he was and he remembered that the deputy had told him she'd packed something for him. For the first time since he'd arrived at the docks the night before, he opened his suitcase. He removed the carefully folded clothes on top—a jacket, a few pairs of shorts and long pants, some t-shirts and shirts—and stored them neatly in the small closet. Finally, he found a bag in the suitcase that he didn't recognize and assumed it must have been put there by Deputy Principal Bulgar. Inside it, he found several sandwiches, a plastic box full of salad vegetables, and another box with his leftover dinner from his final meal at the orphanage. His eyes grew wide and excited when he found another bag filled with candy, but as he reached inside it, his fingers grazed a piece of paper. He unfolded it hurriedly and quickly lost his appetite.

Dear James,

I did everything I could for you to stay, but the principal is adamant. I can't describe to you how I feel and how sorry I am for everything. I know that you are not responsible for all the strange occurrences over the years. Not consciously, at least.

I've packed some food to last you for the next couple of days. I hope you will accept my advice and go to the docks. I know someone who works there, and he told me that the site manager was a good and honest man.

I've also packed the letters from your mother that were left with you when she brought you to the orphanage. Reading them will be challenging; I'm sorry you'll have to do it alone. I should have given them to you sooner so you could have asked me questions.

I hope we meet again in better circumstances. Be careful.

Maria Bulgar

After reading the letter, James examined the smudged stain at the lower right corner and imagined Maria writing the letter as a tear had slid down her cheek and dropped onto the paper.

James dropped the piece of paper and picked up the envelope. The paper had turned yellow with age and it felt crispy as he ran his fingers along the faded lettering on the front that read *St. Benedict's Orphanage*. His mother had written these words. For the first time in his life, it felt like he was occupying the same space as her. Touching them was the closest to her he had ever felt. Somehow, she seemed more real than ever. She was more than just the story the teachers at the orphanage had told him. She had existed, and she had written on this envelope.

With a deep breath, James opened the envelope and was surprised when two pieces of paper fell out rather than just one. He opened the first letter as though he was handling delicate glass that could shatter at the lightest touch.

Dear teachers of St. Benedict's,

My name is Victoria Tanner. This little angel is James. My life is in danger, and so I cannot care for my son, although it is with a broken heart that I leave him in your care. I'm sorry. I know he will be in safe hands.

I have written another letter for him to read when he turns eighteen. I expect you will read it and think I'm mad. Whatever your opinion of me, please do not reveal the details of this letter to him until he comes of age. It is crucial that he receives it, but keep it from him until he leaves. My darling child deserves to enjoy his childhood before he is confronted with the truth about his mother.

Thank you,

V

When James finished reading, he immediately moved to open the letter that he knew was addressed to him...but he hesitated.

Why would the teachers at the orphanage have thought her mad? Was he the son of a crazy woman? Had the teachers kept the letter from him all these years to protect him? To protect his idea of who his mother was in his own mind?

James threw the letter on the bed and dropped his head into his hands. He had no idea who his mother had been. He couldn't even picture her face. But maybe, by not reading the letter, he could keep his invented idea of her unblemished in his mind.

But she is already blemished, he thought. She abandoned me. I owe her nothing.

And for the first time in his life, after so many years of trying to get his hands on the letter from his mother, he unfolded it and read its words.

Dear James,

With a heavy heart, I am writing this letter with the knowledge that, most likely, I will never see you again. Never again will I feel your touch, see your smile, or hear you babbling. I can't expect you to understand, but I need you to know that I am only doing this to protect you. It was not my intention to leave you at an orphanage. It was not my intention to hurt you, to leave you alone, to condemn you a life without a mother. Oh, how alone you must feel. I am so sorry. I wish I had more time to explain everything to you. Hopefully, someone like you will reveal themselves at the right time to tell you more. To answer all the questions that you must have.

You are a very special little boy and you have the power to make special things happen. From the moment you were born, your potential was clear, so I feel confident in saying you must have experienced strange, inexplicable things throughout your childhood, right? It isn't fair that you had to face those experiences alone, but it was for your own safety that you were as far away as possible from anyone who understands them. There are good people out there who could have helped you—explained them to you. But if too many had known where to find you, then the bad people could have found you, too. I couldn't risk that.

You, like me, are an elemental. I know this word sounds weird now and I wish I could tell you more. But you are not the only person who will read this letter. The staff at the orphanage will read this. I cannot say too much or else they may destroy the letter and never show it to you.

I know you must have felt abandoned by me your whole life. Please know that while I am gone, there are others like you—other elementals. Now that you are old enough, I hope you will find them, or that they will find you. They will be able to tell you who you are, what you can do, and why strange things happen sometimes. Most of all, they will keep you safe.

But be careful. I don't know what the future holds but I suspect the bad people will still be out there, looking for you. Be careful who you trust, sweetheart. I know how unfair this must seem, that I tell you that you are in danger but cannot give you any more information. Trust your judgment as best you can. More than that, trust the power that you have inside you. It is greater than you realize. Use this gift—and it is a gift—and do good in life.

I love you more than anything in the world.

Your mother

P.S. Beware the flashes of light.

James read the letter to the end and then stared at the space underneath the final words as if expecting more to appear that would explain what he had read. But the words did not appear; these were the only words he had from his mother, and they made no sense. He reached for the envelope, hoping to find something else—another letter, a code to decipher the true message buried inside the words—but there was nothing.

CHAPTER 3

Beware the Flashes of Light

JAMES HOVERED IN THE air. It was calm and peaceful. Everything was perfect and serene. But then he heard a sound like thunder in the distance, and when he turned his head in the direction of the crashing, he inhaled sharply. On the distant horizon, across the vast ocean, a tornado was forming. But it wasn't a tornado; it couldn't be. The swirling wind was aglow with orange light; fire, even. The frenetic wind was approaching the mainland, which itself was beginning to rise. Was it growing? Or was it erupting from beneath? The closer the cyclone was to the mainland, the higher the earth around James rose. When the storm was only four hundred feet away, everything around James began to tremble. Although James was floating, he felt the vibrations intensify from one second to another. When it was three hundred feet away, the storm accelerated so quickly toward the mainland that it seemed to suck the oxygen out of the air, and James was left gasping for breath and clutching at his throat. But he didn't have time to worry about breathing. The tornado was mere seconds from colliding with the mainland, when it would destroy everything in its path...

James awoke to the sound of an explosion so loud that it caused his ears to ring. Disoriented and with no idea what was going on or where he was, he jumped out of bed and ran for the door. The first thing that caught his sight in the darkness was a ruined gate, bellowing hot flames, and heavy smoke. Where once had stood the guard house, where he had met Alan only the night before, there was now nothing but red-hot metal shards and twisted steel.

"Help!" James screamed until his lungs filled with smoke and he had to cough it out. Heeelp! Alaaan!"

As the fire raged louder and higher and hotter, James shielded his eyes as he tried to peer through the flames for someone on the other side. Maybe for Alan, or to see someone already trying to help. As the flames danced and licked the air around him, James saw, for the briefest of moments, the silhouette of someone wearing a hat and coat on the other side of the burning wreckage.

"Alan?" James cried, but he knew it wasn't Alan. The outline was almost certainly a man, but too tall and skinny to be the guard who had been so kind to him.

James took a deep breath to shout again at the stranger, but just as he was about to speak, the fire reduced to just half its size in an instant. Before James could get a good look, a sphere of...something appeared before him. It almost looked to James like it was made of the fire itself and it started to shine a bright red.

"Look out!" James shouted. In his semi-sleepy, semi-shocked state, James couldn't understand how the fireball had formed and why it was so close to this stranger but he was sure it would start burning him if he didn't move soon.

But the stranger didn't scream. He didn't even move.

James blinked as he tried to see what the man was doing. Was he moving his hands? He couldn't be sure, but the fireball suddenly grew. No, it wasn't growing. Moving! It was moving toward him! But James couldn't get his legs to shift his body out of the way. It was as though the fireball caused him so much fear that he'd forgotten how to breathe; it was as if his brain refused to believe what he was seeing right in front of him.

Before the fireball could reach him, a flash of blue light came from James' right, and a similar-looking sphere started to move into the path of the fireball. Whatever it was made of, the distraction was enough to make James to react. He bent down and covered his head with his hands, waiting for the two spheres to collide. Just meters in front of him, the blue sphere crashed into the red one; each disintegrated into the other, sending red and blue sparks firing in all directions and another explosive bang that shook the ground.

Out of the corner of his eye, James spied another red flash from where the unknown stranger was standing, and his attention was immediately drawn to his right again when another blue flash lit up the night sky.

And then, as quickly as it had all started, there was silence. The only thing James could hear was the sound of the crackling flames in front of him. Despite the warm air and the fire a few feet away, James shook with fear and confusion at what had just happened and he breathed a small sigh of relief when he heard the distant sound of approaching sirens. James was sure that help was coming and he was pleased he wouldn't be alone anymore. But what would he tell them? Looking around, there was no evidence of the two spheres he had seen or what had happened when they'd collided, and the stranger in the hat and coat was nowhere to be found.

A few minutes later, the police arrived, soon followed by firefighters who connected their hose to the hydrant to finish off what was left of the guard hut fire. An ambulance, two more police patrols, and another fire truck arrived a little while later. Once they'd managed to put out the fire completely, James saw a motionless, blackened body on the ruined floor. He was sure it must have been Alan, even though he didn't want to believe it.

When he approached the body, he was horrified and had to swallow down the vomit that he could feel rising in his throat. He had never seen a dead body before, but despite the terrible sight, James couldn't tear his eyes away. It took one of the cops several attempts to get James to snap out of his stupor.

"Are you all right? Are you hurt?"

"I-I'm fine."

"What happened?" the policeman asked.

"Huh?" James looked at the still body. "I don't know."

What will this cop say if I tell him the truth? That I saw a strange shadow throw a fireball at me, but I'm OK because a blue sphere flew in from the opposite direction and stopped it? They'd sooner put me in an institution for the mentally ill than believe me... Although, maybe that would be for the best. Who knows? I might even find my mother that way.

No, he couldn't describe exactly what he had seen. Instead, James explained only what he felt he could explain. How he had been awakened by a big bang and a fire burning wildly. How he had been so petrified that he'd remained almost entirely still until the police arrived. And when the police officer asked if he'd seen anyone else, James quickly replied that he hadn't. It was such a lightning-quick response that the policeman even flinched a little.

After the officer had written it all down, he thanked James and walked over to his vehicle. James took the opportunity to go back to his room, where he sat down on his bed and closed his eyes, though he knew he had no hope of resting. Instead, the backs of his eyes seemed to have horrible images of the night imprinted on them. The abnormal fire, poor Alan's grotesque remains, the stranger in the coat, the two colliding spheres, the lights that had emerged...

As though he had been shocked back to life, James sat up straight and said, quietly but firmly, "Beware of the flashes of light."

He picked up his mother's letter, which had fallen on the floor when he'd fallen asleep earlier. Are those the lights my mother was talking about? James wondered. Is that stranger one of the people she'd mentioned in the letter? An elemental? And who produced the other sphere? And why? To protect me? Or were they both trying to get to me and they just got in each other's way?

Before the questions could overwhelm him anymore, someone knocked on the door. James flinched at the sudden sound so much that he threw his arms out to the side and smacked the bedside lamp. He quickly picked up the lamp with one hand while opening the door with his other. Stanley Walden was waiting on the other side, barely able to keep the tears from falling.

"What happened, James? Is that Alan under that sheet out there?"

"I don't know what happened." James rubbed his wet eyes. "I don't even know if that is Alan. But who else could it be? He and I are the only ones here. If it's not Alan, then where is he?"

As if answering his prayer, James heard fast-paced footsteps approaching, and for a second, he had hoped it was Alan. Instead, as Stanley turned around, James peered over his shoulder to see Terry coming to his hut.

"What the hell's going on here?"

James, whose hands began to shake again, soon recounted everything that had happened. Like with the cop, he left out the parts that he knew would make everyone think he was mentally unstable. After he finished, the three of them stood in silence for a few moments as though they were hypnotized by the flashing lights of the emergency vehicles as the various professionals went about their duties.

"Is that really Alan lying there?" Terry asked, eventually breaking the silence.

"It's not confirmed yet. The body is unrecognizable. I think—"

"No," Stanley interrupted, "you're right, James. Who else could it be?"

After a sleepless night of waking nightmares, and once he was sure all the emergency vehicles had gone, James decided he needed to escape the hut. The day was as gloomy as he felt, and thick gray clouds hovered menacingly over the docks. James headed for the ruined gate where two rather young boys were cleaning up the remnants of the explosion and loading the leftover shrapnel onto a nearby small van. Before Stanley had left the previous night, he had told Terry and James that the docks would be closed the next day, so James decided it was the perfect opportunity to get some space and explore the nearby suburban center to clear his head. But the stroll was anything but relaxing; all James could think about was Alan, the mysterious stranger James was increasingly certain must have been responsible for the explosion, and what, if anything, he could have done to prevent the fire. But most of all, he thought about his mother's letter and the flashes of light.

Maybe Alan is dead because of me, James thought. Maybe they wanted to kill me like my mom described in the letter, and Alan just got in the way. Collateral damage, as they say...

James followed the pedestrian walkway and bicycle lanes of the flat coastal path that he knew from looking out from the docks led to a built-up area a mile or so north. As he neared the suburban center, his exhaustion took the form of hunger, and he ducked into the nearest bakery, lured in by the mouthwatering smell of freshly baked bread. He still hadn't eaten a proper meal since leaving the orphanage, and his stomach started to cramp as he took in the selection of steamed buns, fluffy loaves, and sugary cakes that lined the glass display.

"Two cinnamon rolls, please." James pointed at the bottom row, recognizing the sweet treats from his time at the orphanage.

The saleswoman obliged, put them in a paper bag, and handed them over the counter. "That'll be one dollar fifty, please."

As James handed her the money, he peered into the wall-mounted mirror that hung behind the saleswoman. Through it, he could see across the street behind him, and standing on the opposite sidewalk, seemingly watching him in the bakery, was a skinny-looking man dressed all in black. He wore a long, unbuttoned coat, boots, and a black t-shirt and pants. Even his hair was black, which hung down to his shoulders, falling to the sides of his elongated face and slightly large nose.

James was careful not to stare into the mirror for too long and he took his time arranging his things before he turned around to leave the bakery. But once he was outside again, the stranger was gone. James looked left and right for any sign of the man dressed in black, but the streets were empty except for one elderly lady walking her dog.

He considered going back to the docks and shutting himself in his hut again, but feeling emboldened by the daylight and deciding he was probably safer in a town of people rather than isolated when no one was working at the docks, James continued on.

The main center was paved with decorative stone, and the various nearby shops reflected the low-hanging sun on both sides of the street. The pedestrianized road opened up into a spacious square with a large clock tower that was surrounded by several gold-painted sculptures that glistened in the sunlight. The building behind the clock tower was a curious one; it looked like a small palace or a slightly dilapidated town hall from the colonial era. Above the old, wooden front door was an inscription engraved into the stone that James could not decipher, and just next door to it was a church that also looked like it had been there for centuries. The church has scaffolding on one of its outside walls, so James presumed it was undergoing some renovations, and as he walked past the open front door, James remembered Alan.

He could not close his mind's eye to the images of Alan's distorted, lifeless body, and were it not for the ringing of the church bells a few moments later, James wondered if he would have passed the whole day in the shadow of the clock tower.

Wiping a tear from his cheek, James decided he'd had enough for one day and he started walking back to the docks, stopping to buy some supplies from the supermarket along the way, and to scout for the stranger in black by the bakery one more time. Now midmorning, the street was full of people. Some walked slowly as they talked with companions or took in the warm summer sunshine, while others drank their coffees in nearby cafés. But while James could feel the sensation of someone watching him, he didn't see the strange-looking man in black again, and he got back to his hut at the docks within the hour. He noticed that the spot where the guard house had once stood was now clear. James sighed as he passed it and entered his hut. He fixed himself some food, did his best to block out the terrible images of Alan in his mind, and soon fell asleep.

He awoke a few hours later to the sound of a woman weeping. James got up and peered out the window, immediately noticing how the sun was already getting close to the horizon—he must have slept for hours, he decided. At the site where Alan's guard house had once stood, a tall woman was standing beside Stanley. She wore a black dress, and her black eye liner and red lipstick were smudged. She seemed hysterical, so James decided it was best to stay in his hut. He moved into his bathroom to a window that would make it easier for him to hear what she and Stanley were talking about. However, between her tears, heavy breathing, and hands that she kept using to cover her face, James couldn't make out much.

Instead, James turned his attention to Stanley, who was staring at the floor but nonetheless seemed to be sympathizing with the unknown woman. After a few long minutes, the woman got into her car and drove away. Once he was sure she wasn't coming back, James went outside to greet Stanley. As he approached, he saw his visibly upset boss wipe a tear from his face with a handkerchief.

"It's confirmed," Stanley said before James could speak. "It was Alan's body. They identified him by his dental records." He paused for a moment. "That was his wife, Stacey Brick. He leaves a little girl behind."

CHAPTER 4

Turning Seventeen

DESPITE THE TRAGIC START to James' life at the docks, the next two weeks were, much to everyone's delight, almost entirely uneventful, and James had started to feel at home. He smiled one morning when he looked out his hut window to see the weather was perfect, not a cloud in the sky, and it took a few moments to realize it was his birthday. He turned seventeen today.

As he thought about the occasion, nostalgia seized him. What would he have been doing were he still at the orphanage? A hearty lunch, gifts, games, laughter... His only friends were there. He had acquaintances at the docks now, of course, but he could not yet call them friends, and after what had happened to Alan, James was wary of getting too close to anyone.

When there was a knock at the door, James got up and opened it.

Stanley greeted him with a smile on his face. "Good morning, James."

"Morning," James replied, rubbing his eyes.

"Happy birthday." Stanley extended his hand. In it, James spied a small box wrapped in decorative blue paper.

"Oh, er, thank you," James said, unsure of what to do or say. He couldn't help but wonder if Stanley bought presents for all his employees—which would be a lot—or else why he would buy something for him. James hardly saw himself as one of Stanley's most valuable workers. "How did you know it was my birthday?"

"The contract you signed says September thirtieth. If I'm not mistaken, today is the day. This is just a little something. The real present is that you're invited to dinner tonight. My wife wants to meet you. Unless you already have plans for today?"

"Er, no, I don't," James said. "But I don't know if it would—"

"We won't take no for an answer. I'll come back for you at six. Be ready." Stanley turned away and left for the main gate before James could say anything else, so he just closed the door and went back to bed. Not because it was his birthday, but because he spent a lot of time in bed when he wasn't working. With so few friends and his home being a small hut on the docks, he rarely had much to do in his spare time. Aside from watching the small TV in his room, which had very few channels that suited him, James entertained no hobbies.

On Saturdays, the canteen kitchen was closed, but James was allowed to use it to prepare his own breakfasts, especially as the so-called kitchen in his hut amounted to little more than a broken hob and a microwave. He made himself some scrambled eggs and a tuna sandwich, which he swallowed in an instant. After putting everything back in its place, throwing out the trash, and cleaning the kitchen, he remembered how nice the morning was and went for an easy walk. Passing by the ships, he saw a small boat tied to a pole, and at the same moment, decided to take a ride. James got into the boat, untied it, took the paddle, and pushed off.

He enjoyed every minute he spent on the water. A warm breeze blew through his hair as he rowed lightly, and for once, all his thoughts were scattered. He didn't think about one thing, in particular, so he could instead focus on the beauty of his surroundings. The water was smooth, so he felt like he was flying over it. At first, he stayed near the shore, but after a while, he grew bold and decided to row further out. When he was some three hundred yards from the shore, he lifted the oars into the boat and stopped to take it all in. The beauty of the sea was unlike anything he had ever seen before; a deep blue that had no end, but with just enough light penetrating the water's surface that he could see small fish surrounding the boat and he immediately regretted not bringing anything to feed them. Turning his gaze back to shore, he briefly spied the large industrial buildings at the docks before looking further to the small suburban village up the shoreline. On the coastal path, James spied three people, presumably parents and their son, cycling casually and enjoying the beautiful day, and thoughts of what it means to have a family filled him with a bittersweet sentiment.

Why had he been left alone? Why did he have to grow up in an orphanage? Without a mother, without a father, without a family. Could he ever turn things around? Was he capable of having a family one day?

As he looked out at the inviting view and delighted at the feel of the warm sun on his face, he decided he was happy with the life he had. He recollected some of the funny moments from his time in the orphanage, although it was impossible for him to think about those days and not recall the strange and unusual situations that had occurred near him. He remembered the time the car of an orphanage inspector caught fire after he had caught the man swearing at Deputy Principal Bulgar, when a freak storm had blown off the neighbor's roof after the children inside had thrown water balloons at James and his friends, and the time a pot of boiling water had exploded.

As James submitted more and more to his nostalgia, he lost track of time, and when he looked up to see the sky was beginning to darken, he decided to return to shore. As soon as he started rowing, he felt as if something had hit his boat. James looked into the water, but there was nothing. He felt another blow. Now, in a bit of panic, he rowed as fast as he could, paddling faster and faster when a vortex appeared in front of him; it was maybe ten meters away, right in between his boat and the dock he was heading toward. James tried to paddle around it, first to the left, and then to the right, but the vortex seemed to follow him, and as he got closer and closer, James started to feel the boat being dragged toward it. The boat started to spin as it got caught in the flurry of the spinning water, and when James lost one oar in the vacuum of the whirling sea, he could think of nothing but to paddle with all his strength with the last remaining oar. Sweat built on his brow and he found himself muttering prayers and begging for help as the boat started to tilt onto one side. But just as he was convinced he was going to be dragged to the bottom of the ocean—that he would disappear off the face of the earth and no one would have any clue what had happened to him—the vortex disappeared.

With trembling hands, James did his best to ignore the unusualness of the situation and he, instead, redoubled his efforts to paddle to shore. For a moment, it seemed to him that someone was standing on the shore and waiting for him, but as he summoned the strength to lift his gaze and focus his eyesight, he saw no one. It didn't matter; he'd reached the shore at last, and with great relief, James got out of the boat, tied it to the pole, and quick-stepped back to his hut.

After closing the door behind him, James shut his eyes and gave himself permission to breathe a little more calmly. Another strange event I am somehow responsible for making happen? he thought. Or am I just going mad, like my mother before me?

When he opened his eyes, his gaze landed on the little blue box he had received from Stanley. Unwrapping the decorative paper, he pulled out a black box with a transparent lid. Inside it was a beautiful silver-colored wristwatch with a black leather strap. James had never owned a watch before, let alone received one as a present, and the warmth that flooded through him helped to wash away the last of the uneasy nerves. The new watch read *10:30*, while the clock on the wall read *15:35*, so he wound the dials on the watch until the times matched.

He sat on his bed and admired his present for a while. When he started to grow hungry, he opened the cupboard for one of his snacks, where he noticed a piece of paper with a message written on it in black ink. Taking the paper in his hands, the first thing he noticed was the unusual but very deliberate shapes in the bottom corner. Examining them more closely, he saw that they were pressed into the paper, not written, and he felt the relief on the back of the paper with his fingertips. He didn't know what to make of them, so instead turned his attention to the words written on the paper: *14th October, 6 p.m.*

James turned the page, hoping to see something else; a message, or whatever. The sheet was blank, except for the strange glyphs imprinted on the paper.

What will happen on October fourteenth at six? James thought. And who could have left that message in my room? I always lock the hut whenever I'm out.

James returned his attention to the symbols. He was sure he didn't know what they meant, but there was something familiar about them. More out of hope than inspiration, James reached into his bedside drawer for his mother's letter and looked at the bottom of the paper. In the right-hand corner were the same imprinted signs. The paper of his mother's letter was older and more discolored, but they looked to be about as thick as each other, and James felt a mixture of excitement and fear run through his veins.

Did my mother leave this message? he thought. Is she still alive? Did she find out I got kicked out of the orphanage early and she's come to keep me safe?

But the handwriting wasn't the same. His mother's handwriting was tilted to the right and neat, while the handwriting on the message was upright, shabby, and heavy-handed like the author had been deliberately pressing a ballpoint pen into the paper with all their might.

So, he thought, not my mother. But perhaps someone who knew her?

When James realized he wasn't going to get anywhere by speculating about who could have written the note in his cupboard, he got changed and decided to wait outside in the sunshine for Stanley to come and pick him up. When he heard car wheels rolling across the asphalt, he had turned around expecting to see Stanley, but instead, he saw Terry parking his car. Terry gave him a friendly wave and shouted "Happy birthday" across the space, but he seemed set on going to his office in the maintenance warehouse. James thought about following him to have a conversation and to find out what he was doing at the docks on a Saturday, but as soon as he took a few steps, Stanley arrived and gave James a friendly tap on his car horn.

Once James was inside Stanley's car and they were on their way, Stanley handed him a white envelope. James hesitated to open it, wondering how he could let Stanley down gently for trying to give him yet another gift after the watch and dinner. But before he could say anything, Stanley clarified. "This is your pay with a small bonus for a job well done. I hope you'll be pleased."

James let out a silent breath, then finally accepted the envelope and thanked him.

"You're welcome," Stanley said. "You've earned it."

Moments later, they came to a standstill due to a traffic jam, and the sound of sirens forced them both to turn their heads. Not a minute later, an ambulance passed them, heading back in the direction they'd come.

"They are in a hurry," Stanley said.

"Must have been an accident. I hope it's nothing too serious."

"Could be. By the way, James, you never told me why you had to leave the orphanage?"

The question took James by surprise. He'd been working at the docks for a couple of weeks now and had hoped he'd dodged the question. He thought for a moment before he responded. "I didn't have to leave, I wanted to leave."

This wasn't true, James knew in his heart. He hadn't wanted to leave. He would have stayed forever if he'd been allowed. It had been his only so-called home. But he couldn't say they had thrown him out because of scary and inexplicable situations happening around him. Stanley would only end up kicking him off the docks, too. He couldn't say that. So, he chose the easiest solution and lied.

"But why?" Stanley asked. "You could have stayed for another year and then made your way into the world."

James stared out of the car window, thinking how best to reply. In the next lane, he saw a man sitting behind the wheel as he fought with his wife. A young girl was sitting in the back, holding an ice cream, and watching her parents arguing.

"Because," James said, pausing a little before continuing, "I believe I can take care of myself. I'm not a little boy anymore. Besides, the other children will benefit from me leaving," James lied again and hoped Stanley wouldn't see through him. "More space for a new kid that needs more help than me." It wasn't the best lie but it was all he could think to say at the time.

"Very noble of you, James."

Just then, someone honked from behind to signal them to drive forward. Sure enough, the traffic began to dispel, and after a while, the road was clear once again.

When they reached a beautiful house decorated with flowers and turned into the yard, James realized he was looking at Stanley's home. It was beautiful, and he found himself imagining himself living in a house just like it. At first, with the mother he had never met; and then with his imagined family of the future.

Stanley's phone started to ring, and out of the corner of his eye, James read Terry's name on the screen. Stanley quickly finished parking, picked up the phone, and answered the call. After a few moments, James saw Stanley turn pale. James studied Stanley's expressions as they seemed to cycle through fear, panic, and sadness, and as soon as the phone call was over, Stanley put the car in gear and headed back in the direction they had come.

"What happened?" James asked at last.

"Ted has just been found dead in the warehouse," Stanley replied.

"What?" James cried. "How? What happened to him? Who found him? The police are already—?"

"I don't know, James." Stanley interrupted. "All I know is that Terry found him. Now, we're going there to see what's going on. Terry has already called the police."

There was no traffic going in the reverse direction and they arrived back at the docks in a quarter of the time it had taken them to get to Stanley's house. Deep in thought and not knowing what awaited them, they both flinched when they saw the police lights.

"Here we are," Stanley said, but as they turned into the dockyard, a policeman stopped them at the gate. When Stanley explained that he was the site manager and that his foreman had called him, the officer let the car pass but said that he would need him later for a statement. Stanley parked the car near James' hut, and they both got out and headed for the warehouse. When James realized where they were going, he thought about his earlier trip on the boat and how he'd felt like someone had been watching him. He thought back to the stranger he had seen the night of Alan's death as well, and the man in black who had watched him in the bakery that day. *Are all these people the same man or different people?* James thought. *And are they responsible for Ted's death as well as Alan's?*

James knew they were at the right warehouse when they saw the firefighters coming out wearing looks of dismay. One of them leaned over the side of the dock to be sick into the water. Stanley made his way to the warehouse when a police officer stopped him.

"You can't come in. Who—?"

"I am the manager of the docks. That man you found inside is one of my workers," Stanley snapped.

"I'm sorry. You can't come in while we're examining the crime scene."

"Crime?" Stanley yelled.

"We can't rule it out yet," the policeman said.

Before James could make sense of what the policeman was saying, Stanley spotted Terry near the warehouse and headed over to him. Terry was sitting on a bench with his head in his hands.

"My goodness, Terry," Stanley said. "You look whiter than a sheet. Are you OK?"

"Don't go in...," he said as if talking to himself. "It's...horrible. Impossible...simply impossible. Terrible." James looked down and noticed Terry's hands were shaking.

Stanley seemed to appreciate how shocked Terry was, so decided not to ask any more questions. Instead, he turned back to the scene and watched, hoping for some information to come his way. When the last group of people came out, James and Stanley headed for the warehouse. Still unsure that any crime could have happened, they stopped at the door, took a deep breath, and entered the room. The warehouse was full. To the left were boxes of various sizes on pallets. To the right were parts and machines that James could not recognize. They were neatly arranged, one behind the other, so that there was a passage about four meters wide between the two sides. The warehouse seemed to have no end. Looking down the aisle, some ten meters from the entrance, James saw a yellow strip surrounding a large machine. As they approached, they saw that it was an old conveyor belt, like those used to load luggage into planes. A motionless body lay on it, but James only assumed it was Ted because they had been told he was the victim. His face was covered in pus-filled bubbles as if he had been doused with boiling water, there were spaces in his hair where the flesh was missing, and his hands, too, were swollen and raw. His shoe had slipped off one foot, and James could see bone. It was as if he had been flooded from the inside out with some kind of acid, for while the body itself was ruined, the clothes on the corpse appeared undamaged. James felt his stomach start the clench and the bile rising in his throat so made a quick exit of the warehouse. While outside, breathing in long, deep breaths of fresh air, Stanley eventually joined him.

"I've known him for twelve years," Stanley said softly. "He's worked for me for six."

"HHow do you know it's Ted? That could be anyone,"

"I recognize the ring on his hand." Stanley's voice was trembling. "I don't understand. In the eighteen years I've worked here, there's only been one accident. Just one. And that was something I could explain. And now, in just two weeks, Alan...and now Ted."

"Did the police ever release the report to you about what happened to Alan?"

"Pah, nonsense. They wrote that the gas installation was not maintained properly, which caused an explosion. Besides, the gas was for heating the room during the winter, but it must have been eighty degrees outside the night he died."

While Stanley was speaking, the police officer from the gate approached Stanley and asked him to go with him to give a statement. James decided to re-join Terry, who still looked white and terrified.

"And? Did you see?" Terry said as James took a seat beside him.

"Yes, I saw. Who could have done that to him?"

"No idea. I don't know anyone who would want to hurt Ted. You've worked with him; you know he's a good guy. You haven't seen anything weird lately?"

The strange men James had seen instantly came to mind, though he chose not to say anything. Still, he had to bite his lip to keep a sob from escaping as he again wondered whether he was to blame for Alan and Ted's deaths. Would they have still been alive if James hadn't come begging for work and a place to stay?

"I have to go," James said.

"What?"

"Nothing, nothing," James said. "I'm going to my room. I have to lie down."

"Go. This isn't a place for a young man like you. I don't even understand why you went into the warehouse."

James left Terry talking to himself and headed for his hut. But before he got too far, he saw Stanley answering the policeman's questions, so approached. "I'm going to lie down."

"OK. I'm sorry your birthday turned out like this," Stanley said.

"I think my birthday is the least of the problems here now," James replied and continued walking toward the hut.

"Hang on," the policeman said. "You work and sleep here, too? I'll need a statement from you, as well," the policeman said, pointing to the notepad he held in his hand.

"Please, officer, leave him alone," Stanley said. "Today is his seventeenth birthday, and he has seen far more than he should have. The statement can wait until tomorrow." The officer was considering what to do when Stanley spoke again. "Look, he doesn't have anywhere else to go. He's not going anywhere."

Another moment passed before the officer grunted. Stanley thanked him, then turned back to James and put his hand on his shoulder. "Good night, James. Get some rest."

James didn't say anything but continued to his hut room, and as soon as he stepped inside, he immediately locked the door behind him and climbed into bed. But sleep was elusive as thoughts began to buzz through his head about everything he had been through since he'd left the orphanage. It was too much of a coincidence that he'd had to leave because of strange happenings and that these unusual events had not only followed him here but turned deadly. At last, James resolved that he had to leave to protect the people around him from any more violent deaths. But even that was problematic. If he left now, he would become the prime suspect in a criminal case for sure when it already didn't look good for James; after all, both accidents had occurred within two weeks of James arriving at the docks.

James thought of his mother's letter, hoping for some kind of clue as to what to do next, but all that did was confirm his suspicions that he was somehow responsible. She'd said he would be in danger, and he had dismissed her warnings as the ramblings of a mad woman.

But thinking of the letter also reminded him of the strange message he had found earlier that day.

"October fourteenth. Will something terrible happen on that day as well? Someone will die again?" James whispered to himself. "No, it won't! Nothing will happen because I won't be here anymore. I won't let anything happen to anyone else because of me. I must leave, even if it makes me look guilty!"

CHAPTER 5

Escape

For the next thirteen days, James did his job as best he could. Stanley and Terry would stop him occasionally or visit him in his room to talk, but James would look for excuses to end the conversations early. His only thought was to get as far away as possible before October fourteenth. He had no idea what the strange note he'd found in his hut meant, but he didn't want anything to happen to anyone else at the docks. They were good people, and he could not bear another "accident." The one piece of good news, at least for James' plan to escape, was that Ted's death had been ruled as a severe allergic reaction to an unknown substance that had brought about heart failure. Of course, James didn't believe that; he was sure that the deaths of Alan and Ted were somehow connected to him. But it meant the case was no longer considered criminal, so James was free to leave without raising any suspicions with the police.

While James didn't know where he was going to go next, he knew he'd figure it out eventually. The one thing he needed, however, was money, so James had no choice but to wait until the last possible moment while he saved up his wages. By the time October thirteenth rolled around, James knew he didn't have enough money to survive on his own for long, but he'd run out of time. It was now or never. James asked Stanley if he could stay in his room all day under the pretext that he wasn't feeling very well and he used the time to pack his things in peace, intending to leave in the evening. Sad and disappointed, James slowly inspected all of his things and after packing everything in his old suitcase, he decided to take one last walk around the docks. He headed for Terry's office, meeting workers along the way, who greeted him with a nod. As James smiled and made small talk, lying about the things he and his coworkers would do together in the coming weeks, he felt pressure on his body, like someone was sitting on his chest. The last time he'd felt that way was when he had been forced to leave the orphanage. Halfway to Terry's office, he met Stanley coming out of one of the warehouses, who was carrying some papers in his hand.

"James!" Stanley cried. James raised his hand in greeting and walked over to Stanley. "How are you? Are you feeling better?"

"I'm fine. I needed some fresh air so I decided to take a walk to see Terry."

"I'm just going to see him. We can go together. I have some order returns that I have to leave with him."

"OK," James said.

"You all right?" Stanley asked as they started walking together. "I don't mean today; I mean in general? You haven't been very talkative since...that day."

James knew what day he was talking about. The day Ted died.

"I'm fine," James said, and the pressure on his chest increased. Stanley must have sensed the curtness in James' voice because he gave up asking after that.

As they approached Terry's office, James touched Stanley on the shoulder. "Thank you. Thank you for everything."

Stanley raised an eyebrow before grabbing James' hand on his shoulder. "You have nothing to thank me for. I should thank you for coming here to work. It's hard to find good workers today. I have to go now. I still have a lot of work to do, but we can talk in the evening."

"I can't today. I want to rest. Another time?"

"Whenever you want to talk, you know where I am."

James half smiled, but when Stanley held the door open to Terry's office, James shook his head and made an excuse to stay outside a little longer. After Stanley came out again, he patted James on the back and walked to his office. James felt even more pressure in his chest; it was getting harder and harder for him to breathe. He felt powerless; his life had no meaning, and he didn't know where he was going to go next. All he'd ever known was the orphanage and he'd only got lucky at the docks because Deputy Principal Bulgar had said he should look for work and board there. After he left that evening, he'd be on his own.

Before entering Terry's office, James took several deep breaths. He didn't know what to say, but he needed to visit him before he left. Inside, James saw that Terry was deeply immersed in the papers Stanley had handed to him, but once he spied James, Terry put down the papers. "How are you?"

"Why do you all ask me how I am all the time?" James asked and he instantly regretted the irritableness in his voice. "I'm sorry. I didn't mean that. I'm fine."

"Don't sweat it, kid. When do you think you'll be ready to come back to work? We're going to have to work overtime if Stanley doesn't hire a few more people."

"Soon. I just need some rest," James said. "How are you?" As soon as James asked, Terry's brow seemed to contort. James knew it was a sensitive topic after how distraught Terry had seemed that day, but when Terry didn't say anything, James tried to clarify. "I meant—"

"I'm fine." Terry interrupted with a small sigh. "I don't really like talking about it."

"OK. Just—"

A worker opened the office door and popped her head inside. "Delivery has arrived."

Terry got up from his chair, visibly relieved that the conversation had been interrupted. "I have to go." He patted James on the shoulder.

After returning to his hut and with his suitcase already packed, James had nothing left to do but to wait for sunset. As he stared at the wooden boards on the ceiling, he thought about whether he was going to head north or west, but he didn't know enough about the states or cities in either direction to make an informed choice, so his thoughts just circled back on themselves again and again. Eventually, he decided he'd buy a ticket on whichever bus was cheap enough for him to afford and would take him as far away as possible in any direction.

By eight o'clock in the evening, the sun had set over an hour earlier, and James decided it was late enough to leave. Most of the workers had already gone home for the day, and his hut was near the entrance to the docks, so he figured he could leave without catching anyone's eye. He picked up his suitcase, turned to check he hadn't left anything behind, then left the hut.

It was James' first time in the suburban center at night, and it struck him how much nicer the place looked with the lights on. Not only nicer but also different; kind of magical, even. Every few steps, a low-lit lamp emitted a soft light that seemed to make the surroundings glow. The shops on either side were closed, but window lights, left on for pedestrians to admire the displays, illuminated James' route. Still, it was late and a weeknight, so the center was almost empty, and by the time he reached the main square, he'd passed only a handful of people walking with a purpose or sitting on one of the many benches.

It was late now, and while the darkness had made his journey more beautiful, he'd been unable to find the bus station. After completing his third lap of the square without finding any signs to point him in the right direction, he gave up.

I'll spend the night in the church, James thought. I'm sure I'll get away with doing it for just one night and I'll move on tomorrow. As far away as I can possibly go.

Walking up the steps to the church entrance, James paused and turned his head toward the palace next door. Like the rest of the center, it looked more magical, more magnificent, at night, lit up as it was by the various upturned lights at its base and beneath its many window sills. James moved his eyes from the colorful roof and white-brick walls to a shifting shadow at one of the side doors. There was only a small light at the top of the door, but it was enough to cast the figure in front in darkness. James could only make out their outline, but whoever it belonged to was standing with their shoulders squared at him. James couldn't help but recall the outline of the man in the coat and hat he had seen through the flames the night Alan had died.

"Good evening," James muttered, hoping to reveal the identity of the person staring back at him. Instead, the shadowy figure simply turned and slipped inside the door behind them.

The warmth and ease James had been feeling up until that point disappeared, and he turned the doorknob and pushed open the church door with tension in his muscles that made him shiver. Though old, giant, and massive, the church door opened with such ease that left James feeling amazed. The stale air inside the church warmed his skin, and James listened to the sound of his shoes scraping against the stone floor until he came to a stop between two pillars. He'd never stood inside a church before, other than the small chapel at the orphanage, but knew enough to know the stone bowls in front of him contained holy water. The church itself was a magnificent sight. Some one hundred feet wide and about three hundred feet long, old statues in the aisles and stained glass windows of various saints decorated both sides of the church. After a few moments of admiration, he dipped his hand into the holy water, made the sign of the cross on himself, and moved on. At the end of the church was a large altar covered with a white cloth. On it were two large candles, a book with leather binding, and a golden chalice. Behind the altar, on the wall, was a statue of Jesus nailed to a cross, which was surrounded by small golden doors in which statues of angels had been placed.

If there was ever a time to pray for guidance, now is the time, James thought. But as soon as he kneeled, he heard a commotion behind him. When he turned, he saw two men and three women walking down the central aisle toward him.

"Don't be afraid, James," the woman in the middle said. "We are friends."

James turned to face the group while dragging his fingers along the stone floor for something, anything, he might be able to use to defend himself. There was nothing. "Friends?"

"Yes, friends. If you'll allow me, I will explain everything to you."

James didn't answer right away but thought about his next move. There was only one entrance and exit from the church that he could see, and five people were currently blocking him from reaching it.

"Who are you?" James asked. He was curious but mostly terrified and he wanted to distract the strangers for long enough until an escape plan presented itself to him.

"We're just like you," she said. "Your mother sent us."

"My mother? My mother is...alive? What do you know about her? Where is she...?" James cut himself off as he heard his voice breaking.

"My name is Mary. I left you that message in your room at the docks. I'm assuming you got it as you or else it's a bit of a coincidence that we'd find you here the day before we were due to come and get you. I was there when Allan was killed. I'm—"

"You killed Allan?"

"No, I didn't kill Alan, you misunderstood." Mary held her hands out in front of her as if in surrender. "I have been keeping you safe. I neutralized that fireball you saw. I calmed that whirlpool at sea that almost sucked you in. Ever since you left the orphanage, we've been following you and making sure nothing bad happens to you."

James could feel his legs starting to shake and his knees starting to give out from underneath him. "Where's my mother?" he asked, trying to sound more confident and demanding than he felt.

"I'll explain everything to you, I promise, but we need to move first," Mary said. "It's not safe here. James, you...you look just like your mother did."

"Did? What do you mean 'did?' Did she send you or not?"

"I don't know if your mother is alive, but it was always the plan to come and get you one day. It's just... The timetable had to be moved up. Please, James, come with us."

"Where are we going?"

Mary pointed to the exit. "To the palace, next door. It is a safe place, I swear."

James looked around at the various closed doors on both sides of him. Certainly, one would lead to another part of the church, but he had no idea if the doors were locked, or what the five strangers would do to him if he tried to flee but failed to escape. He took a moment, praying that a priest, a nun, a janitor, anyone, would choose this very moment to walk through one of the doors. He could tell them he felt threatened, and maybe they'd even give him a bed for the night after kicking the five strangers into the street.

But no door opened, and realizing he stood no chance against five people, especially people supposedly capable of neutralizing fireballs and stopping whirlpools, James straightened himself up and headed for the church exit.

As he passed Mary, she touched his shoulder. "We are your friends. You need not be afraid of us."

James paused, looked Mary straight in the eye, and felt a warmth that reminded him of Deputy Principal Bulgar. "All right," he said, doing his best to sound calm.

Once James was outside the church, he waited for Mary to pass him. She led James and her entourage through the gate to the left and to the low-lit door James had seen earlier, and he realized that this Mary had been the dark figure he'd seen.

As they neared the door, Mary stopped and pressed her hand to James' chest. "Before we go in..."

"Yes?" asked James.

"Once you enter, everything you think you know about this world will change."

CHAPTER 6

The Revelation

ONE OF THE MEN put his hand on the stone next to the door. It briefly glowed a warm red, as though it were actually made of plastic with a light inside, and the door opened. James watched as the light from the stone slowly faded away before he allowed himself to be led inside, and after walking through a short brick-red corridor, they emerged into what looked to be a large hall. James guessed the floor space must have approached that of the church he had been in a few moments earlier, although this new room was shaped more closely to a square than the rectangular church, and the first thing to catch his eye was the high, oval ceiling that was covered in colorful paintings.

James sensed Mary's eyes on him, so after giving her a quick glance, he looked up at the soft blue, bright red, shining yellow, and burnished green. "I've seen those symbols before. On my mother's letter and on the piece of paper you left in my room."

"They are the glyphs of the four elements: water, fire, air, and earth," Mary said, her voice almost a whisper, further adding to James' feeling that wherever they were had a holy quality about it. "The one with the flames is fire, of course, and the droplet divided into two represents water. The four wavy lines, one on top of the other, that means air."

"So that green irregular triangle divided into two means earth?"

Mary put her hands on her hips. "Exactly."

Around the rune-like signs were motifs that seemed to represent each of the elements opposing the others: a wave rising over the land; sparks of fire falling to the ground; rocks smashing into ice. And at the dome's center—at its highest point—all four elements clashed with each other. Upon this mix of chaos was a fifth sigil, one painted in gray that James had never seen before, not even on his mother's letter. It resembled the number eight, rotated on its side, like the symbol for infinite, only its edges were serrated. He looked down to ask Mary what it meant, but she had already moved away from him.

As James looked around to find her, he took in the detail of the room. Candles were lit on all four of the walls, but most of the warm lighting came from the four huge chandeliers that were evenly spaced down the center of the room and the fireplaces on either side of the room's center. There was a raised platform between the two fireplaces with a large table, and James realized they were not alone; people were sitting at the table. Although they all had their backs to James, Mary, and her companions, only one of the three people looked to be the size and proportions of a regular man. The man on the left was so small that he was sitting on three large pillows so he could sit with his head above the table's top, and James had even dared to think he might have been a child if not for the man's long beard. He looked like a man who had spent most of his life working in the sun and he had arranged his long, thick, black hair into a ponytail. Meanwhile, James wasn't sure if the person in the middle was a man or a woman; only that they were rather tall, with a slightly elongated face and pointed ears that protruded through their long, straight, silver hair. The three people seemed to be engaged in a serious conversation until the small man interrupted the conversation when he locked eyes with James.

"Greetings," he said. His voice was deep and harsh. He slid off the cushions on his chair and the bang of his heavy working boots hitting the wooden paneling of the raised platform echoed through the spacious room. He was no more than five feet tall. He tugged at his scruffy pants, attached to which James noticed a knife, and shrugged until his old leather jacket sat more comfortably on his shoulders.

"Hello, everybody," Mary said. "I have someone with me who I am sure you want to meet."

As she said that, the other two people at the table stood up and turned to face James. He didn't flinch, despite the vast contrast between the small bearded man on the left and the tall skinny man—James could now see he was clearly male—in the middle.

"Aren't you going to introduce us?" the tall man said. His pale skin was almost as shiny as his silky hair, and his gray, full-body length coat shimmered in the golden light of the fires set around the room.

"We're going to take this slowly, OK, Kymil?" Mary said. She gestured toward the raised table and six chairs but it took her to touch James' shoulder to break him out of his trance. Feeling embarrassed for staring at the tall man and his short companion, James looked at the floor as he followed Mary onto the platform and took a seat directly in front of the fireplace. Mary sat on his left, and, on his right, sat an elderly man, who, before James had interrupted him, had been conversing with Kymil and the short man at the table.

"James, I would like you to meet Kymil," Mary said, and the tall silver-haired guy bowed his head. James stood up and offered his hand across the table. The tall man frowned a little but quickly stood up and took James' hand in his own. His skin was as smooth as velvet, but James decided it would be best for everyone not to say anything.

Meanwhile, the small bearded man walked around the table to James to give him a firm but friendly slap on the back. "I am Dalnur."

"Who...?" James cleared his throat. "Who are you?"

"Are you deaf, lad? I just told you my name."

"I know...but you don't look..." James stopped and wondered how to ask him without offending him. "You don't look like me."

"Of course, I don't look like you. And a damned good thing it is, too," Dalnur said with a deep laugh. "I am a dwarf. Haven't you seen a dwarf before?"

"No, he hasn't," Mary answered on James' behalf. "He doesn't know anything about any of this. He has lived all his life in an orphanage."

"You mean to tell me that—?"

"Yes, yes, yes," Mary interrupted again. "Up until today, he had no knowledge of our existence. This is his first time seeing a dwarf...and an elf."

"You are an elf?" James asked, turning his head toward Kymil.

"I am, indeed," Kymil said, bowing his head proudly while Dalnur returned to his chair and hopped back on top of his cushions.

As James continued to flick his gaze between the elf and the dwarf, James heard a cough to his right and turned to look at the elderly man. "This is Mr. George Cavano," Mary said.

James offered his hand to the man, as well. "Oh, I beg your pardon. My name is James. James Tanner."

"I know who you are," George said. "We all know who you are. Welcome. This might not be home, but it's cozy enough to serve its purpose."

"And where is this," James said, circling his eyes from the floor to the ceiling and back to the floor again to indicate the large hall, "if it's not a home."

"A safe haven," Kymil said.

"More like a safe house," Dalnur said with a snort. "Somewhere to lie low when you're in danger."

"I'm in danger?" James tried to swallow but his throat was dry.

"I know that all of this must be very strange for you and difficult to understand," George said. "No doubt, you must have questions. Ask whatever you wish, and we'll do our best to answer you. Does that sound fair?"

Before James could say anything, Mary placed a hand on his shoulder. "First thing's first," she said, waving to somebody on the other side of the room, "I'm starving and I believe that our guest must feel the same."

James wasn't particularly hungry but a small part of him felt grateful for the distraction when a man Mary waved to approached from across the room. He had been one of the men to accompany him back from the church. Mary asked if he could bring them something to eat and drink. He nodded and walked away, but before James could compose himself to ask a question, the man returned with glasses of water for everyone at the table.

"I know that this is going to sound weird," James said, eyeing Kymil, "but can you tell me, what is an elf? I mean, you kinda look like they are described in the stories...but I thought they were just that: stories." James winced a little, convinced he must have asked his question in the most offensive way possible.

Kymil took a sip of his water, licked his lips, and replaced his glass on the table. "We don't look so very different, you and I. Maybe we elves are a little taller and our lifespan is a little longer than yours."

"Ha!" Dalnur laughed, spitting out his water.

"All right, Dalnur." Kymil had a small smirk on his lips. "A lot longer than yours. We prefer to keep to our own company. Human beings have a history of...meddling where they are not wanted."

"Why haven't I heard of real-life elves before?"

"We prefer the company of the trees of the forests and live in small, easily manageable, isolated tribes according to our own elvish law. It just makes things easier. We want no part in the bothersome lives of humans, and the best way to keep them out of our affairs is to keep to ourselves."

"Are you...? Are you a leader of your tribe? You seem so...grand," James said, his voice shaking.

Dalnur leaned into Kymil and gave the elf a little nudge with his elbow. "I think the lad is in love, don't you?"

James felt his cheeks turn warm but he couldn't help his questions. He had heard stories and watched movies involving elves and dwarfs, but he knew it was all just the fruit of someone's imagination. And yet, he was sitting in a room with both an elf and dwarf, drinking the same water as them.

"No, I am not. I am something like a spokesperson," Kymil said. "There are fourteen elvish tribes left in fourteen different locations. They stay hidden, but we still like to keep abreast of affairs with the other races. For that, they need someone like me to interact with the rest of the world."

James thought with a furrowed brow. "You said there are fourteen tribes *left*. Did there used to be more?"

Dalnur laughed again and even Kymil smirked. "Very astute of you, James," Kymil said. "There were twenty-one tribes once. But four of them were destroyed in the war and three others have...separated themselves."

"The war?"

"Yes. The war. The war dealt a lot of damage to our people. To every species, in fact. The fighting was worse in some places, and by the end of the war, there were too few elves left for the four tribes to sustain themselves. Those surviving elves were forced to integrate into one of the remaining tribes. Meanwhile, three tribes decided our elvish traditions were partly responsible for causing the war in the first place. They rebelled against the law that governs our tribes around the world and formed their own community with new laws. We call them dark elves now."

"Why dark elves?" James asked.

"A silly nickname, really," Kymil said, although his face showed no hint of humor. "Most elves have silver hair, like mine. After they went their separate ways, the elves wanted to be recognized as being separate from the rest of us, so they changed their hair to black"

Mary moved to stop James from asking another question, but James gave her a pleading look. "Why did they rebel?"

"Elves are the protectors of all life, not just the lives of elves. That is fundamental to our law. During the war, we suffered many casualties, and some elves thought that we should focus on protecting only our own; that the rest of the species should take care of themselves. This was the beginning of the rift, and it only grew after the war ended."

In truth, James had even more questions now, but as he shifted in his seat to ask another, the doors opened at the other end of the hall and two men wheeled a cart inside. Immediately, James felt overcome by the delicious scents that wafted their way toward the table and up his nostrils, and where he had once thought himself not too hungry, he was now starved. The men put everything on the table, wished them an enjoyable meal, and walked away. Mary removed the covers from the dishes to reveal fried chicken, cooked vegetables, salad bowls, and a pasta dish. Everyone else at the table seemed nonplussed by the quantity of the food, let alone its golden haze and mouthwatering smell, but to James, he had rarely seen such a feast. Perhaps due to his habits picked up at the orphanage, where he had to wait to be invited to get served at the canteen, James was the last at the table to serve himself. Still, other than Dalnur—who seemed to have an appetite that would shame a hungry horse—James was the first to finish all the food on his plate, and the only one to have seconds.

"That's quite the appetite you've got there, young James," Dalnur said while picking his teeth with a chicken bone. James smiled, stared at Dalnur a moment, looked down at his food, then gazed back at the dwarf. "I presume you would like to know something about my kind?"

James, with his mouth full, gave a sheepish smile.

"I suppose you could say we share some similarities with the elves but we're not really anything alike. We dwarfs live in cities, only they are deep underground. We are hardworking people; very proud and stubborn as hell."

"I've never heard someone describe his own people as stubborn before?" James muttered between bites of food.

"Ha, what would you know about how different cultures talk about themselves? You've been out of your orphanage for what? A few weeks?"

"Dalnur!" Mary snapped.

The dwarf was smirking, but his red cheeks belied the small amount of shame that James suspected he felt. "Ah, you're right, lad. Normally, a dwarf wouldn't use these words, of course, but I have spent a lot of time with humans; I know how best to describe us for you to understand. If, or when, you come across another dwarf, you'll see the difference. We spend our time working, building, and upgrading our cities, building weapons, and training. Like my friend here," he said, patting Kymil on the arm, "we dwarfs have learned that we're better off below ground than trying to compete with the humans above it."

James absorbed every word with interest. The whole night seemed like a fairy tale he could not believe, but still, his eyes did not deceive him. In front of him sat two strange men who were definitely not what he would have described as typically human.

"How come nobody knows about you?" James said eventually, finally pushing his plate away.

"Who are you talking to, lad?" Dalnur said.

"You. Kymil. Both of you, I guess. I mean, obviously, some people know about you, but how did you manage to keep your existence a secret from the rest of the world?"

"Obviously, we didn't. At least, not completely," Dalnur replied. "There are stories about us. Other people have stumbled upon us and our cities in the past but it's very rare; never enough to cause us any worry. Every time a human tries to tell their people about us, they're ridiculed. Nevertheless, it has happened. Everyone has heard stories about elves and dwarfs; that's why you know the names of our species and have some idea of what we look like. In every myth, there is some truth," Dalnur said proudly, turning his head toward Kymil.

"What's stopping someone who has stumbled upon your tribe, Kymil, or your city, Dalnur, and coming back with others?"

James saw Kymil peer at Mary before he looked back at James. "We stay hidden using our abilities. For most of our history, it was easy. Humans didn't move far enough or fast enough to ever cause us any concern. But in this modern age, humans have developed technologies that risk exposing us—satellites, drones, et cetera—and we have had to adapt our methods of hiding."

"And why are you hiding exactly?" James asked. "Are humans really so bad?"

Kymil and Dalnur both smirked at each other while James sensed Mary and George both bowing their heads a little at his question.

"Humans are afraid of the unknown," Kymil said. "They always have been. All that is unknown to them, they tend to either enslave or destroy. With them, everything is about wealth and power, which is not the case with us. Elves want peace and harmony."

"And what about us? We don't want peace?" Dalnur asked, firmly pushing his fist onto the table.

"Of course you do, my friend," Kymil replied calmly, turning his head toward Dalnur. "Don't be so hasty. I was talking only about elves. I would never be so bold as to presume the opinion of your people."

This calmed Dalnur down, and Kymil continued. "Thousands of years ago, our races lived together in harmony. But over time, humans became envious of the powers we possess."

"Powers?" James asked. "You mean the ability to control the elements?"

Kymil nodded. "We possess such power, yes, among other special attributes that set us apart, but now is not the time or place."

"But I still don't know how you are hiding yourselves?" James asked, shifting slightly in his seat. "Which abilities are you using?"

"You already said it," Kymil replied. "We use the elements,"

"And how does that work?" asked James.

Kymil looked at Mary, who turned her chair slightly so that James would face her.

"James, before I try to explain, I can only give you the basics, OK? I'm not the best person to explain," Mary said, staring into his eyes.

"Then who is?"

"He's not here. But you'll meet him soon enough."

James uncrossed his arms and eagerly waited for Mary to continue.

"Your mother left you a letter. In it, she explained the elements and the people controlling them—"

"Wait!" James held up a hand. "How do you know what is written in my mother's letter?"

"Call it an educated guess," Mary said.

James didn't understand, but he also didn't want to interrupt Mary again to keep her from telling him something important.

"As Kymil said before, power and wealth are important things for some people. This trait isn't restricted to your typical human, either. Human, elf, and dwarf elementals can be just as guilty of trying to accumulate power and wealth, and the more they gather, the more they are likely to abuse them.

"In the last twenty years, strange things have started to happen. Earthquakes, tsunamis, floods, volcano eruptions, and so on. Those who don't have any knowledge of elementals call it climate change or global warming. They're not entirely wrong, but we believe that someone—an extremely powerful elemental—is using their power to manipulate world events. We still don't know who is behind this or even why but we are doing our best to find out."

"Wait!" James interrupted. "What does all of this have to do with me?"

"We will come to that." Mary placed her palm on James' knee. "So, you know there are four elements, and as you have started to see for yourself, there are people who can control these elements. Typically, this is a gift you are born with, but concentration and imagination are the key. Without them, even the most gifted elemental cannot control the elements. With them, you can do anything. For example, people who can manipulate the water element can form water from the air by gathering the particles of moisture. They can then use this water in many ways, like turn it into sharp pieces of ice or boil it."

"Huh?" James blinked back the confusion that was beginning to cloud his mind. "'People who can manipulate the water element.' So not every elemental can control every element?"

"That's right. Most of us can only control one, maybe two elements. To control three is extremely rare, and controlling all four is virtually unheard of. First, an elemental needs to learn which elements they are attuned to. Only then can they start to imagine how to combine their elements."

"Can you show me?"

"I was about to," Mary answered with a smile as she pushed her right sleeve up. She looked at one of the fireplaces, and at once, a small red sphere came out and floated gently through the air. It stopped beside James, who was instantly on his feet, his mouth agape.

"Touch it," Mary said. James opened his hand, and Mary brought the sphere into his palm. He felt a small tingling sensation. "You see what I mean?"

James could hardly believe his eyes. No matter how much he tried, he couldn't keep his hand from shaking.

"But that's not all," Mary said, and slowly, she started to increase the temperature of the sphere.

James could feel the temperature rising. It started to burn a little until James finally had to pull his hand away.

"No matter if it is summer or winter, and regardless of whether we have a pile of logs in the corner, our fireplaces are always burning."

"You can make fire from nothing?"

"Effectively, although it is always easier and more efficient to use existing fire than to create one from nothing. It takes less energy."

"Energy?"

"Your energy. Energy from your body, energy from your brain. The brain is working twenty-four hours a day. Non-stop. But your brain needs to rest. That's why we go to sleep each night. You can't function without sleep. By sleeping, we reduce our brain functions; something like a cool-down period. If you didn't sleep, eventually, you would pass out. In that way, the brain protects itself. It shuts down and forces you to sleep. You understand what I mean?"

"Kind of."

"The more energy you have, the longer you can concentrate, and as I said, concentration is the most important thing when it comes to controlling these elements. But you have to be very careful. You have to balance your energy with the, let's call it, output power. If you're using one hundred percent of your energy, you will feel tired very quickly, and, eventually, pass out if you don't stop."

"I see," James said. "So you need to resist the urge to use all your energy at once if you want to do something that requires time, otherwise you'll run out of energy first. But in my mother's letter, she said that I am one of these elementals. That I have the power of using these elements."

"And she was right," Mary interrupted.

"What do you mean? What you just did with that sphere... What I saw happen at the docks... I have never been able to do anything like that."

"But you have." Mary took a deep breath. "I knew your mother, and for the few months you were together when you were a baby, I saw you do something extraordinary. One evening, when you were three months old, Victoria asked me if I could prepare a bath for you. And I did, but the water was very cold because I forgot to turn the hot water on. I put you inside the bathtub, and you started shivering and crying. But almost in that instant, the water around you started to heat up. By the time Victoria came in, you had stopped crying. You had changed the water's temperature to your needs on pure instinct."

"So, you think I can control which element? Water?"

Mary shrugged. "Perhaps. Or perhaps fire. The truth is, with the right amount of concentration, knowledge, and imagination, most elements can be manipulated to achieve similar ends."

But James didn't seem to be listening. Suddenly, he was lost in his thoughts. "You really think that I am capable?"

"I'm positive."

James turned his head to George, who nodded his agreement. He couldn't believe any of this. He just couldn't. This was science fiction; something you might see on TV but not in real life. With so much information, the cloudiness in his head started to turn into pain.

"I'm sorry for interrupting," Kymil said, putting his hands on the table and crossing his fingers. "I would like to see the letter if you don't mind. I must be on my way."

James raised his eyebrows.

"Could you give us the letter your mother left you?" Mary asked, placing her hand on James' in his lap. "Do you have it with you?"

"Yes, I do, but what does this have to do with anything? How do you even know about it?"

"Can you show us?" Mary asked.

James stood up and turned around. His suitcase was nowhere to be seen. Before James started to panic, Mary said that it had been taken to his room by one of the men who had accompanied them from the church.

"My room?" James asked. "I have a room here?"

"Of course! Did you think we were going to make you sleep outside?" Mary said before turning to Kymil. "Back in a minute." And she stood up and led James away from the table.

As they approached the back of the room, Mary pushed open a big wooden door, and they stepped into another long dark hallway with many doors on both sides. Without any warning, candles on the walls started lighting up as they walked. As they passed the fifth set of doors, Mary stopped and pointed to the one on the right-hand side. "This is the bathroom, and your room is a little further down the hall. Number thirty-two. And please, when you're done, bring your mother's letter with you."

James entered the bathroom, locked the door, and faced a mirror on the other side of the wall. "What am I doing here? What is going on?" he asked himself.

Before leaving the bathroom, James washed his face and hands with cold water. As he reached for the door handle, he heard distant mumbling outside. Without hesitation, he stepped outside, but when he turned his head to the left and then to the right, there was nobody there. Deciding he was too exhausted after such a long day and even longer evening and that he must have imagined it, he turned and walked down the hall to the room marked number thirty-two. It was unlocked, so he stepped inside cautiously and looked around. There was a neatly folded bed on the left with a nightstand and a burning fireplace on the right. Beside it was a comfortable-looking chair and a shelf filled with books. The room had no window but that didn't bother James; after spending his whole life in an orphanage and sleeping in a breezy hut for the last few weeks, the room was pure luxury.

Beside the bed was his suitcase. He opened it and retrieved his mother's letter and put it in his pocket. Before heading back to the hall, he decided to have a quick pass of the books on the shelf, but as he approached the fireplace, something caught his attention. The fireplace was burning but there was no heat coming from the flames. He moved closer but still couldn't feel anything. Then he remembered when Mary had sent the sphere of fire into his hand, and he slowly eased his hand toward the flames until his fingers were completely consumed by them; nothing more than a tingling sensation. He felt perplexed—he knew it wasn't normal—but he again reminded himself that he was too tired to process this information properly and it would have to wait until the next day. So, he took his hand out of the fire, moved away from the fireplace, and stepped into the hallway.

Before he could rejoin the others in the hall, he heard them. Dalnur, especially, with his deep, booming voice was yelling, but James couldn't distinguish what he was shouting about. As they saw him enter the hall, everyone went quiet. He approached his seat and put his mother's letter on the table. Mary took it at once and started reading it. After a while, James noticed that Mary's eyes were watering.

Did Mary know my mother? James asked himself. Were they close? Of course, she said something about bathing me when I was only three months old…

Before James could finish his thought, Kymil asked Mary for the letter. The elf stood up, took a flask out of his robe, uncorked it, and poured some of the bluish liquid inside over the letter. James wanted to protest but he stopped himself when he saw new words appearing on the paper. The words were blue, just like the liquid, and vanished after a few seconds, but it was enough time for everybody to read them.

"Who is Wanda Wolgor?" James asked.

But no one answered. By now, everyone who had been sitting was standing. James could see that everyone recognized the name, but they just stared at each other. After waiting for a couple of moments, James repeated the question. But again, no one answered. Instead, Kymil took a sip from his glass, bowed his head, and wished them a good evening.

Dalnur followed a moment afterward, and as the two of them left, Mary slumped into her chair. George did so, too, albeit more slowly and carefully. But James stayed on his feet.

"I asked a question," James said as calmly as he could.

Mary urged him to sit down. As he did, she turned her body to face him. "Listen to me, James. Your mother and I were very close. We had been working together just before she disappeared seventeen years ago. Victoria was the most wonderful person I knew. Everybody loved her. So, when I was fourteen, and your mother asked me if I would help her on occasion, I accepted immediately. James..."—Mary leaned in closer and put both her fingers around James' hands—"I was with your mother the day she left you in the orphanage. You were four months old. That's how I knew she left a letter with you. I watched her write it. At least, I thought I did. Victoria must have added that secret message when I wasn't looking. Believe me, James, I have never seen a person who cried more than your mother did that day. Never."

Mary took a deep breath and slowly exhaled before continuing. "She disappeared three days later. To this day, we don't know what happened to her. She just vanished. I have looked for her ever since but I haven't found a trace of her. The same day you left the orphanage, we received a note telling us where to find you and that we had to look 'closely' at your mother's letter. I don't know who wrote that note, but evidently, it was someone who has been keeping an eye on you. I immediately sent a team to watch over you at the docks. We had wanted to wait until you were eighteen to reveal all this to you; that had always been our plan.

But as you can tell from the terrible things that have been happening, you are in danger. We had to react; we had to help get you away sooner than we'd planned."

James was quiet for a long time after that. Mary asked George to bring her a drink, but everyone at the table knew it was just an excuse to give James space to process.

"You...knew my mother?" he said eventually.

Mary sniffed and wiped away a tear. "I did."

"And...she loved me? She didn't want to give me up?"

Mary shook her head. "Not for a moment."

They sat in silence again for a while longer.

"Thank you for telling me all that, Mary," James whispered. "Of all the questions I should be asking right now, I don't know why this is the one bothering me so much, but can you tell me, who is this Wanda Wolgor? Why is her name on my mother's letter?"

Mary looked at the floor, put her palms together, and rubbed them slightly. "Yes, Wanda." Mary exhaled as she said the name. "She is a special person. Her father was human but her mother was an elf; interbreeding between races has long been forbidden and, as far as we know, Wanda is the only half-human half-elf alive today. We think so, anyway; she hasn't been seen in years."

"OK, but what's the issue? Why did you all react like that when you saw her name?"

"Listen, James, she's one of the most dangerous people on this planet. By mixing races, she has the best traits of the human and elven races. But she also has all the worst of our two races, as well. Elves and humans are very different. An elf speaks of logic, peace, and control, while a human is unpredictable and temperamental. Elves generally live to serve everyone, while humans are fundamentally selfish. Imagine struggling with such different traits as part of your nature. Such people are often unstable and all hell can break loose. It often did with such children, which is why such inter-species relationships were banned to begin with."

"But what does that have to do with *us*?" James said.

"Wanda was born among us. She lived with her father and mother until she was thirteen, when she vanished, but not before promising to avenge her father's death. Long story short, Wanda's father was killed, and she blamed us all for his death. No one knows where she is, but we haven't heard from her in so long that everyone had kind of forgotten what a threat she is. Seeing her name on your mother's letter—"

"Means she might still be out there, plotting her revenge," James said firmly. "I see. But what makes her so dangerous?"

It took Mary a while to summon a response, during which time George returned with some drinks and sat down on the chair where Kymil had been sitting across the table.

"Wanda Wolgor is widely known in our world. By our world, I mean elementals, dwarfs, elves, and so on. Her father was a human by the name of Drago, but her mother was an elf. Their marriage was one of the reasons the war started; many opposed it. Many of the elves, humans, and dwarfs protested against mixing between races because they were afraid of what could happen if a child was born. What powers could it have? What would happen if they produced an unstable child who was too powerful for anyone else to stop?"

"How was it their fault the war started?" James asked.

"I didn't say it was their fault. It wasn't. They simply fell in love. I don't think they ever even planned on having a baby, but one way or another, a few years after they married, she got pregnant. Wanda's mother was and looked like the happiest elf in the world. You know, elves have a far longer lifespan than humans. They live up to eight hundred years."

"Eight hundred years?" James asked, his eyes widening.

"The oldest elf recorded was one thousand and one years old." Mary held an expression that told him not to interrupt. "For elves, the first eighty years of their lives are considered childhood."

"Eighty-two years to be precise," George added while filling their glasses.

"Yes, eighty-two," Mary said. "At eighty-two years old, an elf is considered an adult. The reason why Wanda's mother was so happy being pregnant is that it is very hard for elves to conceive. Some couples go many decades, even longer, trying to have a baby, so for her to be expecting after only a few months was, they thought, a blessing. With time, people in our community started to accept the family, but many others elsewhere didn't approve. One day, we found her father's body in their house, distorted beyond recognition. Meanwhile, Wanda and her mother just...disappeared."

James waited for more information, but it was not forthcoming.

"You should get some rest," Mary said, standing up. "There will be plenty of time to discuss this and so much more tomorrow."

"You think that I'll be able to sleep tonight?" James asked. "My life has changed completely. I want to know more. I want to know everything."

"I know you do. I doubt I'll sleep either. But I believe I have given you a lot today. Maybe too much. You have lived in ignorance for seventeen years. A little while longer won't change anything." She waited for a moment for her words to sink in. "James, I know you're curious. I would be, too. But as I mentioned before, I am not the best person to explain everything. You'll get your answers soon, trust me."

James smiled and patted Mary's hand. "OK. I understand. Thank you."

"It's been a long day, and there will be longer ones to come. Try to get some sleep. If you can't sleep, then just try to rest as best you can."

James excused himself and went to leave the hall. When he opened the door leading to the hallway, he saw a woman dressed in black disappearing into what he was sure was his room. There was something familiar about her, but he couldn't place her. He marched down the hallway quickly, just short of breaking into a run, when he heard a loud bang. Then another one. And another. He dove to the floor as he heard people shouting, footsteps pounding against the floor, then another bang that was followed by three more. James curled into a ball and froze. He couldn't move. He could feel his heart pounding hard in his chest and his legs started shaking violently.

All of a sudden, a door burst open, and George wrapped his arms around James. "Put your head down and follow me!"

George pulled James to his feet and supported him as they walked down the hall. Every time James lost the feeling in his legs and he collapsed to the floor, the old man pulled him back up. “Get a grip!” George slapped James across the face.

As George dragged him down the hallway, James turned his head and caught a glimpse of what was going on behind them. Although the hallway was full of smoke, James could see bodies lying on the floor beyond where he had collapsed. Burned bodies. He could also see a few people dressed in black, and they were walking toward him.

“In here!” George said as they reached the main hall. But just as he pushed the door open, the wall exploded, throwing James to the ground. One of the bricks hit him hard in the chest, and he had to gasp to try and catch his breath. He turned his head and saw George lying motionless on the floor. James tried to stand up but couldn’t; the pain running through his body overwhelmed him. He could still hear distant screams and shouts but couldn’t move.

Just like that, there was a figure beside James. His first thought was that the people in black had caught him and were about to finish the job of killing him. But as his vision cleared, he saw it was Mary standing over him, and she was doing something with her hands. Steam started to build up and he felt himself being pulled to his feet and shoved into the main hall. As they cleared the hallway, James heard another loud bang and then the ceiling collapsed behind him.

“Let’s move!” Mary lifted James’ arm over her shoulders to support his weight.

James struggled to stay on his feet as they ran to the other end of the hall and exited the building. Still gasping, James saw a van waiting for them outside. James, Mary, and three of the people who had collected James from the church earlier that night climbed into it.

"Go, go, go!" Mary shouted.

The driver stepped on the gas, and they were off. Behind them, James could see smoke billowing out of the palace as shadowy figures ran into the square outside.

"Where to?" the driver asked.

Mary exhaled and turned to face forward. "Home."

CHAPTER 7

HOMECOMING

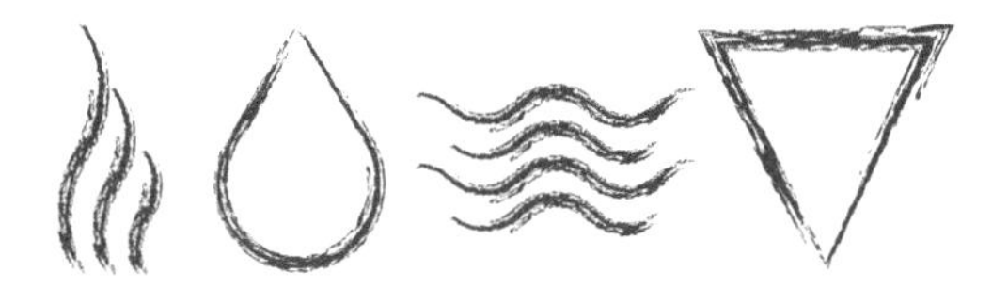

AFTER DRIVING IN SILENCE for what seemed like an eternity, James felt his heartbeat start to return to normal, although he still felt dizzy and struggled to focus as the world went by outside the van window. Still, he had enough presence of mind to recognize the route the driver was taking: they were heading back to the docks.

"How the hell did they find us?" the driver asked.

"I hate to say it, but the only explanation is that someone was either careless and followed, or worse, someone ratted us out." Mary turned to James with a heavy frown. "How are you feeling, James? Are you OK?"

James tried to respond that he was fine, but he could only produce a mumble. Eventually, he just closed his eyes and nodded.

"We're arriving at the docks. We'll be safe soon, then you can rest."

Sure enough, a few minutes later, the driver turned the van into the docks and parked it behind one of the more dilapidated warehouses. Everything was a blur to James as hands grabbed him and bundled him out of the van and onto the wet cobblestones. He felt himself being leaned against a cold wire fence.

"Would you mind?" Mary said to one of her companions.

The man raised his hand toward the fence, and like paper flapping in the wind, the fence started to bend and tear itself apart.

That's impossible, James thought to himself.

A few seconds later, there was a hole in the fence big enough for the group to climb through. The man that had somehow bent and folded the fence stepped through first, and James felt himself being supported on both sides as he was carefully moved through the hole.

"Come on," Mary said quietly. "It's not far."

They walked a few hundred feet, and Mary pointed to the big boat anchored nearby. The group clambered aboard, careful not to drop James in the water as they guided him across the walkway before lowering him onto one of the rear-facing seats. One of the passengers untied the boat, while Mary started the engine. Slowly and quietly, they moved away from the docks and across the dark water, into the night.

Several minutes later, they started to pick up speed. With the roar of the engine and the sound of the boat skipping over the waves in his ears, James felt Mary sit beside him. James was massaging his chest, trying to ease away the pain that was still causing him some trouble with his breathing.

"I'm OK," James said before Mary could say anything. "W-What happened? Who were those people? What do they want from you?"

Mary sighed. "Actually, I believe they were after you."

"Me?" James said, gasping as the cold sea air started to penetrate his burning chest and lungs. "What do they want with me?"

Mary shook her head. "Maybe your mother's letter? Maybe they heard about the secret message and they wanted to know what it said. I'm sorry, James. I really don't know." Mary reached across to stroke James' shoulder. "I'm sorry. I thought I could protect you there. But where we're going now is even safer."

"Where?" James struggled to say.

"You'll see. A little more patience. It's a long journey. You should get some rest in the meantime," Mary said. "You can go below deck and get some sleep."

James woke up in one of the small cabins a few hours later. The bed was the same width as the room, so he had to roll over it to get to the door, but he was grateful he had managed to get some rest. He hovered by the door for a moment. In the small space, he could marvel at the beauty of the blue wasteland outside the small, round window that stretched for as far as his eyes could see. He could breathe in the cool morning air that seeped under the door and soothed his screaming chest and lungs. And he could pretend everything he had seen and learned the previous night had been a figment of his imagination—the sphere of fire, the explosions, the men and women that had tried to kill him, George... But he knew it had all happened. Somehow, his world had turned upside down, and there was no going back.

As James made his way up to the main deck, he had to shield his eyes from the strong morning sunlight that shone brightly in a cloudless sky. The sun felt hotter than usual. He felt the ship sway beneath him and had to adjust his balance until he found his sea legs. He closed his mouth and took a deep breath in through his nose, smelling and even tasting the salt. It was wonderful. He had tasted the air every day while working at the docks, but it had never tasted as good; it had always been mixed with the harsh flavor of petrol and diesel fumes from the ships on the water, and the stink of hot solder and grinding metal in the warehouses and shipyards. Out here, in the middle of nowhere, the air was pure. No land, no cars, no boats. The nearest human beings were above him, where he saw a single plane gliding through the open expanse of the sky, leaving nothing but a white trail in its wake.

"Good morning," Mary said.

James turned his head and saw Mary coming up the steps behind him from below deck. "Morning," he replied as he seated himself in one of the plastic seats on the port side. He tried again to fill his lungs with the fresh breeze, but this time, a sharp pain caused him to cough and squirm in pain.

"You OK?" Mary asked.

"Where are we going?"

"An island in the Bahamas. One on which our ancestors built a safe haven, a home, and one we've managed to keep hidden all these years. A place where you can rest and learn."

"Learn?"

"Yes. Learn." Mary replied. "Every elemental has to learn about the powers they possess. Only by learning can you really control elements in the right way."

"Can you please show me again?" James asked. "Please?"

Mary looked at James, almost as though she was studying him, then she stood up. "I can show you but I cannot teach you how to do it. For that, you must wait until we arrive." She signaled to someone James couldn't see to stop the boat, rolled up her sleeves, and approached the edge of the boat. She closed her eyes, and moments later, the sea around the boat began to freeze. James didn't know what was more shocking: the waves coming to a halt in mid-flow or the ice steps that slowly started to form at the side of the boat.

One by one, Mary stepped down each step and onto the ice, where she then gestured for James to do the same. James couldn't help but feel unsure, so he didn't move at first, but then Mary outstretched her arm, and he took it. They both stepped onto the ocean's solid surface carefully, planting their feet wide to avoid slipping.

"Don't be afraid," Mary said, still holding his arm. "My elements are fire and water. I can manipulate them however I want."

James looked around and saw that the stairs had already melted away. The only ice left was the few square meters around their feet while, just beyond, the ocean continued to ripple and roll as usual. Mary's smile calmed his nerves, and with every step she took, new ice formed beneath them, and James shuffled behind her before the old ice melted away behind them. James felt like he was creeping forward at such a slow pace that when he turned around to see the boat, he had expected it to be within touching distance still. Instead, it was almost one hundred feet away, and the dark expanse of undulating deep blue ocean between them and the boat made James feel sick. As he started to ask something, a strong cold wind started to blow, and seconds later, a thick, lingering streak of forked lightning scorched the sky and struck the sea a mile away. James fell down to his knees in fear, but he was soon overcome with confusion at the sound of distant laughter. He turned to Mary, who wore an angry expression that she was directing at the boat.

"Enough!" Mary screamed, and the laughter from the boat immediately died away. "Marcus, stop acting like a child! Have you forgotten how you felt the first time you found out about your abilities?" She pulled James to his feet, and they walked back to the boat, all the while the ice formed beneath their feet and vanished behind them. As they clambered onto the boat, Mary shot an angry look at Marcus, who silently slipped away without saying a word. Turning to James, she apologized.

"For what?" James asked, grabbing onto the same seat he'd been sitting in earlier as if his life depended on it.

"That was Marcus. He created the lightning that scared you."

"Why?"

"Because he thinks it's funny and because he is a child," Mary answered, raising her voice.

"But I thought there were only four elements. You didn't say anything about lightning."

"This is why it's important to learn about your elements from someone who knows how best to teach you. Elements can combine in different ways to create unique effects. Marcus can control water and air, so he can manipulate clouds, moisture levels, and air temperature to create bolts of lightning. Lightning is not hard to create, but it's very hard to control where it's going to strike. Marcus happens to be pretty good at it. He's one of the best, in fact. Unfortunately, he knows this."

Soon enough, Mary and James were aboard, and the boat was moving again, so James started to relax now he was back among things as they should be. The ocean was flowing, no one was summoning lightning, and he could just rest his eyes and enjoy the warm sun as it grew hotter and hotter as they neared the Bahamas. He drifted between thoughts of his mother, the powers he supposedly possessed, and how his life had changed to more mundane questions like how the weather could be so clear during storm season in the Bahamas. As he decided, like everything else it seemed, it must be down to magic, he drifted to sleep, only to be startled awake when Mary tapped him on the shoulder.

"We're nearly there," Mary's voice was soft and apologetic. She pointed to the horizon ahead, and James spied a tall albeit faded island that rippled in the rising heat. "Welcome to Leilani Reef."

"We're in the Bahamas already?" James asked. "As far as I know, the Bahamas is a very populated place. I thought we were going somewhere more secluded."

"Our island is well hidden. It doesn't belong to the Bahamas but it's in that area."

"Hidden how?" James asked, raising his eyebrows. He wanted to scoff at the idea of hiding an entire island, but he'd had enough surprises over the last twenty-four hours than to think he knew better.

"We, that is, our ancestors, used our powers to master ocean travel long before regular humans managed it. After they founded Leilani Reef, they used the elements to manipulate what people can see and sense when they approach it. If a ship gets too close, for example, we summon a storm to force it to change course. And above our island, we maintain a perfect mixture of air and water to reflect the surrounding water, something like a mirror. When anyone looks down from above, be it by plane or satellite, they see only water. Only those who reside there know about its existence."

"And how come I can see the island now?"

"Because we've allowed it," Mary said. James sighed and rested his head in his palm. "What's wrong?"

"What's wrong? What do you mean what's wrong? I lived in the normal world yesterday. With normal people. Literally overnight, everything has changed. Elementals, dwarfs, elves, hidden islands. Yesterday, I touched fire with my bare hand and it didn't burn me. Today, I walked on water."

"Hey, slow down," Mary said, calmly grabbing him by his shoulder. "Look at me. I know it's a lot to digest, but there was no other way. We didn't have time to introduce you to our world slowly. And I'm really sorry about that. I know how you must feel."

"You know nothing," James said, turning away. He watched the land coming closer and closer and he could feel his heart pumping in his throat. As the island came into sharper focus, the first thing he noticed was the thick forest that lined the tops of the steep cliffs that formed the coast. Nearer still, James coves of beautiful sandy beaches with palm trees. And finally, as the boat slowed as they approached a small jetty, he noticed the small collection of people waiting to welcome them. He recognized the first figure at once; it was the elf named Kymil. With his silver hair tied back and hands crossed in front of him, he seemed to stand even taller in the bright Mexican Gulf sunshine. Beside him were a boy and a girl, both of whom were waving excitedly. Apparently, the men and women aboard the boat were just as pleased to see everyone waiting for them; their voices became louder, the laughter picked up, and the boat started to sound with the banging of hurried footsteps as everyone on board hurried up and down the steps to bring their belongings onto the deck, ready to depart.

"Come on, James," Mary said. "You are home."

James, feeling thrilled and scared at the same time, stepped onto the pier after her. As he did so, the boy and the girl walked over to him.

"My name is Mike. And this is my sister, Venessa."

"Hi," Venessa said with a smile on her face. "Welcome to Leilani Reef."

"Hello, Mike. Hello, Venessa," James replied, turning his head from one to another.

"We heard you were attacked," Mike said enthusiastically. "Do you know who did it? And why? What do you have that they're after? Has the palace hideout been demolished? Are you staying with us? Are you going—?"

"OK. That's enough," Mary said. "Let's get James to the village first, then he should get some rest. It's been a tough journey. Lead the way, Mike."

Mike agreed, albeit with a little discontent on his face, but when James smiled at him, his disappointment vanished at once. James turned around and found himself before the elf; when he bowed his head, James did the same.

"How did you get here before us?" James asked.

"We drove," Kymil replied calmly, and James could swear he saw his lip twitch slightly.

"What do you mean? Like in a car?"

"In a jeep, to be precise," Kymil replied.

"Yeah, right, a jeep that drives on water." James made no attempt to hide the annoyance in his sarcasm.

"But we did. In this case, it's not about the vehicle; it's about the surface."

James' eyes widened as he understood what Kymil meant. "Ice," he said with a heavy breath. "You froze a path across the ocean and drove on it."

Kymil looked at James with contentment in his eyes. "You'd best get on, James. There will be more time for us to chat."

James hurried off after Mary, Mike, and Venessa, who had started walking into the forest. They walked in single file as they followed a small, barely discernible path.

"Go on," Mary said, inviting James to follow Mike and Venessa while she brought up the rear.

He slipped through the trees and, after only twenty feet or so, found himself standing in a basketball court-size clearing with two off-road vehicles parked on each side. On the other side of the clearing was a dirt road that seemed to only lead deeper into the island's thick forest.

"Can I ride with you?" Mike asked, looking at James.

"Erm, I guess."

And so, they all clambered into one vehicle: Mary behind the wheel, Venessa riding shotgun, and Mike and James in the back. Mary started the car and off they went, the light growing dimmer as they drove deeper and deeper into the forest. Big trees covered up the sun, and it looked like early evening although James knew it was a little past noon. For a while, the road got steeper, too, and after about fifteen minutes, and a lot of questions from Mike, something caught James' eye. The forest started to clear, the road started to level off, and James spotted people further in the forest, working on both sides of the road. It looked like they were planting something, but before he could ask a question, Mary stopped the car, and a man approached them.

"Hi, Jimmy," Mary said.

The man raised his hand and made a couple quick hand movements before looking at the back seat of the car.

"Yes, we did," Mary said, turning her head toward James.

With another few hand movements, Jimmy smiled at James, and Mary drove on.

"Jimmy can't speak. He said thank god you're OK, and that he is glad you are here."

Barely a moment later, Mary pulled over again. They had reached the other side of the forest, and what James saw through the windshield took his breath away. Mary had put the car into park just a few meters from the edge of a steep cliff that marked one side of a big, wide chasm. On the other side of the gap was a high plateau surrounded by a big wall with double wooden gates. Behind the wall, he could see a large stone building that resembled a castle that had been renovated and modernized. An old wooden bridge connected the two sides. It swayed ever so slightly in the wind but otherwise looked secure, wide, and strong for three cars to cross at once, side by side. Eventually, James stepped out of the car at last and joined the others at the edge of the deep chasm, his heart pumping and legs shaking as he looked down. He couldn't see the bottom; the trees lining the steep cliffs simply disappeared into the fog below.

"You should see the look on your face," Mary said with a wide grin. "This is our sanctuary. An island within an island. Here, we live, learn, and try to keep the balance in the world."

Everyone jumped back in the car, and as soon as the front wheels touched the bridge, James felt his heart pound every time he heard a crack from the bridge or felt a wheel slip off one of the planks. But they reached the other side without incident, where James found himself up close to the thick wooden gates that were much larger than he'd envisioned on the other side of the bridge. He saw strange engravings on the door made of gold and silver color.

"What do they mean?"

Mary looked at the gates and then back at James. "There is no element strong enough to conquer another; only the mind can conquer another. It means that every element is as important as the next. Water can extinguish fire just as fire can boil water. Do you see what I mean? In short, there is no strongest or weakest element. They are all only as strong as the person using them. Thus, it is your imagination and concentration—your mind—that make all the difference."

As James pondered this, the gates started to open, and Mary started to edge the car forward slowly. Once they were through and into the small clearing on the other side, the gates started to close behind them, and Mary parked the car.

A few hundred meters away, James saw small wooden houses arranged into neat rows. People sat outside them, talking and laughing, reminding James of the barbecue he had seen on his way from the orphanage to the docks. But unlike the Miami family that had eyed him suspiciously, these people waved when they saw James, Mike, Venessa, and Mary, and greeted them as they approached. A few kids were playing on the basketball court nearby, and as they followed the path, James saw it branched off in many different directions, with some leading deeper into the ever-present forest. Flowers of all possible sizes and colors lined the stony pathways and filled the many gardens James passed, broken up only by the tall, Victorian-era-looking street lamps every twenty feet or so. Despite the pathway twisting and turning, James noticed how the largest path, the one they were following, was leading them on an uphill incline. At the top, looking over everything, was the old stone castle-like building James had seen from across the chasm.

"That's where we're going." Mary tapped James on the shoulder and then pointed at the enormous stone building, shortly before they left the rows of houses behind and entered another small patch of forest.

"What is this place?"

"Your new home." Mary took his hand and squeezed it gently. As she did so, James felt her warmth and kindness. There was no question she had made this whole terrible experience that much easier to bear, and with each passing moment by Mary's side, his attachment to her grew. She made him feel relaxed and safe in this new strange new world, so he allowed himself to get excited. Excited to explore the colossal building and the rest of the plateau. Excited to learn more about these people, the power of the elements, and his past.

The forest grew slowly thinner and the building loomed larger as they emerged back into the warm sunshine. It rose up some sixty feet in the air, James estimated, and must have been at least three hundred feet wide. Large wooden gates had been left wide open, instantly making the imposing structure appear so much more welcoming. Despite the gesture, James walked slowly to the entrance, his stomach clenching in time with his every step.

Mary invited him to enter first, and Mike and Venessa stopped short of the entrance as well, so James leaned his head into the large lobby slowly. The building seemed spacious inside. A stone staircase occupied the middle of the foyer, which led up to the other floors, while James could see the lobby branched off into several corridors on both the left- and right-hand sides. Whether she grew impatient, James didn't know, but Mary took his hand and led him down a wide corridor behind the stairs and to the back of the building. On the way, they passed a kitchen and a large, spacious living room before they arrived in a dining hall that could comfortably seat over two hundred people and probably many more if people were willing to squeeze in. James was accustomed to living with lots of people since he had grown up in the orphanage, but this hall made his old canteen look like a quaint café.

"Come on," Mary said, looking at her watch and pulling James further into the dining hall. "It's almost two. You have to eat something and then you can rest."

"Rest?" James asked. "I don't need rest. I don't need to eat. I need answers! I need somebody who can tell me what is going on."

"Look. First, we eat because I haven't eaten anything since yesterday and I am starving. After that, you can decide for yourself if you want to rest or not. OK?"

James looked into her eyes and felt his frustration diminish. When he looked away from her, his attention was caught by Mike and Venessa. They had grabbed a table for six and were ushering Mary and him over to join them.

"Come, sit here, James," Mike said. "You don't mind if we join you, right?"

James sat down, suddenly eager for food, and he felt a little guilty for snapping at Mary as he had done. She was right; he was starving, as well.

As soon as they sat down at the table, a young man approached them with a cart full of various drinks and juices. James felt overwhelmed by the options, so he only chose water, but after Mary, Mike, and Venessa each chose some exotic fruit juice James had never heard of before, he asked the young man to replace his water with freshly squeezed orange juice. The young man obliged, and James thanked him before he wheeled his cart off to the next table.

James took his first sip, closed his eyes, and sighed at the sheer pleasure washing over his taste buds. When he opened his eyes again, he almost jumped out of his skin; Mike was staring at him with wide eyes and a curious grin. "When are you going to see the old man?"

"Old man?" James asked.

"Mike, please," Mary said. "Let's at least have lunch in peace and then we can—"

"Old man?" James asked again, this time with more certainty in his voice.

Mary shot Mike a hard look, who seemed to recoil. She let out a long, slow sigh. "The old man, as many of us call him, is a walking encyclopedia of knowledge. His name is Arick. Do you remember I told you I wasn't the best person to teach you all you need to know? Well, Arick is that person...not us!" Mary raised her voice while looking at Mike.

The young man with the cart came back around, only this time it was loaded up with plates and metal trays filled with a vast array of food. James smelled it before he saw it, and when he turned to look at the selection of buffalo chicken wings, tater tots, barbecue ribs, pot roast, meatloaf, and various side dishes and salads, he could feel his saliva glands going into overdrive. He had never seen such a variety of food in one place. There were more kinds of sauces than he knew the names of, spices that he doubted he'd be able to pronounce, and the desserts looked so good that he had to ask the young man not to show them to him until after he'd eaten a hot meal.

But what distracted him more than the slices of apple pie, banana splits, and peach cobbler, together with ice cream and chocolate chip cookies, all of which were neatly arranged on small plates, was how only he seemed to be appreciating the food. The others picked out a plate like it was nothing, while James could barely process what he should eat, and he felt guilty for having so much choice.

Everyone was patient with James, however, and he eventually did eat until he couldn't take another bite. He'd forgotten what they had been talking about by the end of the meal, but Mike was quick to remind him.

"So, you've eaten," he said, smirking at Mary, whose face fell. "Will you go and see Arick now?"

"He's not here?"

"No," Mike said, "he doesn't live in the Castle or any of the houses we passed on the way up. He lives on the other side of the island."

"You call this building the Castle?" James realized it made sense as he saw Mike and Venessa nodding.

Mary rolled her eyes, got to her feet, and grabbed James by the hand. "Fine. If it means you three will give me a moment's peace." Mike and Venessa moved to get up, as well, but Mary pointed a finger at them. "No, just James."

As they exited the dining hall, James glanced at the others and saw them still talking and laughing. He saw how happy they were and became distinctly aware that it was something he had never experienced before. His life had never been so comfortable and carefree to allow time to sit around and joke.

Rather than lead James back out the way they had come, Mary walked him over to a side door that opened out to the back of the Castle. "His house is at the back of the plateau, right at the very edge and overlooking a bay. It'll take us about ten minutes to walk there. A few tips. Arick knows the best way to explain everything to you so that you can understand. Interrupting him will only slow him down. If he offers you tea, don't refuse. And one more thing, the old man sometimes wanders off, so to speak; he gets a bit lost in his thoughts. Just be patient with him."

Walking down the dusty path, they met several people who greeted them. Mary exchanged a few words with some before continuing, while James admired the various homes, communal buildings, and gardens.

"This is beautiful," James said. "The island, the nature. It's so peaceful."

"I'm glad you like it," Mary said, grinning slightly.

"How long have you been here?"

"Me? I was born here. So were you, James."

"Really?" James felt his lip quiver.

Mary nodded and smiled a sad smile.

"And what about the rest of them?"

"We elementals have been here for a very long time. Some of these people were born here, like you and me, while others have migrated here from other communities over the years."

James considered this information carefully. "So, there are more places like this around the world?"

"Several," Mary replied. "And they're all just as well hidden." James opened his mouth to speak, but Mary closed her eyes and silenced him by raising her hand. "James, your questions are relentless." She smiled again. "Fortunately for me, that's Arick's home; he can have his turn with you." She pointed toward a small wooden house built into the side of a few large boulders with no sound nearby but the chirping of birds and the rustling of leaves in the wind. "Don't be fooled by the size of the place. What you see is just the part of the house that leads to the lower, more spacious sections with a sea view. Arick likes to be isolated in some way where he can think in silence."

Together, they entered the house, and immediately, James noticed how the salty and fresh air was replaced by the musty smell of wood and dirt. They found themselves in a room that contained almost nothing but stairs leading to a lower level, a few paintings on the wall, and a hanger on which hung several jackets, sweaters, and vests. Under the hanger, James saw small shelves with shoes and slippers.

"Please take off your shoes and put on a pair of those slippers. Arick likes his house clean. And when you're ready, go downstairs."

"You are not coming with me?" James asked.

"I'm afraid not," Mary replied. "You don't need me down there. I'll be back for you later."

James watched Mary leave the house. He changed his shoes for a pair of slippers, took a deep breath, and went down the stairs. They ended in the middle of a large hallway that stretched in both directions.

Mary was right, James thought. The house is a lot bigger than it looks from the outside.

The walls were rough-hewn stone, while the floor was made of stone tiles. Every few feet, small lamps burned on the wall, giving a special, even magical reflection to the space. There was complete and deafening silence in the hallway, and it took James a few moments to get used to it. Only then did he hear the sound coming from the room opposite from where he was standing. It was the sound of a low, barely audible, crackling fire. James took a few deep breaths, approached, and lifted his fist to knock when he heard someone's voice from the other side of the door.

"Come in, James."

CHAPTER 8

ANSWERS

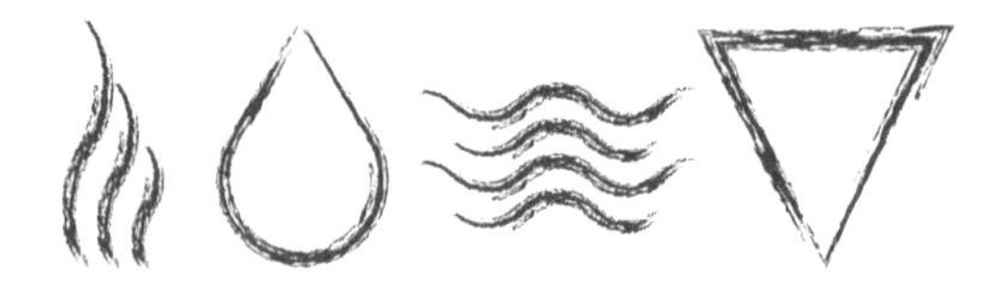

JAMES PUSHED THE DOOR to reveal a small room with a large desk in its center that was buried beneath piles of paper and strange objects. On the front of the table, James recognized the engraved symbols of the elements. Like those he had seen on the dome of the palace, he noted the mysterious fifth carving, the jagged infinite sign, at the center of the four he now knew well. On the left wall was an antique-looking world map that stretched from floor to ceiling. In front of the desk were two chairs, and sitting behind the desk, James saw an elderly man with gray hair scribbling some notes in a leather-bound book. The two lamps on the wall behind the desk were the only light in the room; there were no windows due to them being underground, and the space reminded James of a dungeon, albeit an extremely clean one with a leathery fragrance.

"Hello," James said.

The man sitting at the desk raised his head, smiled at James, and offered him to sit in one of the chairs opposite him. "Let me just finish this," the man said with a quiet but strong voice.

James sat down and waited for the man to finish his scribbling. Meanwhile, he observed the room. The brickwork was punctuated with enormous pieces of stone that seemed to erupt into the space, and James concluded the house had been built against and into the existing stone, almost as if it had been as much excavated as it had been built.

The man stopped writing, closed his book, and turned to James. "So, you are James Tanner. I wasn't expecting you until tomorrow. I thought you'd want to settle in first. Welcome."

"Thank you. And you must be Arick?"

"I am. You know, the last time I saw you, you were this big." He held his hands out in front of himself about fifteen inches apart.

A small nervous smile escaped James, then a question came to his mind. "If you remember me when I was little, then surely you knew my mom, too?"

Arick maintained his friendly smile, but his eyes looked sad. "I did. Victoria Tanner lived here, on this very island. Your mother was a very special person; always helpful and putting the needs of others ahead of her own. We missed her when she left. We still do."

"So everyone keeps telling me. Why did she leave me in the orphanage, then? Was she more interested in others' well-being than mine?"

"No, you meant the world to her. She brought you to the orphanage to keep you safe."

"Safe from whom?"

Arick took a sip from his cup. "Kymil has told me about the secret message you all read hidden in your mother's letter."

"Wanda Wolgor," James said, reciting the name that Kymil had made appear with his mysterious potion.

"Wanda was very close with Victoria Tanner, and even more so when she found out your mother was going to have a baby. Wanda was an only child, you see; perhaps she hoped to be an older sister to you. Victoria let her help look after you. Wanda would visit her on a daily basis and she looked forward to the day you would come into this world. She would put her lips to your mother's belly and sing songs to you while your mother rested. The bond lasted until Wanda's father died, when she disappeared with her mother, never to be seen again. Both left under the impression your mother had killed Wanda's father, and Wanda swore vengeance.

"Now, it is only my presumption, but I believe your mother was afraid Wanda would avenge her father's death by taking away something she cherished more than anything else." Arick pointed a bony finger at James. "You."

Arick was quiet for a moment. James thought he was giving him time to respond, but before he could speak, Arick continued. "I realize this is all very confusing for you. A few weeks ago, you assumed your mother had simply not wanted you. A few days ago, the world looked very different. But the truth is, only Victoria knew the full truth as to why she left you at the orphanage, and who she thought she was protecting you from. So, instead of looking into your past, let's concentrate on your future." Arick's smile was warm, and James nodded. "I believe you have already learned something about our world."

"Mary has told me the basics, she says. She said she was not the right person to go into detail."

"And she was right," Arick replied while stroking his chin. "When it comes to the elements, you have to learn the right way. Everything you do, you must do the right way because doing something wrong can be catastrophic. I'm talking about the skills you possess. Your power to manipulate elements."

James didn't even blink and he could feel Arick's eyes boring into him.

When Arick seemed satisfied, he continued. "You see, there are four basic elements in life."

"Earth, fire, water, and air," James added at once.

"Correct. These four elements are the foundation of life on earth, but you probably knew that already. But what you didn't know, or at least, not before a few weeks ago, is that these elements can be manipulated. *You* can bend these elements of life to your will, James Tanner. To do good or, should you so choose, to do ill."

"Yes, Mary said as much. So, for example, if I can control water, I could summon waves in the sea. But people without this ability cannot."

"Not in the same way, perhaps, but it is possible to create waves without manipulating the water element. An air elemental might generate strong winds to whip the sea into a frenzy, for example. Or an earth elemental might generate a tsunami by causing an earthquake at the bottom of the sea. Of course, some of these require more energy and concentration than others, but all things are possible with the help of a medium."

"A medium?" James asked.

"Mary didn't explain mediums to you? She didn't tell you I was a medium? One of the most powerful, once upon a time."

"No," James said, his cheeks feeling hot.

"Never mind. Indulge me for now, and we will return to the subject shortly," Arick said. "Sticking with elements for a moment longer, the most important thing to know when manipulating the elements is to know when to stop. It requires an extraordinary amount of concentration and energy to control an element, and if you drain yourself before you're ready, it can lead you to collapse. There have even been cases of elementals dying from exhaustion while using their powers."

James felt his face pale and the hairs on his neck stand on end.

"You will begin your training in the coming days and weeks, but always remember, if you feel something is wrong, stop immediately. If you get blurry vision, stop immediately. If your element doesn't submit to your will as easily as you feel it should, stop immediately. These are some of the signs that your energy is running low. Controlling your element is not something you can 'push through' when you feel tired;

rather, it could cost you your life, or if you make a mistake, it could cost the life of someone nearby.

"The second important thing to understand about the importance of energy is that it's more important to be steady than forceful. Let's take a car, for example. If you're driving at full throttle, the car uses its gas much more quickly, so you deplete the tank faster. If you drive at a steady pace, you can drive further without stopping to refill. The same is true of your energy while controlling the elements. You have to temper your power. If you give it all the energy you have at once, you will soon be on your knees. Of course, give too little and you probably won't achieve anything. It's about finding the right balance, understand?"

"I think so," James replied.

"You don't," Arick said with a wink. "But I wouldn't expect you to. Not until you've tried to control the elements for yourself. For now, just try to take it all in and understand how important this is."

At that, Arick stood up. "Follow me," he said, then he walked out of the room and down the hallway until he led James through a big set of wooden doors. James' eyes watered at the sight of shelf upon shelf of leather-bound books that filled the left side of the room; books that looked simultaneously both ancient but in perfect condition. To the right, James could see a desk and a big low burning fireplace with an old sofa and two very comfortable-looking armchairs in front of it. There was a small coffee table that looked old and handmade between them, with two cups and a teapot on top of it. On the far side of the room was a wall made almost entirely of glass, with a panoramic view of the warm, blue sea and coast of the island. The view was entirely unobstructed, and James realized Arick's house must have been built into the side of a cliff edge that overlooked one side of the island.

Arick sat down in one of the chairs by the fireplace and gestured for James to do the same. With his eyes fixed on the magnificent view, James barely paid any attention to the teapot until it started to shake and steam began to rise out of its spout. It was just a normal porcelain pot and too far from the fire for that to be the source of its sudden increase in temperature, and James realized it must be Arick who was using his power to heat the water inside.

As if reading his thoughts, Arick gave James a wink. "Very good, James. You're learning." Arick then took out two tea bags from the box beneath the coffee table, put one in each cup, and poured some of the steaming water on top of it. "I know much of this must still seem impossible to you. But try to think of it this way: everything you have ever heard that seems like fiction or fantasy to you is, in one way or another, based on something true and possible. Every myth, every legend. For example, have you ever heard of a sorcerer?"

"Sorcerers are people who can do magic." James spoke slowly while eyeing Arick suspiciously.

"And wizards?" Arick asked.

"The same," James said.

"What's the difference?"

James shrugged. "Sorcerers use dark magic while wizards use their magic to do good. I don't really know. Why are you asking me? I am here to learn, aren't I?"

“Patience, James, patience.” Arick leaned on the table and took his cup of tea. “Without patience, there is no concentration, and without concentration, you will achieve nothing in this world of ours.”

James bowed his head.

“I am asking you because you wanted to know about mediums, correct? And I promised to tell you. Sorcerers, wizards, warlocks, whatever you want to call them, don’t exist. Those are myths that non-elemental humans invented to explain what we call mediums. Mediums are people born with a special ability: the ability to concentrate harder and for longer than anyone else. They can also channel the elements from elementals.

“It’s important to understand the difference here. Mediums aren’t technically elementals; they cannot manipulate fire, move rocks, or create waves on their own. Their power is that they can clear their heads and concentrate on only one thing. But they work in harmony with elementals to channel their power and energy to allow for more powerful phenomena. We talked earlier about earthquakes. No single elemental is powerful enough to create an earthquake strong enough to cause a tsunami, but if a strong medium can channel enough energy from many elementals at once, then it is possible.”

“I think I understand.” James watched the steam rising from his tea cup, but he was too busy thinking about everything Arick was saying to drink. “A medium on their own wouldn’t be of much use. But when they can channel the energy of elementals, they become more powerful than any one of them.”

"Precisely," Arick said, and James thought he sensed a hint of arrogance in the old man's tone. "If you ever come across a medium who you suspect is your enemy and who is not running away from you, then turn and run as fast as you can in the other direction."

"How—?"

"How can you recognize a medium? Normally you can't because they look like ordinary people. But when they are channeling energy from elementals, they enter a kind of trance. This is because, other than the small movements they might make with their bodies, they are utilizing their ability to concentrate; they are blocking out all other distractions to focus on their task. Ironically, while this is when they are at their most dangerous, it is also when they are at their most vulnerable."

Arick moved his gaze to the fireplace, and for a moment, seemed lost among the flames. James actually appreciated these moments when the old man would drift off briefly; they gave him time to process what he was being told.

"Arick?" James whispered when he was ready to speak again. "Arick?" he repeated, louder this time.

"Hm?" The old man blinked his heavy eyelids and turned his face away from the fire.

"What did you mean, every myth and legend is true in some way?"

"Well, let's put it to the test, shall we? Can you name a well-known wizard? One who has existed in literature for centuries?"

James shrugged. "Merlin?"

"Exactly! Well, Merlin was as real as you and I, but he was no wizard. He was a medium, and he is so well known because he was one of the most powerful mediums ever he ended up making quite the impression. Non-elemental people called him a sorcerer because they couldn't explain the magnificent, sometimes terrifying things he could do. He never traveled alone; he was always accompanied by at least two elementals, although he was always careful to keep them hidden from view. He drew from their power but made it look like he was doing everything alone." Arick laughed a little and leaned in closer to James. "In all honesty, the man was a bit of a show-off."

James listened closely and envisioned everything Arick said. In between Arick's short pauses, James delighted at the sound of the wood crackling in the fireplace.

"If mediums can only draw their power from others, how do they discover their abilities in the first place?" James asked.

Arick's face lit up. "You're a shrewd lad, aren't you? The answer is that many never realize what they're capable of. You see, elementals almost always discover their powers by themselves."

James immediately thought of the strange events that had occurred throughout his childhood in the orphanage. The in-door clouds, the shaking ground... He *had* been responsible for those events; it had been his abilities starting to manifest, only he'd had no one to tell him what was happening. James frowned a little. The principal had been right to get rid of me, he thought. I was a danger to everyone there. Who knows what damage I could have done if I'd stayed?

"Mediums, however," Arick continued, "must draw their power from somebody else. Without an elemental to lend them their power, or from whom they can otherwise forcibly take it, they simply cannot know of their abilities. Merlin was lucky; his father was an elemental who was able to help train and guide Merlin. But there are probably thousands of mediums out there in the world who will never know their true potential."

"Sorry," James said. "Did you say they can forcibly take an elemental's power?"

Arick swallowed hard. "It is a difficult task, but yes, for a skilled medium, it is possible to take an elemental's power without their consent. It is dangerous for all involved."

Again, Arick drifted into one of his trances, as if lost in some haunting memory. James remembered when Mary had told him to be patient with Arick, so instead of trying to snap him out of it, James stood up and moved to the other side of the room. In one corner, in front of the vast bookcase, James saw a large glass marine exhibit perched on four wooden legs. The floor of the tank was covered in small sharp-edged stones and a thin layer of grass. A thick wooden branch dominated most of the space and separated into several smaller branches. It was brittle and covered in moss, and there was a hole in one side that looked to be full of dead crickets and mealworms. Guessing they were the dinner for whatever creature inhabited the terrarium, James tapped the glass with his finger, and sure enough, the resident poked its head out of the hollow branch. He had several yellow spots and stripes on his body that made James think he was likely poisonous. A moment later, the small creature emerged from its hiding spot entirely, and James saw it was about eight inches long.

"A fire salamander," Arick said from just a couple of feet behind James, causing him to flinch. "You know that this tiny creature has no natural enemies? But it doesn't use its abilities to overstep or upset the natural ecosystem. It simply does what it can to survive and to live in peace."

James watched closely how the salamander used its small but powerful jaw to chew up one of the crickets before escaping back into its hole.

Arick put his hand on James' shoulder, walked him back to the chairs, and they sat down again.

Arick put his elbow on an armrest and leaned his head on his palm while gazing into the fireplace. "I believe that's enough for today. But it is just as important to think about the information you are given here as it is to acquire it. Some things require time and experience before we truly understand them."

James couldn't argue. He had questions, of course, and was eager to see if he really could manipulate any of the elements. But he could see how much the conversation was wearing on Arick, too.

"Thank you, Arick. But before I go—"

"Trust your elders, James. We have been training elementals for longer than you've been alive."

"This isn't about elementals or mediums," James said quickly. "Well, not really." He waited for Arick to ease himself back into his chair. "What can you tell me about Wanda? About what happened between her and my mother?"

"Did anyone tell you about Wanda's parents?"

"An elf mother and human father."

"For as long as we have written records, there have been people who opposed mixing the races on account of the powerful offspring they can produce. The first such child about whom we have any information was a boy called Arbane. His mother was human and his father was an elf. According to the stories, they were a happy family for many years. The father often traveled, leaving Arbane alone with his mother, and the two developed a close bond. So, when his mother died of a stroke, it...changed him. He became angry and obsessed with finding a way to bring her back. He was thirty-eight when she died—an adult by human standards, but a child according to his elf heritage. His father treated Arbane like an elf, ignoring his son's more human tendencies, and he forbade him from studying advanced magic until he was older.

"Well, Arbane wouldn't accept this, and he found a way to teach himself dark magic he had no business knowing. One such magic was necromancy."

"Necromancy?"

"Yes," Arick replied. "Necromancy is a practice of dark magic that involves using the dead to foretell future events, discover hidden knowledge, or reanimate decaying corpses."

"Arbane wanted to bring his mother back from the dead?" James surmised.

Arick grunted, and James noticed how pale the old man was suddenly looking. "He knew his mother would not be the same but he convinced himself enough of the woman he knew would be there. He was so obsessed with the idea that he did not think about the possible consequences of meddling with necromancy."

"And?" James asked, leaning forward in his chair.

"And he succeeded. His mother came out of the portal he created. But she was...different and she was not alone. Those who witnessed it and managed to escape described how someone who looked like Arbane's mother shuffled through the portal barefoot, wearing only a tattered, stained dress. Her long greasy hair obscured her barely visible white eyes, her skin was pale and gray, and she spoke with her spine-chilling voice."

"What did she say?" James asked, noticing his voice cracked as he spoke.

"'The dead have no place among the living.' As soon as she said it, several more of the dead came through the portal and began attacking everyone witnessing the event. We don't know the details. Those who survived were the ones clever enough to flee at the sight of the creatures; they didn't hang around to see what happened to those who weren't so quick to run. The story goes that Arbane wasn't prepared to send his mother back to the realm of the dead, and when several other elementals tried, Arbane went mad and used his immense powers to stop them. Rumor has it, it was Arbane's own father who ended up killing him."

The story had James feeling on edge, so he stood up and started to pace back and forth in front of the fireplace. "I'm missing something. Why forbid all mixed relationships based on what Arbane did? Aren't these the actions of just one mad person?"

Arick hummed in acknowledgment. "Before his father died from the injuries that his son had inflicted on him, he confessed that Arbane had suffered his entire life from the conflict he felt between his human and elven aspects of his personality. Arbane seemed to possess the power of two elementals, but also, he was constantly in conflict with himself. His mother's death may have pushed him over the edge, but Arbane was on a trajectory toward madness from the day he was born."

James stopped pacing and leaned against the mantelpiece above the fireplace. The crackling embers helped to calm his nerves. "And this always happens? The children of mixed races are always powerful and always go mad?" When Arick was slow to respond, James turned to look at him.

"Truthfully, we don't know. But it was agreed between the elders of all the races at the time that elf, dwarven, and human elementals should no longer be permitted to have children with each other in case they should produce a child capable of so much destruction. Over time, mixed-race relationships became frowned upon, as well."

"So," James said, trying to put the pieces of the puzzle together, "Wanda was condemned before she was even born. Just her parents being together was enough to trigger a war?"

"And while no one saw any signs of madness in young Wanda, her abilities as an elemental far exceeded even the most experienced of us. I have never seen a more powerful elemental in all my long years."

James was about to ask Arick to bring it all back to his mother, but there was a knock on the door. As James looked up, his eyes glanced past the window overlooking the island, and he saw the sky was darkening. How long have I been here? James thought.

"Come in," Arick said without turning his head.

The door shifted, and Mary entered the room, though James hardly recognized her. She wore a black formal dress with matching high-heeled shoes. Her long hair hung loosely and onto her shoulders, where James spied the twinkling of a golden necklace.

"Is there a party somewhere?" James asked.

"You mean because of the dress?" Mary replied." A friend of mine had a birthday party..." She then turned to Arick. "Are you done for today?"

"Yes," Arick replied. "That's enough for today. I'm tired. Tomorrow is a new day, James. We will talk more. For now, you should get some rest, too."

James was feeling tired, too, it was true, but he still had so many questions. He wanted to know more about the world he'd stepped into. More about what was going on. More about the elementals and himself.

But he knew his questions were going to have to wait, so he thanked Arick one for time and wished him a good night before following Mary through the hallway and back up the stairs to the surface.

CHAPTER 9

In a Perfect World

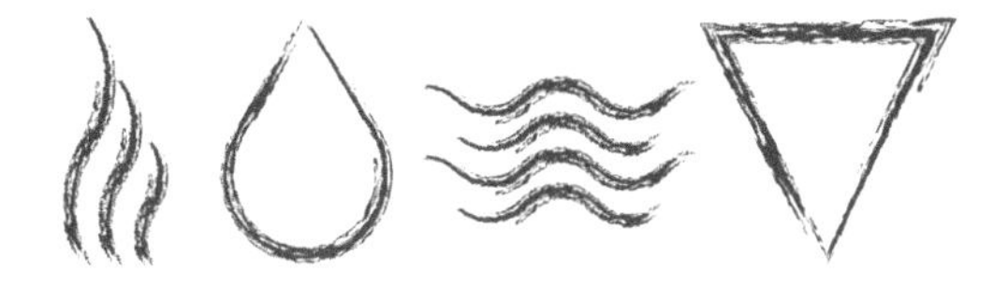

After dinner in the hall, Mary had taken James to one of the upper floors of the Castle, where a dorm-like room had been arranged for him. It was small—a bed on one side and a large desk on the other—but cozier than anywhere else he'd slept, especially in comparison to the old communal room at the orphanage and his snug, breezy hut at the docks, and James was delighted with it. He said goodnight to Mary and went straight to the bathroom, which consisted of a toilet and shower. Above the sink was a small white cabinet with a mirror, so after splashing some water on his face, James looked at his reflection for the first time in days. He looked older and a little tired and decided he needed sleep.

James thought his head had been on the pillow for a matter of moments when he heard the knock on the door, but after rubbing his eyes, he saw sunshine pouring through the gaps in the blinds. Another knock on the door made him get up. He opened the door to find Mike standing behind it, wearing his characteristic smile.

"Oh, er, good mor—"

Before James could finish, Venessa poked her head around one side of the door. He flinched and took a step back.

"I'm sorry, I didn't mean to scare you," Venessa said, although James could see she was holding in a laugh.

"It's OK," James replied. "Didn't see you there."

"What are your plans for today?" Mike asked.

"Er, I don't know. My head's still swimming with everything I learned yesterday."

"Great!" Mike bounced on his toes. "We can show you around! It'll help clear your mind a little."

James looked at Venessa, who shrugged. "Sure. We can give you the tour. Do you want to know any specifics or...?"

"Well...yes, I want to know it all," James replied, grabbing a jacket and following the siblings away from his room. The hallway was dark and carpeted, but as they reached the large open space above the main staircase, light poured through the looming windows. From the outside, the dark, imposing building deserved its nickname of the Castle, but inside, it was much more modern, with wood paneling and freshly painted plastering. There was no one else on the upper floor, but as they descended to the first floor, James started to see other young adults and older teenagers walking about the site.

"Well, let's see, our dad's the boss," Venessa said, and James couldn't help but notice her lift her chin a little. "He runs things. Last I heard, there are about two hundred adults and around forty children right now."

"The population changes?"

"Of course," Venessa said, raising an eyebrow. "People come and go. This is no prison. Nobody is being forced to stay."

James bit his lip as they walked through the main entrance and out into the bright sunlight. The Castle stood on a hill in the middle of the clearing that seemed to form the vast majority of the Leilani Reef community. As James followed Mike and Venessa down the stony path that cut through the neatly trimmed grass on either side, he couldn't help but smile at the teenagers gathered in their groups to gossip, eat, or study.

"How do you power the place without the outside world noticing?" James asked as they reached the tall street lamps on the rows of houses he had walked through the day before. Instead of going back along the route that led to the chasm and the bridge, Mike and Venessa turned off the path and started climbing a small hill. "How do you get food and supplies?"

"We grow everything we can ourselves," Venessa said. "For everything else, we sail to the nearby islands. For the electricity, we have solar panels spread throughout the island and generators in case of an emergency. And if we ever need an extra boost, we just move the clouds aside for a little while." As she said this, she swept her hands across her face, as though shifting the clouds.

"What do you use to get the supplies you need?"

"Money," she said with a laugh. "Like everyone else. You are forgetting our abilities."

"You've lost me. What do our abilities have to do with money?"

Mike invited James to come closer as if he was about to share a secret with him. "We magically print fake money." James looked from one sibling to the next, not knowing what to say, when they both burst out laughing. A few passersby turned to see what was going on, but the trio ignored them. "That was a joke, I'm sorry. I couldn't resist."

"We are elementals," Venessa said. "Our earth elementals summon precious metals, like gold and silver, which we then sell. You wouldn't believe the wealth under our feet."

James felt his cheeks start to glow. "But then any earth elemental can summon gold to make themselves rich." They both nodded. "And you don't see any problem with that?"

"Not really," Venessa said. "Wealth means nothing to us. We have everything we need; we wouldn't know what to spend it on. We can build using our powers, we can demolish using our powers. We grow our own food, make our own clothes. It's really just tools and tech—"

"And games!" Mike said.

"And games that we need," Venessa finished.

James contemplated her words. "What about weapons?"

"What about them?" Venessa asked.

"Do you buy them to defend the island? Or are there other elementals that use that wealth they can conjure to buy weapons to use against other people?"

"You mean like tanks, airplanes, bombs? All that is useless against us. Your mind is the greatest weapon there is. With proper training, you can fold tanks like paper, disable the engines of aircraft, and deflect or disarm rockets before they ever become a threat. Our powers are our greatest form of generating what we need to live comfortable lives and our most effective form of defense against any threats."

When they reached the top of the hill, Venessa pointed into the distance. The brick houses and stone-walled barns and outhouses made way for a huge expanse of fields. A handful of them was busy with activity as people idly tilled the soil, pulled legumes from the ground, or sauntered in and out of greenhouses while laughing and conversing with one another. On one side, James spotted a two-story building that stretched along the edge of the many sanded-down tree trunks that served as the staves of the large outer wall. Although James couldn't see it, he knew the giant chasm he had crossed the previous day would be just the other side.

"That's the school," Venessa said.

"School?"

"Yeah. We have to learn somewhere, you know."

"Do you learn how to control the elements there?"

"Not just that," Mike said. "We learn everything. Math, history, biology, chemistry, physics, science... Knowing how the world works helps us to better use our elements."

"Plus, you know, it's important to know these things, anyway," Venessa said.

"And who are your teachers?"

"Depends. The experts who live here, like Arick, who teaches about the elements and history. Every person who lives here has a role and contributes to the community in their own way," Venessa said.

"Plus the people who are passing through, especially if they are a real expert," Mike added.

"Like Dalnur and Kymil?"

"Dalnur knows a lot about materials and construction, so he tends to teach physics."

"Speaking of," Venessa said, pointing a finger at the dwarf, who was approaching them from the direction of the school. He was side by side with a barrel-chested man who appeared to be almost as thick as Dalnur was tall, and three times the dwarf's height. He had a bushy beard that although it was nowhere near the length of Dalnur's, was nonetheless neater and better maintained. Beside him, holding his hand, was a small girl with long golden hair tied in a ponytail. She sang a song James didn't recognize while jumping on one foot, then another, all the while gripping the man`s hand for support.

"James!" The large man thrust an enormous hand toward him. "Nice to meet you. Welcome to our humble home. I'm John, and this is my daughter, Tanya." The man gazed

down at her while she grabbed her father's leg and squeezed it tightly.

"Er, hi..."

"Everything OK?" he said with a raised eyebrow. Then he rolled his eyes and let out a small sigh. "Of course, we haven't been introduced yet. I've heard so much about you, I'd forgotten we haven't said hello yet."

Dalnur pointed at the large man. "James, this is John. He is one of the leaders of Leilani Reef."

"I'm also the unfortunate soul to sire those two chatterboxes that have been following you around," John said, peering over James' shoulder at Mike and Venessa. He still had his hand outstretched and pointed forward. "We're delighted to have you here."

James returned the handshake, and as John's calloused hand enveloped his own, he felt a bead of sweat fall down the back of his neck. "Thank you for taking me in. I'd be dead if not for Mary and her team."

"This place was your mother's home, James. Heck, you were born here. We're not taking you in; we're bringing you back to where you belong."

"Good to see you're getting to know the place," Dalnur said. "How do you like it here?"

"I don't know what to say. It's beautiful," James replied.

"I'm glad to hear that," John said before directing his attention to Mike and Venessa. "You two, come with me."

Mike shook his head. "James asked us to show him around."

"And you will. But I need your help with something. It won't take long and you can meet up with James after. It was great to meet you, James. I look forward to a longer chat."

Mike lowered his head but obeyed his father. Shortly after, he and his two sisters disappeared with John into the woods, and James found himself alone with Dalnur.

"Walk with me," the dwarf said in his raspy voice as he turned away. "I know this is all new to you and the very knowledge that you can manipulate the elements is exhilarating, but don't take it lightly. In a perfect world, we would only use our powers for good. To disperse the clouds when our crops need sunlight or gather them when they need rain, so we can grow all the food we need to feed the world twice over. To put out forest fires and hold back floods.

"But alas, the world is not perfect. Strange and difficult times are coming. Not everything will always be as it is now. You will have to learn to use your elements to defend yourself; the responsibility you carry is not a light burden, but you must act like a warrior. Keep that in mind." Dalnur stumbled over a root protruding from the ground, but before he could fall, James shot his hand out on instinct and grabbed him by his arm. "You see what I mean?" Dalnur said, laughing. "You must never relax completely. Always stay vigilant."

"Why do you think hard times are coming?"

Dalnur twisted his face and appeared to chew the inside of his cheek. "I honestly don't know. A feeling, I suppose. The things we talked about—the floods, earthquakes, tsunamis—I think someone is behind them. I hope I'm wrong,"—the dwarf leaned into James, touched a stubby finger against his own bulbous nose, and gave a wink—"but I rarely am."

"But you must have a reason for thinking something like that," James said.

"Only in my gut."

"If you keep thinking that way, then something bad is definitely going to happen," James said with a smile, trying to cheer Dalnur up.

"Maybe you're right," the dwarf said with a quiet sigh. "Maybe you're right."

"What do you mean?"

"Everyone thinks I ponder about such things too much." Despite not actually falling to the ground, the dwarf dusted himself off. "You know, James, if you like it here, you'll love our dwarven abodes underground. You'll have to come with me sometime. I'd like to show you my city."

"I would love that," James said.

Dalnur looked up at him with a wide smile that creased his eyes and lifted his thick whiskers around his mouth. "Then it's settled. I'll arrange for you to accompany me when I next leave."

When they reached the training area, they parted ways. Dalnur set off first, and James followed him with his eyes until the dwarf disappeared out of sight, when he turned back to return to the school entrance to wait for Mike and Venessa. He couldn't help but feel fond of his new friend. Whether this threat about which Dalnur spoke was real or imagined, it was clearly troubling him.

I hope you aren't withholding from me to spare my feelings, Dalnur, James thought as he headed off in the other direction. There are already enough people keeping secrets from me.

CHAPTER 10

ELEMENTS 101

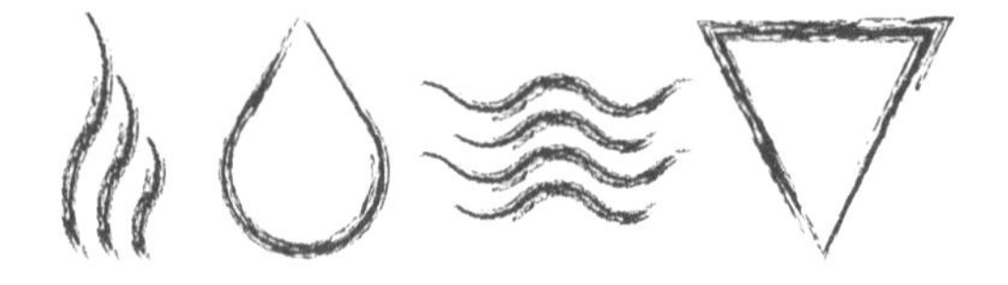

MARY WAS SITTING AT the same table as before, and when James entered the dining hall, she signaled to him to join her. She was in the company of several others, but Marcus was the only one James knew. He held out his hand and offered the seat next to him, which James accepted.

"I'm sorry about what happened on the boat," Marcus said. "The lightning? When you and Mary were on the water?"

"Oh, yeah, don't worry about it," James said with an uneasy smile. "You scared me, but I can't say I wasn't impressed, even if I still don't really get how you did it."

Everyone at the table started laughing, and for the first time, James felt like he was part of something. Part of a society that accepted him. Something akin to a family. He had always told himself the teachers and his friends at the orphanage were his family, but he'd never really felt it—not like he was feeling it now. As he watched everyone at the table smiling at him and each other, James couldn't help but grin from ear to ear.

As the laughter subsided, Mary leaned into James. "You'll find out how it all works today, I promise. Arick is a man of his word. Your practical training begins now."

James nodded. He knew he'd been pushing for answers ever since Mary had first taken him to the palace hideout back in Miami, but now he was about to learn how to manipulate the elements for the first time, he couldn't help but feel butterflies in his stomach.

Mary seemed to sense this, and as a cart of breakfast options was wheeled by, she grabbed an egg sandwich and threw it into James' lap. "Have some breakfast, and we'll go to work."

James was about to take a bite when he saw Kymil sitting alone at the next table. He excused himself and walked over to join him. Kymil gave James a short, almost imperceptible nod, and James sat down.

"How are you?" Kymil asked. "Have you settled in?"

"I'm fine, thanks," James replied. "Actually…I have. For the first time, I feel like I belong."

"You do belong," Kymil said, putting his fork down. He had three dishes in front of him. A bowl of lettuce seasoned with pumpkin oil, scrambled eggs mixed with vegetables and avocado, and a plate of apple pie. He sipped on his glass of freshly squeezed orange juice.

"I'm sorry to bother you while you're eating your breakfast, but since I'm about to start my training, and with you being an ambassador who travels a lot, I don't know when I'll get another chance to ask you about your kind."

"Don't apologize, James. I understand. If only more of your kind were so direct with their curiosity, perhaps humans would face fewer misunderstandings. What do you want to know?"

"I don't really know. Let's start with your rulers or government. You said there are fourteen tribes, but you also mentioned laws all elves—or most, anyway—follow. Who leads at that level?"

"Her name is Bedisa. It means fate or destiny."

"Your leader is a she?" James asked.

"Most of our leaders are female. They are far more logical than us males."

"And she rules over all elves?"

"Not quite. She and her kin handle inter-tribal laws and disputes, but each tribe chooses its own leader for its own concerns. And then there are those who have separated themselves from the rest of us since the war."

"The dark elves?"

Kymil's face lacked any emotion, as seemed to be the norm with him. But James could have sworn the elf's eyes had darkened a little. "Their self-proclaimed leader is an elf named Besola. He was a good community member until he lost a child in the war. He accused the rest of us of inaction. Unfortunately for all of us, he is not only a powerful elemental but a charismatic leader, and he attracted huge numbers to his cause."

"Hi, James."

James turned to the side to see John.

"Arick tells me he's already had his introductory chat with you and that you're ready to begin your training." John sat at the table and started scooping large spoonfuls of his breakfast into his mouth. "Nice to see you don't hang about. These are trying times, and we need people who take action like you."

"Well, I don't know if I'd call myself—"

"But just make sure you dedicate yourself to your studies as much as you do to questioning this one," John continued, winking at Kymil. "A piece of advice, don't take everything that Kymil tells you at face value. Don't get me wrong, he's not going to lie but he won't tell you everything about his people either."

"What do you mean?" James asked, looking from one to another.

"Elves are beings with so many abilities and powers, they make the rest of us look like amateurs. Throw in their long lives, too, and they're damn well near smarter than most of us humans, as well. But Kymil is humble, so he'll dress down whatever he tells you about his people."

Kymil tried to reply but John wasn't done. "If you really want to know all about elves, talk to anyone but an elf," he said, smiling.

"You are amusing yourself, are you?" Kymil asked.

"It's the truth." John raised his glass. "Cheers."

As the upbeat John munched on his breakfast, James turned to Kymil again. The elf was watching John like an onlooker might observe a rhino in a zoo enclosure.

"Ah, you've met John, then." It was Mary, moving over from the table she'd been sitting at. Mike and Venessa followed, and they both grimaced when they saw how their father was shoveling down his food.

"Kids!" John said. "Thanks for telling James, here, all about me. Embarrassed myself before, didn't I?"

"I think you're doing that yourself," Mike whispered, loud enough for everyone to hear.

"You haven't touched your breakfast, James," Mary said.

James looked down at the egg sandwich in his hand. "Oh, right..."

"Eat it on the way. Let's get a move on."

"Oh, OK," James said, then turned around. "It was nice to talk to you both again."

"Not so fast, kid," John said. "We're coming with you." He'd already polished off all the food on his plate, and when he got up, he made such a screech with his chair on the polished floor that half the hall turned and stared. "Oops," he said with a shrug, then set off to leave the hall. Kymil followed closely behind, then at Mary's urging, James, Mike, Venessa, and she all did the same.

In the clearing outside, James watched as John and Kymil approached the dwarf, Dalnur, and three men.

"These ugly souls are our mediums," John said when he had deemed James as being close enough to hear him. "This is Tony; he's also one of our best cooks. And this is Alex." James shook hands with both of them. "They help me look after the fine people of Leilani Reef,"—John looked at Dalnur and Kymil—"and its guests. They're also going to help with your training. Everyone here will do so, as well as Arick, whenever he deigns to leave his house for two minutes."

"They help you manage the affairs of the island?" James repeated. "Doesn't that mean they have better things to do than to spend their time helping me?"

"Mediums aren't as common as us elementals, and Alex and Tony are our only two at the moment. It'll be some time before you're ready to work with a medium, but I saw no harm in introducing them to you now." John placed each of his enormous hands onto one shoulder of each of the other two men. "Anyway, for now, you need to learn the basics. For starters, we need to find out which element, or elements, you can harness by the end of the day."

James almost sneered. "The end of the day? I only learned all this stuff is even possible two days ago. How could I possibly...?" But James stopped talking when he saw John's thick beard turn upward upon his large grin.

"You are no different from any of the other late bloomers that came to us not knowing a thing about elements. You're far from the first elemental to have been forced to grow up without a guide."

As John finished, Marcus came bounding up from behind James. He still had the crumbs of his breakfast in the corners of his mouth. "You haven't started without me, right?" he said, his cheeks red from the short run he'd taken from the dining hall to the clearing. "I've been looking forward to this, what about you?" Marcus grabbed James by his shoulder and gave him a little shake.

"Looking forward to what?" James replied. "I don't know what's about to happen."

"Well, then, allow me," Marcus said, rolling up his sleeves and clapping his hands together.

Before James' heart could beat twice, the blue sky began to darken as clouds appeared overhead, and the trees started to bend and sway. Loud rumbling thundered through the sky at the same time that flashes of lightning appeared on all sides. Before James could interpret what was happening, heavy rain, the likes of which he'd never seen before, was lashing at his arms that had, just a moment earlier, been bronzing in the warm sunshine.

James looked at Marcus, who seemed to sense James' eyes on him because he opened one of his own, saw him, and grinned. As quickly as the storm had appeared, it disappeared again, and for the first time, James understood why concentration was such an important component of casting elemental magic.

When James could feel the hot sun on his face again, he thought about breaking the silence to say something. But while he looked at Marcus with admiration at what he had just done, the others looked at him with impatient frowns and bored expressions. It seemed to James that they wanted more from him, and Marcus was happy to oblige. The air around James began to vibrate. He could hear it from within the very depths of his ear canals and feel it on his skin. It seemed the wind had ceased all of a sudden, but then, James saw the air gathering in one place, forming a sphere a few feet away from him and Marcus. Once the sphere had grown to the size of a volleyball, Marcus stretched out his arms and, with open palms, made a shoving motion as if he wanted to push the sphere away from him. The sphere flew through the air like a speeding bullet; James lost sight of it, but he saw the damage it caused as it crashed into a large rock, causing it to shatter, and James ducked as stone debris rained down toward them, falling just short enough that no one was hurt.

After collecting himself and looking up, James saw that everyone was grinning at him. He could feel his heart pumping as he rose to his feet.

"And that's not all," Marcus said, obviously pleased with James' reaction. "The limit of what one can do is one's imagination."

Then Mary took a step forward, held out her hand, and a high flame arose from her upturned palm. She closed her palm, and the fire disappeared, then she summoned a small ball of fire in one hand and a small ball of water in the other. "This is who I am," Mary said to James as the spheres hovered a few inches above her hands. "I am fire. I am water." She then put her palms together and both balls vanished.

"And now for my contribution," John said.

James had been too dumbfounded by Mary's display to look away, but when the ground beneath his feet trembled, he realized that John was an earth elemental. Cracks began to appear all around them, and the dust from the ground started to rise. James felt vibrations throughout his body and he had to twist his knees to keep his balance.

And then, as with Marcus' storm and Mary's flame, the earthquake ceased.

No one said anything after that, and James got the sense that everyone was waiting for him to react.

“What are you looking at? You think I’m capable of any of that? I can’t do anything of the sort! Mary, tell them what you saw me do when we were attacked at the palace? I didn’t throw fireballs or strike those people in black that chased us with lightning. I trembled on the ground like a coward. George died saving me. And for what? You would have all been better off if he’d saved himself.” There was anger in James’ voice, though it was not enough to hide the emotion that caused his words to break and his breathing to falter.

“It’s natural to doubt yourself,” Mary said. “But we all felt that way once, too, and you just saw with your own eyes what is possible.”

Marcus gestured toward a shelter a few hundred meters away. Underneath it, James could see a wooden bench with in-built chairs. “Follow me, James,” he said, leading the way. “We’re going to start slow.” Mary, Mike, and Venessa followed, while John hung back to exchange hushed whispers with Tony and Alex.

After reaching the shelter first, Marcus lifted a box up from underneath the bench and pulled out a couple of dirty glass bottles.

I hope we don’t have to from drink them, James thought.

From the same box, Marcus pulled out chalk, parchment, and pencils, as well as a variety of small vials filled with powders and liquids of different colors. Mary sat at the head of the table, Marcus sat next to James, and Mike and Venessa sat on the opposite side of them.

"Now, let's see what you can do with these objects," Mary said, looking at James and rubbing her hands. Mary took one of the dirty glasses, placed it in front of her, and covered the glass with the palm of her hand. Instantly, water formed inside the glass. "You have to imagine what you want to do with water. In this case, think about the moisture in the air around us and visualize pulling it into the glass. There's no shortage of it; there is more water in the atmosphere than in all the rivers and lakes on earth. Alternatively, you can pull it up from the ground. You have to focus on water and water alone. It may sound complicated now, but it's not."

"And what if water isn't my element?" James asked, his eyebrows furrowed in confusion and worry.

"We'll start with water and work our way through the others until you feel a connection with one of the elements. But we have to start somewhere. As both Marcus and I can manipulate water, it's a good one to start with because it's one we both understand. We can explain what to look for; which sensations are important and which you can ignore.

"Now, try," she continued, holding up the small bottle in front of James' face. "Think of water. Don't think of the glass containing the water. Only the water. Look past the glass. If it helps, close your eyes and try to imagine it in your head. See only the water; block out everything else. When you feel your concentration is entirely focused on the water, imagine doing something with it. Your imagination is the only limit."

James had been around water his whole life, and for the last few weeks, while living at the docks, he had been beside it every day, yet he had never felt anything like what Mary was describing. Still, he didn't want to disappoint her, so he set out to do his best. He stared at the glass, took a deep breath, and closed his eyes. In his mind, he saw his surroundings as they were, only Mary, Marcus, Mike, and Venessa were absent. He saw the table, he saw the items on top of it, and he saw the bottle of water. He tried to reach for the water, but the glass stopped him from touching it. Eventually, James opened his eyes again. The glass bottle remained on the table, untouched, with the water still inside it, and James bit his bottom lip.

"Don't rush it, James." Mary's soft voice instantly eased his frustrations. "Remember what John said: you'd use your elements by the end of the day. The *end* of the day! As I see it, the day has barely started."

James went to close his eyes again, but just before he did, Mary reached out and grabbed his hand. "Focus only on the water. Strip everything else away."

Once again, James conjured the scene in his mind. At first, the breeze on his skin distracted him, reminding him that he was standing in an open clearing with three people he barely knew as they tried to teach him to use magical powers. But as the seconds became minutes, the image in his mind became less and less. He stopped feeling the wind and hearing the rustling of the trees. The grass underfoot faded to black, and the shelter overhead disappeared like a ghost vanishing through a wall. Then, one by one, the objects on the table were no more, and then the table itself. Just like that, there was nothing in the dark void of James' imagination. Nothing but the small glass bottle floating before him. He tried to grab at the water again in his ethereal form, but doing so kept pulling him out of his focus. So, instead of bringing the water out of the glass, he did to the bottle what he had done to everything else. Keeping the water where it was, James willed away the glass. Bit by bit, it disappeared, leaving the water hovering in the middle of nothingness.

A sudden crack made James' heartbeat quicken, and he opened his eyes in surprise.

"What happened?" he said. No one seemed hurt. On the contrary, Mary had a wide smile on her face.

"You did it," Mike said, throwing a fist into the air. James looked at the table where he'd last seen the bottle of water. Instead, he saw a pile of broken glass lying in a wet patch on the table's surface.

"You did what exactly?" Marcus asked. "Broke some glass? I thought you were trying to move the water?"

Mary snapped her gaze at Marcus. "That's still progress."

Marcus' cheeks turned red faster than Mary could summon fire. "Of course, it's progress, I'm just messing with you." He reached over to James and patted him on the back.

"What does it mean if I can break glass? Did I do that with the wind element? Maybe earth? I suppose I might have vibrated the molecules in the same way John moves the ground, no? I couldn't seem to grab the water, whatever I tried."

"Calm down," Mary said, breathing slowly and indicating for me to do the same. "You can break glass with any element; it doesn't mean anything. Ignore the glass completely. There is no glass anymore. Instead, focus on lifting up all this spilled water. See what you want to do with it in your head. Concentration...imagination..."

James closed his eyes and imagined the scene in his head again. As before, he stripped away the details until there was only the puddle of water before him. This time, without the glass bottle, it felt easier for him to reach the water. He pictured it rising from where the ground had been before he'd made it disappear. He saw in his mind's eye as the water folded over and weaved in and out of itself. He could feel it without getting wet and taste it without quenching his thirst.

As he concentrated on the water, he heard a gasp, and then another, and then another. Somehow, he knew he was doing it; he was controlling the water. He wouldn't open his eyes; he wouldn't allow himself to be distracted but he also knew the water was floating. It was as Mary had said; he could feel it.

Finally, he opened his eyes, slowly and carefully. The ground was dry, and James had to lift his gaze to see the blob-like mass of water floating a few inches above the table. But what was even more wonderful was the great feeling running through his veins. He felt like he was personally connected to all the water everywhere. It was like touching a living thing, and he felt the coolness and softness of it inside him. He wanted more, and he realized he could have it, so he outstretched his hand, palm facing up, the way Mary had done with fire, and with his mind, he brought the water to him until it hovered above his fingers.

"Yeah! You got it!" Mike shouted, pumping his fist in the air as he jumped off the bench.

Mike's shout was too much, and James' mind suddenly flooded with everything he had been trying to keep out. The water in front of his eyes fell in an instant, spilling all up his arm and over the table.

"Oh, er, sorry," Mike said when he realized what had happened. Venessa scowled and punched her brother in the shoulder, but James was too excited to care.

"I felt it!" James said with more enthusiasm than he could ever remember having in his voice before that day. "I felt it. I felt the water. I can't describe it but I know. Please, Mary, put more water in the glass. I want to do it again."

Mary shook her head from side to side. "*You* put it in." She looked at Marcus briefly, who pulled forth another glass bottle from the box beneath the table.

James stopped for a moment, put his right-hand palm on top of the glass, closed his eyes, and tried to visualize the water in the air. He felt the water on his palm slowly begin to form but it was not enough to fill the glass. "I can't. It's not working. There is not enough water."

"There is," Mary whispered. "You just need to expand your visual space. You are only looking for water around this table."

"Go bigger," Marcus said. "You have to occupy more space. Imagine yourself drifting upward and away from this place. Imagine all the water in the air in this clearing. Go further still; visualize the whole island."

He understood the principle of what they were saying but he couldn't fathom how he was supposed to occupy so much space with his mind. Eventually, he got tired, and he shook out his wrist in frustration. "I can't," James exclaimed, exhaling sharply. "It's too hard."

"You're acting like a child," Mary said, and for a moment, James felt like he was back in the orphanage again. "Do you think elemental magic is easy?"

"What? No, of course not—"

"Then why do you think you should be able to learn to control water on your first try?" Marcus asked.

"What you have done today in such a short time is extraordinary in itself," Venessa said in her soft voice.

"Maybe you just need some freshening up," Mike said and he summoned a few drops of water to sprinkle over James' face.

"That's just mean," Venessa said, letting out a guttural laugh, and James couldn't help but crack a smile. He suddenly realized why Mary had been so keen for James to wait to get to the island to ask his questions. Why John had asked four people, not just one or two, to train him during his first session. Mastering the elements required patience and balance, and that's what his new friends were doing for him now. Every time Mary pushed him, Mike offered him a moment of respite. Every time Marcus made him reach for the next goal, Venessa reminded him of everything he'd already achieved.

"I appreciate what you're all doing for me," James said, putting his hands on the wooden table and feeling the rough and bumpy surface, "but really, I can't."

"Only because you tell yourself that," Mary said. "I promise you that you can. But there's no need to force this. Why don't we take a break?"

When James had insisted the best way that he could relax was to explore Leilani Reef so he could take in the fresh air and let his thoughts wander, Marcus, Mary, and Venessa had headed back in the direction of the Castle. Mike, meanwhile, had offered to stay with James to show him around and, with no fixed destination in mind, he'd led James across the clearing and up a bank where they took shelter under a tree. The dazzling sun passed through the canopy, creating a dance of shadow and light on the floor as the branches and leaves swayed in the gentle breeze. Freshly mowed grass glistened in the sunlight, and James enjoyed the distinct smell of it as he listened to the distant chirping of birds and the playful squeals of the girls playing jump rope nearby.

"How long did you need to master your elements?" James asked eventually, turning his head toward Mike.

"Master?" Mike scoffed. "I didn't master them. It takes years, even decades." James raised his eyebrows in surprise. "If anybody ever tells you they've mastered their element, they're almost definitively lying."

"What do you mean?"

"To be a master of one element, you must be able to produce anything imaginable with it, and to do so almost effortlessly."

"Says who?"

"Arick. Actually, those were his words, not mine."

"I see." James smiled and rested his head against the tree. After a few more moments of enjoying the warm weather, he jumped to his feet. "OK, I think I'm ready to try again. Help me summon water."

"No way!" Mike exclaimed. "You cannot do this yourself."

"What do you mean? Why not?"

"Because you are not skilled enough. You could hurt yourself, or even worse, you could hurt me! The hardest part about controlling the elements is not handling the element, but maintaining your concentration and stopping your mind from making you act out something crazy or dangerous."

"Huh?" James rubbed the back of his neck.

"Our minds think up crazy things sometimes. Normally, it's entirely meaningless and harmless. But if I'm in the middle of conjuring a lightning strike and I suddenly get distracted and think about that lightning bolt hitting Venessa... Well, there's a strong chance I might kill her. And if she survives, there's a strong chance she'll kill me."

"What's stopping me from doing that even with someone standing next to me?"

"Nothing, but people who know the signs for these sorts of things might be able to counter you."

James thought about what Mike was telling him. "You are with me, and I trust you, Mike. You can stop me."

"Yeah, right," Mike replied sarcastically. "I'm still not allowed to use my abilities when nobody is around and I've been conjuring the elements for years. I can do small things alone, but when I want to train, somebody has to stay by my side. I told everyone not to worry—that I don't need babysitting—but Arick and my father insist."

"And why is that?"

"Arick says that young people and old people can't concentrate properly. I don't know what he means by that but..."

James thought for a moment, looked around, took a few steps, bent down, and grabbed a thick wooden stick. "Take this." Mike narrowed his eyes. "Take it!" James repeated firmly, thrusting the stick into Mike's hands. "I'm going to try again, and if you see something isn't right, strike me over the head with this."

"Are you mental?" Mike asked. "No way. My dad will ground me for a year."

"C'mon. What can happen?"

"What can happen?" Mike said, raising his voice. "I'll tell you what can happen. In the best case, you are going to kill yourself, and I'm going to be grounded for, like, ever. In the worst case, you're going to kill me, yourself, and everything on this island."

"Relax." James patted the air with his hands to encourage Mike to calm down. "That's why you are here. And you have the stick." His smile was broad. "C'mon, nothing is going to happen. Help me out here; I don't want to wait until we've marched all the way back to the Castle, and that's assuming Mary, Marcus, and Venessa are all together. We might have to look for them, and that could take hours."

Mike closed his eyes and squeezed the stick until his knuckles went white. "Please don't make me do this."

"Look, I'm going to try with or without you, but if you leave and something happens, people are gonna ask why you left me alone."

At last, Mike threw his arms up. Gripping the stick in one hand, he shook his fist at the sky with the other. "Argh. You're going to get me in trouble... OK, how do you wanna do this?"

James chuckled, sat back down, and leaned his back on the tree while Mike stood beside him, holding his stick with two hands like a baseball player waiting to strike. James looked at him and laughed before he closed his eyes and tried to concentrate. He thought about everything he'd learned from Arick and remembered the advice Mary and Marcus had given him. He then took a deep breath and exhaled slowly. Sure enough, as he visualized water droplets in the air around him, he felt their presence. He imagined he was outside of his own body, looking down on himself from the branches above. Sparkling all around him were the tiny droplets of water. Then he pulled back, like a bird taking flight but keeping its nose pointed down, until he could see the whole clearing; still, he could see the sparkles of light as beams of sunshine bounced off the water particles in the air.

Slowly, steadily, he pulled back further and further, higher and higher. He could see the Castle and the nearby residential homes and streets. He could see the woods that led up to the great chasm that surrounded the town, and the larger forests beyond. Up and up he soared until he could see the entire island.

As the water in the air sparkled all the more intensely, he realized the full extent of the quantity of water he could harness, but more than that, he could feel it. He felt a connection between the water droplets and finally understood that he wasn't flying through the air; he was hopping from one water particle to the next. He had been moving slowly because he'd been jumping between neighboring molecules, but now he knew he could concentrate on any single droplet and instantly transport himself to its location. Through his thoughts, he traveled from one end of the island to the other in a fraction of a second. He was everywhere at once, observing everything.

He remembered his goal and concentrated on gathering as much of the water as he could, and with his thoughts, he pulled it all in front of his vision of his own body, still resting against the tree. Before long, the momentum of the water moving toward James' body seemed to take care of itself, and James allowed himself a moment to celebrate as he watched the growing sphere of water as it grew and grew and grew.

Suddenly, the vision in his right "eye" started to blur. He felt a tingling sensation in his arms and legs. An invisible weight pressed against his chest, and he remembered what Arick had told him about balancing his energy.

James broke his concentration immediately. When he opened his eyes, he saw an enormous wall of water in front of him, as tall as the tree he was sitting underneath. It lasted for the briefest of moments and then came crashing down over James and Mike.

Soaked through and lying in a pool of muddy water, James lay on his side for a moment while he caught his breath. There was a buzzing in his ear, and he struggled to breathe, let alone move. Mike was kneeling beside him, his mouth moving, but James couldn't make out what he was saying. But as the water disappeared into the saturated soil, and James' energy returned to him, the buzzing subsided. With Mike's help, he sat back up and smiled.

"What's wrong with you?" Mike snapped. "You think this is funny? I almost peed my pants. Another few seconds and I would have hit you with the stick so hard you would have thought everything you've seen the last few days had been a weird dream." But James could only laugh all the harder. "I asked you what's so funny?"

"I did it," James said between laughs. "I controlled water!"

"If almost killing yourself was your goal, then yeah, you succeeded," Mike said, lowering himself next to James and resigning himself to getting dirty in the large pool of mud. James peered at Mike out of the corner of his eye, still with a wide smirk on his face, and Mike quickly fell into a fit of laughter, as well.

Their laughter was interrupted by a forced and obnoxious cough. Turning their heads, they saw Mary, Marcus, and Venessa standing not far from them, all with their arms crossed. Mike jumped up to his feet and started explaining how he'd had no choice and how James had made him do it.

"Please, don't tell Dad," Mike pleaded.

"Traitor," James said, pulling himself up while smiling.

"It's not funny, James," Mary said. "You could have hurt yourself."

"But as you can see, I'm fine," James said, even though his legs wobbled as he tried to hold himself upright.

"You were lucky," Mary replied. "But I'm glad you managed to manipulate the water."

"I can't believe how much you pulled in on your first morning," Marcus said, his mouth agape.

"But you're messing with powers you freely admit you don't understand," Mary continued. "You're not the only person who lives on this island, James! And you owe it to the people who care about you to protect yourself."

Everyone went quiet, and James could see the tears welling in Mary's eyes. Why does she care so much about me? he thought. Do I remind her of my mother?

"I'm...I'm sorry, Mary. You're right."

Mary wiped a tear from her eye. "Just... Next time, when you have the urge to end your life, please let us know beforehand."

At that, Venessa laughed, and Marcus and Mike joined in.

James was silent at first but he started to chuckle, as well. "I am sorry about this mess. I guess it was a bit too much water."

"Just a little," Marcus said sarcastically, bringing his thumb and index finger together.

"Can we go and change so we can continue?"

Mary frowned. "Why do you want to change?"

He started to laugh, thinking she was joking, but quickly stopped when it became clear everyone else was taking her seriously, as well. "Erm, in case you haven't noticed, Mike and I are soaking wet. I don't want to catch a cold."

Mary shook her head from side to side. "You still have a lot to learn."

"Wha—?" But before James could finish, Mary had closed her eyes and, moments later, James saw the steam slowly rising from his clothes. In a matter of moments, he was completely dry; even his hair looked like he'd used a hairdryer after showering. He turned to Mike and saw hundreds, perhaps thousands, of tiny drops of water separating themselves from his clothes and body. Marcus then turned those little drops into balls of ice before allowing them to fall to the ground.

"You see," Mary said, opening her eyes again. "Concentration and imagination. That's all you need. All elements work on the same principle. It all comes from your brain. The more you can concentrate and the more you understand how the elements truly work, the stronger your ability to control your element will be."

CHAPTER 11

THE BLUE CAVE

"YOU KNOW, I'M ON kitchen duty after your little stunt," Mike said, stepping over a broken boulder. James hung back slightly to peer over the side of the cliff edge; it was a straight drop to the sharp rocks being pounded by the rough waves, and James felt a combination of awe and queasiness. They were about half a mile from the Castle, and James still had no idea where Mike was leading him. "Dad said I should have known better than to let you practice water magic alone."

James shrugged. "Well, he's right."

Mike turned sharply, his face a combination of betrayal and fury. "What do you...? It was your idea. You made me do it!" James snorted so that Mike knew he was teasing him. "Unbelievable. The shy newcomer learns to control a little water, and all of a sudden, he's Emperor Elemental!"

As Mike stepped off the well-trodden dirt path they had been following and onto the rock, the wind picked up and blew a branch under his feet. He tumbled head first into the bush.

"What the...?" he said, picking himself up as quickly as he'd fallen and pulling a twig out of his hair. "Was that you?"

James winked. "After dinner last night, I was too excited. I mean, come on, I'd just learned to control water. Who can sleep after they realize they can do that?"

"James, how many times have we told you now that you cannot practice on your own? Not yet."

"I know, I know, I won't do it again. I just couldn't resist last night. Anyway, there are only so many water tricks you can do in those dorm rooms before you get bored, so I decided to give the other elements a try. Earth and fire—"

"You tried to conjure fire last night, on your own, in your bedroom?" Mike put one hand on his hip and another over his eyes. "James Tanner, you'll be the death of me."

"Don't worry, they were a no-go. But then I tried air. It didn't take half the amount of time or energy before I was lifting my bed and clothes around the room. I even managed to hover at one point."

Eventually, Mike relented. He walked over to James, punched him playfully in the shoulder, and smiled. "I'm pleased for you, man. It seems you've figured out your elements in record time. Just—"

"Yes, yes, no more practicing alone, I promise." James stepped closer to the cliff edge and peered over the side.

"That's a long way down, and those rocks in the sea look pretty sharp. I hope you're not taking us down there."

Mike's characteristic grin returned. "Actually, I am. What's the matter? Don't like heights? Good, consider this revenge."

James tongued the inside of his cheek as he followed Mike through a bush and along a barely perceptible path until it merged with a set of steps that had, by design or by accident, been worn into the side of the rock. "I've got no problem with heights. It's falling to my death off the side of a steep, crumbling cliff face that scares me."

They carefully zig-zagged down the uneven stairs, which were wet with the spray of the sea. So as not to slip, they moved slowly and deliberately, and by the time they reached the bottom, James' thighs were screaming in agony, his shoes were soaking wet, and he could barely hear Mike speaking to him over the roaring waves; James only knew his friend was telling him to keep going by the exaggerated way Mike was swinging his arm toward the entrance of the large cave before them.

Most of the cave's entrance was submerged in deep water, and as they followed the walkway inside from the left-hand side, James estimated the huge spherical-shaped space was big enough to harbor one large ship or several smaller ones. He traced the outline of the space and its features and concluded that an elemental must have carved the cave into the rock for a deliberate purpose. Nothing in the cave was man-made; it was all hard limestone with the gentle sheen of seawater and algae. Yet, the curving ceiling was almost entirely smooth, the walkway that Mike and James were using was flat, with just enough of a rough surface to give them a good grip, and the same walkway jutted out into the water in such a way as to function perfectly as a dock for any ships. There were even columns of rocks that jutted out of the ground at the ends of these docks to which sailors would be able to tie their boats.

To the left, the walkway split off to form a small access strip that led deeper into the cave. Mike stepped onto it. "Come on."

The deeper they entered the cave, the quieter the waves behind them became, and the darker it got. Finally, just before James lost sight of Mike altogether, he turned on a switch on the wall and small lamps sparked into life, illuminating the passage. Like the harbor they had come through, the "corridor" they were standing in was perfectly spherical, as though it had been drilled by an enormous machine, and a few yards further on was a steel door blocking the rest of the way.

Mike pushed on the door, and James covered his ears as the sound of grinding, screeching metal echoed off the walls around them.

"What is this place?" James asked, stepping through the open door. Like the rest of the cave, it was carved entirely out of the rock, but this new room was far more intricate. Several pillars supported the ceiling from collapsing. The dimly lit dwelling was almost empty except for two rusty chairs, a table with two lanterns underneath, and several tools that hung on a wall-mounted peg board. On the far side was a large metal cabinet that covered the wall from the floor to the ceiling.

"It's called the Blue Cave. Most people on the island only go in and out of the harbor we just passed through. But Venessa and I got bored a while back and we went exploring and found this room." Mike wiped the dust off the table and then sat on one of the metal chairs beside it. "Pretty cool, huh? No one uses the room anymore, as far as I know, so I like to come here now and then when I want to be alone."

"Why are you showing it to me?" James asked as he slowly walked the perimeter of the room.

Mike shrugged. "Training is important. So is taking some time to relax. I figured you've been through a lot these last few days and it might all be a bit overwhelming. If you ever need some peace and quiet, you can come here."

James was grateful for the dim light. It meant Mike didn't notice when he wiped away a tear. Mike was a little over-energetic at times for James, but he was also a good friend. He'd never had good friends before meeting Mike, Venessa, and Mary.

James ran his fingers along the edges of the cabinet. It was ice cold to the touch. It didn't take long for his curiosity to get the better of him, and he pulled one of the drawers open. It was full of various bits and pieces, from screws and nails to old rusty keys and door hinges. Coupled with the tools on the wall, James assumed the place had once been used as a workshop that was abandoned long ago.

He started to open and shut the other drawers in turn, peering in just long enough to get a sense of the useless junk inside each one, until the contents of one drawer made him pause. James pulled out a few scrolls, took them to the table, and unrolled them, one by one.

"Are these...maps?" Mike pulled one of the lit lanterns closer and squinted.

"I think...this is Leilani Reef, right? The entire island?"

Mike pointed at the dried parchment. "Yeah, look, this is the chasm around town. And this is the coastline you can see from Arick's library." Then he lifted a smaller parchment on top of the one they'd been examining. "This is a map of where we are at the moment."

James wiped his nose on his sleeve. "The amount of salt in the air is incredible. It unclogs everything."

"You see here," Mike continued, dragging his finger slowly over the map. "These are the stairs we came down. This is the entrance to the cave, and this marks the door to this room."

James pointed at another spot beside the room. "And what's this?"

Mike leaned over to have a better look. According to the map, there was some kind of passage at the other end of the room.

James turned the map to orient himself so he was facing where the space should be. When he looked up from the map, he was staring at the cabinet. "Behind that, maybe?"

Mike checked the map again before nodding. "Looks like it."

James had already moved back to where he'd found the parchments and he leaned his shoulder into the large, heavy cabinet. "Give me a hand."

Mike rushed to help James, but no matter how hard they pushed, the cabinet wouldn't budge. James was about to suggest they start emptying the drawers to make it lighter when he crouched down to discover the closet was bolted into the rock floor. He ran his fingers along the base of the cabinet and discovered another large bolt in the opposite corner.

"Mike, is there a heavy-duty wrench hanging on the wall over there?" James said, pointing to the tools on the peg board with one hand while refusing to let go of the bolt with his other.

"Erm, do you mean this?" Mike grabbed the first tool he could reach and threw it at James.

"Mike...," James said, picking up the tool and pocketing it, "that's a screwdriver."

"Well, I don't know!" Mike said, sounding exasperated. "We're elementals. If we need to fix things, we use our powers. I don't know what any of these things are."

James chuckled.

"What's so funny?"

"It's just...for the first time since I've arrived, I feel like I know something you don't. It's nice! Working at the docks has paid off."

Mike laughed and turned back to the peg board. "Which one is a wrench then?"

James spied the wrenches to Mike's left and pointed.

"There are loads."

"These bolts are pretty big," James said. "Just bring me the biggest one, and we'll work our way down until we find one that fits."

A few minutes later, the two had taken it in turns to loosen both bolts until they could unscrew them with their hands. The metal bolts had been so rusted that James' fingers were sore from using so much strength to loosen them, and Mike pressed his palms against the cold rock surface to cool them down.

"Are you ready?" James asked Mike a few moments later. Once again, they pushed against the cabinet, this time managing to shift it away from the wall.

"What the...?" Mike said. "There's nothing there. All that effort for nothing?"

Sure enough, there was nothing but rock. As Mike walked over to collapse into one of the chairs, James stepped closer to the wall. There was something unusual about the strip of limestone they'd exposed. A few feet over, the rock was rough and jagged, like it was everywhere else in the room. But where they had pulled the cabinet away from the wall, it was smooth and glassy.

James reached forward to touch the wall. It reminded him of the images of cooling lava he'd seen while watching documentaries back in the orphanage. "Doesn't the rock here look strange to you?" As soon as James' fingers grazed the surface, he felt a warm tingle shoot up his arm and into his core. Even as he pulled his hand away, the rush of energy warmed his torso before flowing back to his extremities again.

"Woah," Mike said, seeing James react, "are you OK?"

"I'm fine..." James looked from the tips of his tingling fingers and then back to the wall. "Mike, I...I think I can..." He rotated his hand toward the wall, closed his eyes, and when he pressed his fingers to the rock again, the glassy surface became soft like butter melting on low heat.

"Er, James?"

But James ignored his friend as he focused on what he wanted the rock to do. Using his mind, he imagined the wall folding back on itself, slowly pulling apart from one side to the other until there was a gap just wide enough for Mike and him to fit through.

When he opened his eyes, James let out a single laugh. He had done it. He had peeled back the rock to reveal a small passageway—the passageway marked on the map.

Mike stumbled up behind James and grabbed his shoulders with both hands. "Holy... James, you can control three elements? That puts you right up there with some of the most powerful on this island. Do you have any idea how incredibly rare this is?"

"Really?"

"Heck, yeah! Dude, the others are going to freak when you surprise them with air and earth." Mike grabbed James' arm as though he was holding on for dear life. "Promise me, I'll be there when you tell them?"

But James was already focused on what lay ahead. The passage was dark, but there was just enough light coming from the small bulbs behind them to see the thin tunnel opened into a large space a few meters in. The closer they edged to it, the more they could smell the stale air that made them turn their heads away.

"Think we'll fit?" Mike said.

"We need some light," James said, but Mike had already retrieved the lanterns from the table. He gave one to James, who immediately ducked and entered the passage. It was cramped, but it wasn't long, and they soon found themselves able to stretch out again in a new room. It was smaller than the workshop, but had less furniture in it, as well: just a metal table with a few burned-out candles and a pencil worn down to the nub. Behind the table was a wooden tripod. Like everything else in the Blue Cave, it was losing its battle against the elements; its hinges were so rusted that they were practically falling off, and the wood looked brittle and cracked.

James decided not to risk sitting on the chair by the table, so stood beside it instead. One of the table's three drawers was empty, but he pulled a small leather book out of the second and started flipping through the pages. "What the...?"

"What?" Mike asked.

"This is a diary."

"Really? Who would keep their diary here?"

"It's... I think it's by someone called Drago. Why do I know that name?" James frantically searched his memory. He'd learned so much over the last few days, it had all started to blur. "I'd never heard of someone called Drago except in stories until recently. Kymil! Kymil mentioned this Drago when he was talking about...?"

Just as James was about to curse his failing memory, Mike stepped forward to get a closer look at the diary.

"Wanda," he said, his voice cracking. "Wanda Wolgor. Drago was her father."

James looked at his friend and noticed how Mike's almost limitless enthusiasm and energy seemed to be failing him at that moment. "This is the human who had Wanda with an elf, right? One of the events that sparked the war?" Kymil's history lesson and the discussion James had had with Arick were starting to come back to him. "He died, right?"

"That's right," Mike said. "Wanda blamed your mother."

"Why? Why my mother? Arick told me that she and Wanda were close."

Mike shrugged. "I'm not sure. I think someone told me that your mother was the one to find Drago's body. I guess Wanda saw your mother standing next to him and decided she was his killer. Wanda vowed she'd have her revenge before she disappeared, or so my parents tell me. This all happened so long ago. I can't believe he kept a diary. I can't believe it's...here!"

"Look at this," James said, pointing to a passage on one of the pages. *"I've made a terrible mistake. My child will suffer because of my decisions, or we will all suffer."*

"What mistake do you think he means?" Mike asked. "Having a child with an elf, maybe?"

James flipped the page and read some more: *"I have no choice. I have to end this. I will use the ring."*

"We have to bring this diary to my father."

James mumbled his reluctant agreement, and Mike moved to exit the room.

"Wait," James said. "There is one more drawer but it's locked. Give me a second." He pulled the screwdriver out of his pocket and shoved it into the lock. With one hard pull, he wrenched it open. The only thing inside the drawer was a small black leather box covered with dust, and when James opened it, he lifted out a golden ring. James turned it over in his hand as he examined it. It had a pointed tip that protruded on one side.

"I guess this is the ring he mentions in the diary?"

"Be careful," Mike said. "I've heard about these. You see that tip? It's designed to scratch people with poison or whatever."

James carefully placed the ring back inside the box and closed it. "Why would Wanda's father have had this?"

Mike shrugged again. "Could just be a coincidence."

James shook his head. "I doubt it. This room was hidden deliberately, and we found his diary in the same desk as this ring. I think he used this cave to get away from the trouble he'd caused and to try to think of a solution."

"Either way, it's giving me the creeps," Mike said. "Let's get back before anyone starts to wonder where we are."

James followed Mike through the tight passageway and back into the workshop. Mike ran to the large metal door and prepared to close it behind them, but just before he did, James grabbed the maps from the table.

"We found one secret passage without even trying," James said, smiling at Mike. "Who knows what other secrets this island holds."

Mike clicked his tongue as James passed him and then he started to close the door. This time, James was carrying too much to cover his ears, so he could do nothing but flinch at the terrible squeals of the old door's hinges.

Before long, they could hear the crashing of the waves again, and when they saw sunlight, it blinded them so harshly that they need a minute before they could keep moving.

Stepping out of the cave, Mike looked up at the steep steps before them and let out a soft sigh. "You ready? This is always the worst part about coming here. Or are you going to be a pal and use your fancy new powers to lift us to the top of the cliff?"

James laughed. "I thought you said I couldn't use my powers when it's just the two of us."

"Ha, then you are learning," Mike said.

"I don't think I could even if I wanted to, anyway. I'm feeling exhausted." But before Mike could take another step, James shuffled to get his friend's attention. "Don't say a word to anyone about this, yeah?"

"We should show my dad. He knows more about Drago and everything that happened than we do."

James couldn't explain why he wanted to keep the diary and the ring a secret for now, but he also knew Mike was probably right. "We will, I promise, but maybe we can wait a bit? If this really is Drago's diary, it's been in that cave for almost two decades. Another few days won't make a difference."

Mike closed his eyes and pinched the bridge of his nose. "You're going to get me into trouble again, James Tanner, I can tell." He let out a long sigh. "Fine! But only a few days. End of the week, we take everything to my father."

James smiled and thanked Mike, then the two friends began their long, slow, and difficult climb.

CHAPTER 12

Coup de Main

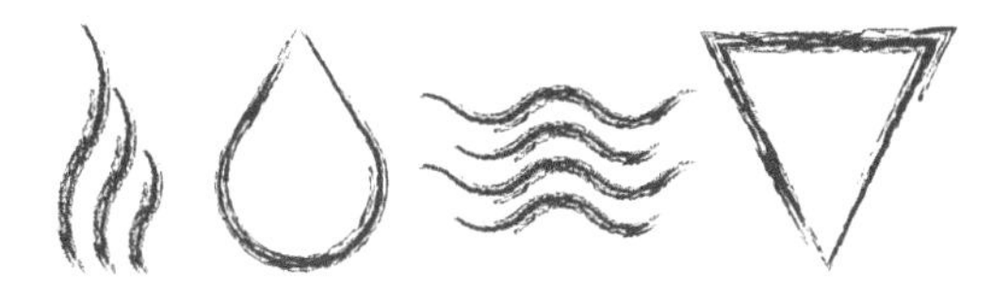

THE LIGHT-GRAY CLOUDS WERE spitting tiny drops of rain, wetting James' cheeks, as he made his way to Arick's house for his lessons. He didn't know how he was going to get through his classes without giving anything away to Arick about the maps or Drago's diary. His mind was swimming with questions. What had Drago planned? Who had he wanted to poison with the ring? Why was he killed first? Had James' mother truly been responsible?

He was so lost in his thoughts, that he almost entered Arick's house without realizing the old man was waiting for him outside. He was standing a few yards past his house, gazing into the woods.

"Isn't it beautiful?"

James blinked at the sound of the voice. "The view? Yes, it is, very."

"I don't just mean this view, but this world in general," Arick said, exhaling a long sigh. "I have never taken for granted that there are people who want to destroy it—who refuse to coexist with the rest of the world—but I don't think I'll ever understand them. It's sad. So very sad."

Instead of verbalizing his agreement, James stayed quiet and stood beside Arick for a few moments to enjoy the sounds of the birds in the trees. Arick seemed to appreciate this, and with a small smile and a wave of his fingers, he invited James inside the house and down into his library. As before, they settled into the library's comfortable armchairs beside the fireplace, and on the table between them was a teapot with two cups. James pressed three fingers to the teapot, and a moment later, the water inside began to boil.

"You're a fast learner," Arick said.

James felt his lips curl and his cheeks flush with heat as he poured some water over the tea: first, for his teacher; and then, for himself. "That's not all." James used his air abilities to lift the wooden box from Arick's desk and floated it over to them. A gust of wind opened it, revealing to Arick his own selection of teas. "I can also manipulate earth, although I'd rather not do that in here until I've practiced some more."

"Three elements! James, that is very impressive. Everyone will be overjoyed." Arick picked out two tea bags before James used his power to close the box and set it back down on the desk.

"I'm glad you've managed to master the basics so quickly. Now we can move on to more advanced theory.

"In the letter Victoria left for you, she warned you about colorful flashes. We call them pointers. Every time an elemental uses his abilities with the intent of doing harm to another living being, a flash appears. It's a curious thing. The flashes don't appear when we use our powers to, for example, heat water in a teapot. We don't know why this happens—our best guess is something to do with intent, but this theory itself poses a far deeper philosophical conundrum about how we interact with the universe. For whatever reason, there is resistance on the element's part when our power is used to harm others, and this resistance generates a flash of light, or pointer.

"But pointers are just the tip of this mysterious iceberg. This brings us to today's lesson. The golden rule when using your elements is that you must never, and I do mean *never*, summon an element inside someone else. For to do so could be to forfeit your own life."

"I don't think I understand?"

"What would be a quicker and surer way to kill an enemy with, let's say, fire? You could cast a flaming ball at them or set fire to them from the inside?"

"Well, obviously, the second one."

"Right. But just as the universe seems to be able to sense the difference between an elemental using their power for a simple task and to harm someone, at which point we see a pointer, so, too, does the universe have a response if an elemental attempts to cast magic inside another person."

"Which is?"

"Curiously, while the victim will suffer the consequences of this terrible act, the caster will also suffer the same fate."

Arick then pulled a small gray folding knife from his pocket. He gently pushed on the blade and it sprang open. "Think of this knife as an element. With it, you can do something useful, like sharpen your pencil or use it to stir your tea. When you do so, there are no other consequences. The element will comply." James watched closely as Arick twirled the knife slowly in his hand. "But if you, let's say, throw the knife at somebody to hurt them, the element resists and produces a strong flash, almost as if it is giving the other person a split-second warning about what's coming.

"But there is a third possibility." Arick leaned forward in his chair and thrust the knife toward James so quickly that he had to slink back in his chair to avoid being cut by the blade. "Instead of projecting the knife at someone from the outside, you conjure it inside another living being's body. For whatever reason, the element retaliates in an instant against its caster, causing the same damage that is inflicted on the victim."

"So, you're saying that you cannot use any of the elements to harm someone directly from the inside, or else you will be harmed, as well? I can dump enough water on someone that they struggle to breathe, but if I conjure water directly into their lungs, the same would happen to me?" Arick nodded, although there was no smile on his lips or in his eyes. "But why would I—?"

"You are a good-natured young man, and I am sure you'd never wish any harm on anyone," Arick interrupted. "If you were so inclined, we would never have brought you here.

"But not everyone is so kind, James; you already know there are people out there who want to harm you. What if you are forced to face such a person? What if their skills with the elements are greater than your own and you sense you are losing the fight? It would only be natural to defend yourself if your life is under threat. But you must *never* give into the temptation to use your power to harm someone internally. Doing so will only harm you, as well. Put simply, James, any attacks must always come from outside of the body. Try to stop a person's heart, boil their blood, suck the water from their skin, and you will suffer the same fate.

"But drive away the air immediately around their bodies and you will suffocate them. Lift the earth at their feet and you will destabilize them. Set fire to the trees and bushes around them to engulf them in flame. As we have discussed, this will create a certain amount of resistance, so any power you cast will be indicated with a pointer, a flash of light, but giving away your position is the price you must pay. Just never start the attack from the inside." Arick played with his teacup without sipping from it. "This lesson is important because, in the heat of battle, when emotions are running high and we are scared for our lives, it is easy to do the thing that seems most instinctive to us. We want to preserve our lives, so we do the thing that will remove the threat as fast as possible. With elements, the quick thing is not always the safest thing."

James looked into the fireplace. He remembered times he had been scared as a child and retreated to his room at the orphanage. He remembered how terrified he had felt when gazing upon the flames that had killed Alan. How he had done nothing to help poor George, who had died to save him. "I…I don't think I would be strong enough to resist. I…I am a coward."

Arick sat back in his chair. He folded the knife and placed it on the table. "No, James, you aren't a coward. Good people do not contemplate harming others; rather, we fear ever being forced to do so. But you will learn. By practicing your powers, you won't just learn how to manipulate the elements; you will also train yourself to use them in ways that are safe for you and those around you. This is why the training we do here on this island is so important; it is why we must all take it seriously." Then, as if the old man hadn't been talking of death and murder and ill intent, he relaxed into his chair and sipped his tea with a satisfactory sigh.

"What if someone else tries to do that to me? What if they don't even mean to but think it as a passing thought?"

"Try not to worry about it," Arick said. "You will learn from your training how much concentration is needed to manipulate the elements to attack another, especially while you're under attack. It is not possible to summon an element inside someone else to the point of killing them without an expressed wish to do so."

"But there are people who do it, right? Or else, why tell me all this?"

Arick ran his fingers down his cheeks. "Have you ever heard the word kamikaze?"

"A few times on television," James said. "I know Japanese pilots would deliberately crash their planes into the enemy in World War Two if it meant fulfilling their mission."

Arick raised his thick, bushy eyebrows. "That's right. These were people of strong conviction and character who wanted to achieve their desired goal at all costs. They gave their lives for what they thought was right. People with similar characteristics still exist in our world today." Arick finished his tea before standing up and walking over the wall of glass, where he gazed out over the beautiful view of the open sea. "James, we elementals are the same. In every group, in every community, there are those who are unsatisfied with the status quo or who crave power. Having power over someone else is an addiction for them. The more power they have, the more they want and the more they will do everything to get it. They'll use fear, force, blackmail… They will even take someone's life if they have to.

"Such people use kamikaze elementals to accomplish their selfish goals, James. The terrifyingly powerful ones will force people to commit heinous acts in their name. But the truly dangerous ones are the charismatic ones. They don't need to force other elementals to commit suicide for them; the elementals will do so willingly. Just like those Japanese pilots."

James rotated himself in his chair to get a better look at Arick. "I feel like you're talking about someone specific. Who are you talking about?"

"The governors."

"Who are—?"

"That's a good question. We do not know. Ever since the war ended, strange things have started to happen. To non-elementals, they look like natural phenomena. Tsunamis, earthquakes, floods, et cetera. But we believe someone is behind them. Someone who wants to create instability around the world. These governors might have something to do with it."

"Why would anyone want that?" James asked. So Dalnur was right, after all, he thought.

"Power? Revenge? Who knows? All we know is that our allies have captured a handful of elementals and dark elves committing terrible acts around the world, and they have never shared their missions with us. Only that they work for their governors."

"Governors? As in more than one?"

"We don't know how many there are or how they are organized, but we are assuming they are working together as their missions and titles are the same."

James searched his memory for a moment. "You said dark elves, right? Kymil told me about them. They're led by an elf called Besola. He turned on his kind when he lost his child in the war."

"Not only his child; his wife, too. We don't know much about him except what Kymil has told us. He was well respected once...before he went rogue."

"And he is one of these governors?"

Arick smiled. "You are a bright lad, James. Yes, we think he is. As for the governor who leads the rogue elementals, we know more about him. But unlike Besola, who has revenge and reform in mind, Damyan is only interested in power. He has turned many of our people from around the world to his cause and he now commands hundreds, if not thousands."

"How? What's his goal?" James asked.

"For as long as elementals have existed, some have thought they should not hide from non-elementals, but use their power to establish their superiority. To rule the world, if you like. Some of the greatest warlords in history were elementals who believed as Damyan does. Fortunately, common sense has always prevailed. A world in which non-elementals are treated as inferior is a world doomed to segregation, slavery, and second-class citizens.

"Unfortunately, Damyan is proving to be particularly charismatic and convincing, or else he possesses some power or weapon that we don't know about that is helping him win so many to his side."

A distant rumble shook the rock around the house and dust and wood chippings fell from the ceiling and onto James' head. The shock of it made James drop his cup, which shattered on the floor, and books fell off the shelves that encircled the room.

"Quickly, James," Arick said, suddenly moving like a man half his age, "follow me." At once, they both rushed to the door, up the stairs, and into the open.

"An earthquake?" James asked.

"No. Most certainly not. Go, James! Go and hide!"

Did he really say I should hide? thought James. "I'm not hiding!"

As he said it, another bang echoed across the island, this time much louder, and, James surmised, much closer. The dust rose from the ground and they both coughed. Seconds later, shouting reached them as a red ball of fire came hurtling through the sky and slammed into the nearby the forest. In seconds, the trees began to burn. Flames rose high up in the sky, followed by thick smoke that rose even higher. People shouted in the distance, but the only word James could distinguish was the name Jimmy. James turned to Arick, but he was nowhere to be seen. James ran through the woods as fast as he could, turning his head from one side to another searching for somebody he knew; somebody who could explain to him what was going on. Reaching the edge of the forest, he felt the heat on his left arm and shoulder from the blazing fire. The fire was growing bigger and hotter by the second and was so close to the path that he had to cover the left side of his face with his hand to protect his eyes. When he was safely out of the woods, his brain started to function normally again.

What the hell just happened? he asked himself.

Remembering his powers, James turned to face the burning woods behind him. He tried to concentrate on pulling the moisture from the atmosphere to douse the flames, but the air was already too dry. He tried to conjure wind, next, but every snap of the trees made him jump and stopped him from concentrating hard enough.

“You’re useless,” he muttered under his breath.

Realizing he couldn’t put out the fire alone, James got back onto his feet and turned around when he saw a woman dressed in black running in the opposite direction, but before she disappeared in the tree line, she turned her head just enough for James to recognize her immediately. Alan's wife? James thought. What was her name? Ah, Stacey. Stacey Brick. I saw her at the docks the day after Alan died. But why is she...?

Then it occurred to James and he felt his skin turn cold, even with the fierce fire still at his back. She was there during the attack on the palace. She is one of them!

Before James could make sense of anything, he heard someone call his name.

"You OK?" Marcus asked, jogging across jutting rocks and singed grass to reach him.

"Yes, I'm fine," James replied, still with one eye on the woods where he had seen Stacey disappear. "What's going on?"

"We have to get somewhere safe. To the school."

"Safe?" James asked. "But the fighting... We have to help."

But Marcus didn't hear him. He made a few gestures with his hands, lifted them into the air, and a second later, black clouds appeared over the trees. Heavy rain, the likes of which James had never seen before, began to fall; not raindrops, but small waterfalls falling straight out of the air, as if someone had opened hundreds of taps and let the water flow. Immediately, the fire began to subside.

"I'm here to protect you," Marcus said. "Those are my orders. Like it or not, you're not ready. Let's go."

James wanted to argue but he didn't know what he could do or say to convince Marcus otherwise. He still felt weak after trying to stop the fire; something Marcus had managed with what had looked like a passing thought. So, when Marcus ushered him to follow and started running, James had no choice but to follow him.

The school wasn't far, and after reaching the brow of the hill and following the snaking stony path, James spotted the clearing where he had practiced the day before. Two groups of people stood facing each other, and even though he could only see the backs of his friends and allies, he recognized those he knew best. John's massive frame was clearly visible at the head of the group, and Alex and Tony and some dozen others were standing behind him. Among them was Mary, who flanked Tony and Alex, while Mike and Venessa were right at the back. But despite being so close to the black-clad attackers, some of whom were mere meters away from John, no one seemed to be doing any fighting. James slowed his pace, almost coming to a complete stop, and squinted until he noticed a thin, almost invisible barrier between John and the man in front of him. It looked like liquid glass with tiny waves that shimmered on the surface. The barrier reached so far into the sky that James couldn't make out its end, and off it stretched off to the sides in both directions, well beyond the wooded borders of the clearing.

"What are you doing?" Marcus called out. He had already reached the school entrance. "We have to go inside!" When James shook his head, Marcus ran back to grab him by the arm, but James shrugged his shoulders, freeing himself.

"No," James said calmly. "My friends are out there."

"And you think you can help them?" Marcus asked. "Besides, they don't need any help. Do you think this handful of losers could hurt any of them?"

"Why on earth should I hide, then?" James asked with a determined look and he started walking toward his friends, coming to a stop beside Venessa and Mike. Sensing his arrival, the others turned to acknowledge James, while John glared at Marcus, who just shrugged before coming over to stand at James' shoulder.

"Mr. Tanner!" the man on the other side of the barrier exclaimed. "Welcome. So nice of you to join us. I was wondering if you were going to show up."

Although the barrier blurred the image of the man speaking to him, James could see he was tall and slim, with greasy, shoulder-length black hair. His face was as pale as a corpse, accentuated by his all-black attire: a long coat over a t-shirt and trousers, and thick, heavy-duty boots.

"Who are you? How do you know my name?" James said.

"Wow, I didn't know I needed to be introduced. Please, forgive my incivility." The man bowed his head a little. "My name is Damyan. At your service."

James felt dizzy. How was this possible? He had only just learned about this so-called rogue elemental, and now he was here, attacking them?

"Enough with the drama, Damyan," John said. "I'll ask once more, what do you want?"

"I just wanted to say hello to my old friends," Damyan replied in a girly voice. "Is that so bad?"

"You have no friends here. Be gone."

"Now, now. That's not something you should say to an old friend." Damyan turned his head to look at James again, and as he smirked, his blue lips pulled back over his long, rotten teeth. "James, your mother says hello. She was very disappointed when she heard who you're hanging out with. It breaks her heart." He cupped both his hands against his chest and put on an exaggerated frown.

With a light step, James tried to approach the barrier, but his legs had lost their strength and he had to lean on John for support. "My...mother? She's alive?"

"But of course," Damyan replied. "How do you think we figured out where to find you in Miami? She told us all about the orphanage." His smile fell. "Of course, somehow, she managed to get a warning out before we could get to you. You were gone by the time my team arrived."

"I-Is that why I was told to leave? I wasn't kicked out... It's because you were coming for me? But that means—"

"That someone at the orphanage knew the truth about you? Absolutely. We found them and we...persuaded them to talk, which led us to the docks."

"Persuaded...?" James whispered to himself. He raised his gaze to Damyan's black eyes. "Who did you hurt? Tell me!" But James knew there was only one person it could have been; the only person who had ever shown him any kind of attention and kindness beyond just keeping him alive. Deputy Maria Bulgar. "Where is she? Is she ok? Is she—?"

"Shut up, Damyan! You don't know what you're talking about," John said, widening his stance and squaring his shoulders. "Victoria died seventeen years ago."

"My-my, for some self-proclaimed leader, you sure don't know a lot about the people you're supposed to be protecting." Damyan put his right hand in his coat pocket and pulled out a gold necklace with a glittering pendant. He brought it closer to the barrier and waited for James to step closer. Engraved in calligraphy were the letters M and J, separated by a heart. "Do you recognize this, James? I suppose you don't, but John certainly does."

James' mind was swimming with questions, so he felt a small sense of relief when he noticed Mary approaching John.

She looked him straight in the eye. "John, what does this mean?"

"Nothing. He could have got that from anywhere," John said, his gaze still firmly on Damyan. "He could have conjured it out of thin air for all we know. Damyan, you are never going to pass this barrier. Even if you could, you know it wouldn't end well for you and your companions."

"Maybe not. But I also may not have to. Or maybe I already have," Damyan said with a childish grin.

John scoffed. "There's no chance—"

"No," James said, recalling Stacey Brick. "I think...I think he's right." James felt the hairs on his arms start to rise. "John, I saw someone, a woman. She ran toward the settlement."

"We have a lot of women here, James. Now is not the time to—"

"I saw a woman running toward the Castle. She is not one of us, I'm certain. I saw her at the docks in Miami. She was married to a man who worked there as a security guard, or so she claimed anyway. He-He was killed. Her name is...is...Stacey. Stacey Brick."

John squinted at James, then nodded at Tony and Alex. He spun on his heels and opened his mouth to say something to Damyan when a deep growl suddenly rumbled through the ground. James couldn't tell if it was coming from the other side of the island or right under his feet, but when the ground started to shake, everybody flinched. Everybody except Tony and Alex, who remained calm and focused, and James realized they were probably the ones maintaining the force field that was keeping Damyan at bay. As James looked for something to hold on to, several blunt explosions sounded through the air in quick succession, and he turned his head to see a black cloud of smoke in the distance.

John unleashed a cry of fury while raising his hands before abruptly bringing them down toward the ground as if to strike it. As he did so, a green flash of light sparked in midair, then cracks in the ground opened up on the other side of the barrier and beneath the feet of Damyan and his followers. James watched in horror as the black holes swallowed those who couldn't react fast enough to save themselves. Those who didn't fall into the chasm still lost their balance and had to jump to the side to hold on to the crumbling soil. At the same time, Alex and Tony raised their hands in front of them, and the barrier started to move toward Damyan, forcing him and those closest to the force field to step, roll, and jump back.

Once they were able to scramble to their feet, Damyan and his group retaliated. James saw a flurry of flashing lights on the other side of the barrier and he immediately remembered what Arick had told him about pointers; about how they appear only when somebody is trying to use the elements to hurt someone. He noticed his hands shaking violently while several attacks from Damyan and his group were deflected by the barrier. Boulders and fireballs crashed into the force field, exploding on impact, and a large icicle in the shape of a spear flew directly at James' face, only to shatter into a million pieces, as well.

Just as James was about to let out a long sigh of relief, a young man behind Damyan conjured lightning in a way he hadn't even seen Marcus manage. The streaks of electricity flew out of his hands and slammed into the barrier, causing it to shake, shimmer, and vibrate. The blow was followed by a roar of thunder so loud that it forced almost everyone to their knees and to cover their ears with their hands. Alex staggered, briefly causing the barrier to flicker out of existence, but he quickly straightened himself and the barrier was restored.

Throughout it all, John was giving orders to everyone on James' side of the barrier. Despite his initial fury, John spoke with a calmness that conveyed his confidence and battle experience. One of those orders was for Mike and Venessa; he told them to find this Stacey and remove her from the island.

"Go with them," John said to James. "You know what she looks like. And watch out for each other. We will handle this."

James ran after Venessa and Mike as fast as he could, catching up with them at the entrance to the school.

"Wait up!" James cried, and the pair turned around, each holding the other's hand. "Your dad told me to go with you. To help."

"Perfect!" Mike exclaimed while Venessa smiled with sad eyes. "We'll cut through the school. It's the fastest way to the other side of Leilani Reef."

They were hardly inside the building when Venessa held up her hand to order James and Mike to stop running. "Do you hear that?"

"Someone's in trouble," James said.

"Or fighting," Mike added.

"Either way, we need to help them," Venessa said. She rotated on the spot a few times as she tried to locate the direction of the sounds of crashing, tumbling, and grunting. "This way!"

As they reached the end of the long, polished hallway, James saw thick smoke coming through the gaps in the door of one of the classrooms. The air was acrid with the smell of burning wood and plastic, and he started to sweat in the hot, stifling air.

"In here!" Venessa cried as the first of them to reach the inferno that had engulfed the classroom.

James ran up to the door. Despite the smoke and fire inside the room, the glass in the door was somehow still in place. He tried to press his face against it to squint through the smoke, but the heat made him snap his hands away. "I think... I see Dalnur! He's in trouble!"

Occasionally, amid the thick rolling smoke and flickers of flame, James spied the colorful flash of a pointer or two.

Dalnur was only a few feet from the door, ducking behind an upturned desk, only peering over the top to project chunks of flooring and ceiling tiles at his target using his earth elemental power.

Fear gripped James' throat, and it hurt to swallow. "Dalnur's an elemental, too, isn't he? Why hasn't he put the fire out?"

"He can't control fire or water, James," Venessa said with biting impatience. "Anyway, I think there is someone else in there with him. He can't put out the fire while he's fighting for his life."

"Then we need to do it for him! We need to help!" James wanted to summon something, anything, to kill the fire to save his friend, but as his mind jumped from one imagined solution to the next, he couldn't focus on a single idea. Every time he tried to conjure water, he thought of Dalnur running out of time and the idea slipped from his mind; when he tried to summon a wind to blow out the flames, he could only produce a blow of air more useless than if he had used his mouth. He fumbled with his hands and his thoughts to try to help, but every crack from the collapsing classroom made him jump and snapped him out of his thoughts.

"I can't... Why isn't it working? I can't summon the water."

"Try earth," Mike said.

"He can manipulate earth?" Venessa said.

"Earth? And do what?" James snapped. "I'll bring the whole building down on top of us."

"Air, then," Mike said, preparing to do exactly that.

As Mike focused on creating a wave in the air to enter through the gaps in the door to clear away the smoke,

James saw Venessa looking at him curiously; apparently, Mike hadn't told her James could control three elements. She shook her head to focus on what was happening, and a moment later, Venessa summoned a stream of water to douse the flames.

With the confidence he got from his friends managing the fire, James finally came to his senses. He tried conjuring another stream of air like Mike had done, and he felt the wind on his back, which pushed the door off its hinges and filled the classroom.

"James, no!" Venessa cried.

Somehow, the wind he'd summoned didn't douse the fire, but fed it; so quickly, in fact, that the flames inside the classroom where Dalnur was fighting exploded outward in every direction, forcing James and his friends onto their backs.

"No!" James cried, picking himself back up.

"Dalnur!" Mike and Venessa yelled in unison.

CHAPTER 13

A Departure

"IS HE ALIVE? Is he OK?" James said.

Seeing what he had done, James fell to his knees in defeat and watched the raging fire continue to consume everything around it. A hand touched his shoulder. James was about to tell Mike and Venessa to withhold any empty words of comfort when he looked up and saw Kymil.

"What are you doing here?"

James blinked back the tears and looked into the fire again. "Dalnur is in there. I...I..."

Kymil stepped in front of the room, and with a few hand movements, the fire died out as easily as if the elf had blown out the candles on a birthday cake. The elf's mastery of his power made James feel numb. Without pausing, Kymil summoned wind and water to cool the embers by the classroom entrance, he peered inside, then retreated almost immediately. "It's empty."

"Wha—?" James said, accepting Mike's help and getting to his feet.

"He got out," Venessa said with a smile.

"There's a gap in the wall," Kymil said, walking back inside the blackened shell of the former classroom. "Perhaps he escaped that way. Come with me."

Together, the four headed through the crumbling school wall and into the settlement. Walking at a brisk pace, James struggled to divide his thoughts between Dalnur's well-being and the battle they had left on the other side of the school. He stopped for a moment and looked back. He couldn't see John or any flashes of pointers, but the barrier had disappeared from the sky and the sounds of thunder, water, fire, and earth crashing together had only intensified. He could only imagine what was happening.

When they got close enough to the settlement, James stopped, not believing what he was looking at. It was as if a tornado had cut everything down; street lamps were bent to the floor, houses leveled to the ground, and even the surrounding trees had been uprooted. Some cottages were still engulfed in fire as the grass around them withered, changing from green to yellow to black.

"Divide into two groups. Mike, Venessa, you take the left side, and James and I will take the right," Kymil said with urgency in his voice.

"W-Where is everyone? All the people who lived here?"

"Fear not, James," Kymil said, leading them in the other direction to Mike and Venessa. "Everyone was evacuated to the Castle at the start of the attack. It's not just a nickname; the place is a fortress. Now, keep your eyes open. If there was someone in that room with Dalnur, they might still be here, and from the looks of this place, they're not friendly."

They walked through the rubble; the remains of houses, furniture, and other household items were scattered all around them. At one of the cottages, James bent down and picked up a picture of a family of four: two children hugging their parents. He thought of what it would have been like if he'd grown up with his parents and maybe a brother or sister, then he remembered what Damyan had said back in the clearing.

My mother is alive? She's been out there, all this time, and Damyan has her. I have to find her… I have to help her…

"Over here!" Mike shouted.

James dropped the picture, and together with Kymil, ran toward Mike and Venessa, finding them behind a nearby pile of rubble. As he rounded the backs of Mike and Venessa, James felt a lump in his throat as he caught sight of two bodies. Stacey was lying on her back with a knife protruding from her chest. Her eyes were open and she didn't show any signs of life. Close by, Dalnur was leaning on his side and breathing deep, labored breaths. He was badly burned all over his right side, and his right arm was so severely broken and twisted as to not look like an arm at all. He was so lost in his pain that he seemed not to have noticed us approaching until Kymil touched the top of his head. There was relief in his eyes when he opened them, but he promptly shut them tight again. He wanted to say something but he couldn't mutter anything but unintelligible grunts through the pain and blood.

"Venessa," James whispered, "look at him. Did I…? Back at the classroom…"

Venessa walked over to James and held his hand. He could tell from her wide eyes that she wanted to reassure him, but James knew the truth. He had tried to use his powers, and in so doing, he had made things worse and seriously injured Dalnur in the process.

"I'm…I'm so sorry, Dalnur," James said. The dwarf opened his eyes again, but he struggled to look at James for long.

"He's losing a lot of blood." Kymil pulled Dalnur into a sitting position, so he immediately began to breathe easier. "He might not be conscious for much longer." The elf then turned his gaze to Mike. "Go! Find Victor and bring him here."

Mike immediately took off, and James was convinced he'd never seen someone run so fast. Venessa kneeled beside Dalnur, who was looking up at Kymil, and held his hand.

"I…got her," the dwarf said to Kymil, his voice raspy and weak. "She thought she was a…match for me."

"Rest, my friend. Help is on its way."

"When the attack…started, I hurried here to warn everybody… Brought them to safety," Dalnur said between bloody coughs and bouts of breathlessness.

"Try not to talk," Venessa said. "Save your strength."

James couldn't bear it. Dalnur looked up at him again and tried to smile, but it only made James more desperate to turn away, and he disappeared back behind the pile of rubble. As he did, he heard shuffling and the moving of stone behind the wall of the half-ruined house. James turned abruptly to see a man emerging on the other side, his eyes fixed on Kymil, Dalnur, and Venessa. It was clear he was an elemental, as he walked with his hands in front of him, cupping a column of swirling flame in each one.

No! James thought. He'd been helpless back on the battlefield alongside John and the others, and now Dalnur was dying because of him. No one else was going to die today; he had to do something!

But the elemental was fast approaching his friends. Kymil and Venessa were too distracted trying to help Dalnur and they had their backs to him, and the dwarf could barely see straight. As the assassin drew nearer, James focused on the flames in the man's hands, the power of them, the unyielding intensity. For a moment, it was as though he could feel the fire; like he was connected to it.

"No!" James cried out, climbing onto an upturned cabinet, alerting the elemental to his presence and making himself the target instead. As he summoned his courage, he felt warmth rising through his legs, stomach, chest, and arms. "No more!"

When James opened his eyes, he didn't know what was worse: the stabbing pain in his head or the burning sensation in his palms. Once his vision had adjusted to the light, he saw Venessa was kneeling beside him, while Kymil was standing just a little further back. She pulled on James' arm, and he barely managed to get up. His whole body ached as if he had been laboring all day; it reminded him of his work at the docks back in Miami.

"What happened?" James asked, looking around frantically. "Wait, there's someone here. We need to get out of here!"

No one spoke; Venessa just stared at him with her mouth open, while Kymil stood upright, his expression wary and alert. James looked around to discover they were still among the ruined settlement. His eyes retraced events from where he had stood on the upturned cabinet to where he had seen the man conjuring fire. A three-foot-wide trail of scorched earth ran from his feet to the edge of the woods, far in the distance. At the end of the trail, there was a body, motionless, the clothes upon it still smoldering.

"W-What happened?" James repeated. His chest felt like it was being crushed. "What have I done?"

"You saved us," Venessa said, trying to calm him down. "That man was about to attack us, and you stopped him. He tried to take cover behind the wall, but your stream of fire obliterated it completely and, as you can see, threw him into the trees."

"My what?" James asked. "I can't control fire."

Kymil stepped closer. "Apparently, you can, Mr. Tanner."

"And what about...? Is he...?" James said.

"Yes," Kymil replied at once. "Better him than us."

"I...killed a man?" James said slowly, almost as if talking to himself. James sat back until he was resting against some exposed brick. "Why am I still alive? I thought casting an element with the intent to harm or kill another meant you suffered the consequences as well?"

"You didn't summon the fire from within him. You summoned it from without and projected it at him. That's very different."

A small pickup came speeding along the dusty road and came to a stop right beside them, then Mike stepped out of the driver's seat. John and Mary hopped out of the backseats, and an older gentleman walked around from the passenger's side. John and the older man went straight to Dalnur and kneeled beside him, while Mary stumbled when she saw James. After raising her hand to her mouth, she let out a short sigh when she looked up to see James was OK, then she peered at the scorch marks on the ground by his feet with a raised eyebrow.

The old man, meanwhile, checked Dalnur's vitals. "We have to get him inside. Bring the stretcher from the car."

Mike did as he was told, and together, Mike, John, Kymil, and the old man carefully placed Dalnur on the board and lifted him into the back of the pickup. Mike jumped back into the driver's seat, while the old man and John stayed in the back with Dalnur, and they drove off.

James looked at Kymil, who was watching the vehicle disappear in the distance with a sad expression on his face.

"He's going to be OK."

"No, he won't." Kymil wiped his hands on a handkerchief. "He is too badly hurt. Dwarfs are the toughest of us, and none showcase their strength and resilience like Dalnur. But his insides are crushed. He'll probably be dead before they even arrive."

"Don't say that. You should have some hope."

"Hope? There is no hope when the outcome is known. He is going to die, and we can do nothing about it. Dalnur is my friend. My very good friend, and I would like to hope that he would survive, but we elves do not live by hope but by the facts."

"I'm...I'm so sorry. The explosion in the school... Just before you found us... It was my fault."

Kymil moved closer to James and leaned in. "Save your self-pity, Mr. Tanner. You may be one of the rare elementals in this world who can control four elements, but you are still a beginner, and no beginner could ever have harmed my dear friend."

"But—"

"But, nothing, Mr. Tanner. It was not the explosion that gave Dalnur his wounds. That woman he fought against was clearly stronger than any of us could have anticipated. Just look at all this destruction around us."

James didn't know whether to feel relief or anger. Was Kymil just saying this to make him feel better? Was he saying it to make *himself* feel better?

"We should go," Kymil said.

"What about them?" James looked at the dead bodies of Stacey Brick and the fire elemental.

"Leave them. I'll send someone to remove the bodies." Kymil slowly started walking in the same direction the car had driven, while Venessa and Mary followed at a distance, consoling one another over Dalnur's condition.

"Who was the man with Mike?" James asked.

"Victor? He is Leilani Reef's head physician. You didn't meet him before?" James shook his head. "As gifted a doctor as he is, he is an even more powerful medium."

Before long, the four companions reached the Castle. Once inside, it was clear from the commotion that the vast majority of the island's inhabitants had been told to gather in the large dining hall.

"Dalnur saved them all," Kymil said to no one in particular as he walked in ahead of James, Mary, and Venessa. "True to your word, my good friend."

A melancholic hush had descended over the enormous space; despite the crowds, there was no laughter, conversation, or socializing. Everyone moved as though in a hurry, yet few spoke with more than a whisper. There were still leftovers from breakfast on the tables, a few broken glasses on the floor, as well as several overturned chairs. James picked one up and sat down at the table where Mike was waiting, and Mary and Venessa joined them.

"Did you hear anything about Dalnur?" James said, keeping his voice low. "Will he be OK?"

Mike raised his head from the table and rubbed his eyes. "We don't know yet. Victor is with him."

"What happened to the others after we left to find the woman that...hurt Dalnur?"

"They tried to destroy the barrier but failed, so Damyan tried to lead a retreat," Mary said. "John ordered Tony and Alex to lower the barrier and for the rest of us to attack. Damyan and two others got away."

"And the others?" James placed his hand on top of Mary's to try to stop it from shaking.

She shook her head. "You know, I've always been against violence, but now that I've seen what they did to Jimmy and Dalnur, I can see why John, Tony, and Alex do things the way they do. They are ruthless...but maybe that's what we need to be to survive."

"Who's Jimmy?" James asked.

"Jimmy, a mute, dark-skinned boy. I'm sure you saw him the day you arrived."

James thought for a moment. "You spoke with him and he replied using his hands." Mary wiped her tears away. "What happened?"

"It must have been Stacey. All the others were behind the barrier. They couldn't get through. She burned him alive."

"What did you mean when you said you now support Tony and Alex?" James shook his head. "I'm sorry, now isn't the time for my questions."

Mary let out a short laugh and quickly lifted her sleeve to cover her runny nose, brought on by her tears. "It's OK. I'd rather answer your incessant questions than think about Dalnur and Jimmy right now. As for John and his team, the ends always justify the means with them. They are ruthless because they believe it is the only way to survive our even more ruthless enemies. But having no boundaries means they will sometimes try to justify the most awful of methods to get what they want. There are a lot of people here who are afraid of them and don't support their way, and until today, I was one of them. But not anymore. How else can we win against people willing to harm poor, poor Jimmy?"

James wasn't sure if he agreed, but as Mary continued to wipe her eyes and nose with her sleeves, he knew now wasn't the time to challenge her opinions. Instead, the four sat in silence, sharing in the somber moment, supporting one another merely by sharing the space.

After some time, Mike sat up and looked at the dining hall entrance, causing James, Mary, and Venessa to do the same. John and Kymil entered together.

"Dalnur didn't make it." Kymil's voice was quiet, gentle, and steady.

Mary covered her mouth with her hands. "No!"

In some way, James had been expecting the news. Dalnur had looked so close to death before, and Kymil had seemed so sure his friend had had no chance.

But what good is all this magic if we can't save the ones we care about? James thought. It was naive, he knew, but a thought that came to him again and again, no matter how his mind justified things.

From the look on Mary's face, she was contemplating something similar. James considered comforting her, as Mike and Venessa were comforting each other, but Mary's warm and gentle features quickly twisted into a fierce and serious expression.

John stepped forward with his gaze fixed on James. "Kymil told me what happened."

James dropped his head. "I'm sorry. I was just trying to help. Venessa and Mike had it under control, and I just made things worse. If I hadn't exploded the classroom, perhaps Dalnur wouldn't have been injured. Or perhaps we would have got to him sooner—"

John held up his hand, then peered at Kymil.

"I already told the boy he need not blame himself. Dalnur was a warrior. He would not have been defeated by an accident." Despite Kymil's condescending tone, James appreciated his words.

"No," John said, "I was referring to how you saved everyone's life. You conjured fire."

Mike slowly turned his head toward James. "You what?" He pulled out of his embrace with his sister and gave her a playful punch on the shoulder. "Why didn't any of you tell me?"

John gave Mike a sideways glance, frowned, then looked back at James. "Not only did you exhibit great bravery today, James, but you have the potential to master four elements. This is an extremely rare talent, and a huge boon for Leilani Reef." He stepped closer and put a hand on James' shoulder. "And when our enemies find out, it will also make you a target. Do you understand?"

James swallowed down the many questions on the tip of his tongue. "I think so."

"Good. Now, normally, we would encourage you to explore your ability to manipulate the elements slowly and while under careful supervision. Unfortunately, today's attack means time is a luxury we cannot afford.

"From now on, your only task is to learn and train to use your elements. Nothing else matters. Do you understand me?" John didn't wait for a reply. Instead, he turned to the others at the table, pointing at Mary then Mike then Venessa. "And your job is to help him any way you can. Got it?"

John turned and walked away, but James called after him. "No, wait!" When John stopped, James stepped closer. "My mother is alive. You heard what Damyan said. We have to find her. We have to save her..."

John's expression twisted into a sad frown. "All the more reason for you to master your elements as soon as possible. This was not the last battle, today, but the first of many to come." He then reached into his pocket, grabbed James' hand, and pushed a cold object in between his fingers. "I found this after Damyan fled. He was right... It's real."

As John turned to leave, James looked into the palm of his hand. It was the necklace Damyan had shown him. His mother's necklace.

The sun shone brightly through the high windows of the dining hall, causing the walls to glow the color of gold. But the beauty of the early evening did little to offset the overwhelming feeling of sadness that was shared by the crowd who had gathered to pay their respects to Dalnur. Like everyone else,

James had arrived back into the hall with a clenched stomach and red eyes. He sat at his usual table in silence, his busy fingers intertwined, exchanging only the briefest of hushed whispers with anyone who acknowledged him.

Fifteen minutes later, music started to play, and when Marcus stood up, everyone else in the hall, slowly, one by one, raised themselves out of their chairs as well. John opened the dining hall doors, and James realized the music was coming from outside. The large man indicated for everyone to follow him through the doorway, down the corridor, and into the low, orange sunlight outside. As James stepped onto the grass, he saw Kymil standing next to a steel coffin in which Dalnur had been laid to rest. The elf had his eyes closed, and he seemed to sway softly to the sound of the music, the corners of his mouth flinching at every beat of the drums. Mary, like so many others, sobbed soundlessly, and husbands and wives, brothers and sisters, cousins and friends all embraced one another. Eventually, the music stopped.

After a few minutes of respectful silence, James winced when the musicians started banging the drums again, this time harder, faster. This was not a somber rhythm, but the sounds of war. Out of the trees, a dozen dwarfs wearing shining gold armor and carrying steel weapons marched toward them, their footsteps matching the beats of the drums. They stopped next to the coffin and bowed their heads. One of them placed a silver knife on Dalnur's chest, uttered some indistinct words, then indicated for the other dwarfs to work together to hoist the coffin onto their collective shoulders. The dwarfs led the rest of the islanders on a slow march to the edge of the island. They stopped next to a huge boulder, and James immediately noticed the hole that had been cut into its side.

Every member of the funeral ceremony was invited to walk up to the coffin to say their farewells. When it was James' turn to approach, together with Mary, Marcus, Venessa, and Mike, he placed his palm on the dwarf's mighty chest, and it comforted James to see that, even in death, Dalnur had a small smile on his pale face.

"You never got a chance to take me to see your city," James whispered. "But I will visit one day soon and think of you."

Mary couldn't stand it anymore and again burst into tears, so with Venessa's prompting, James led her back to the side.

After everybody had said their goodbyes, the dwarfs lifted the coffin carefully into the hole, then proceeded to place smaller stones on and around the coffin until Dalnur was completely covered. Kymil then walked over and stopped in front of the tomb. He outstretched his left hand, and with his right, made a circular motion. Instantly, the stones covering the coffin melted into molten rock, and a fraction of a second later, they cooled again, becoming solid, and thus, sealed Dalnur in his tomb. Some of the onlookers gasped as the steam rose from the boulder and wafted high into the air, but what followed was only silence, except for the waves crashing into the cliffs below, the high-pitched mewing of seagulls, and eventually, the shuffling of feet as, slowly, little by little, the crowd began to dissipate, leaving only Kymil and the dwarfs.

James and his group moved away and sat down under a nearby tree. The sun slowly began to set, casting shadows all around them, while the wind blew from the sea, bringing in the fresh and salty air. Once the sun had set completely, they saw Kymil walking beneath the silver light of the moon, and invited him to join them.

"I have known Dalnur for a long time," he said, sitting down on a thick, arching tree root. James thought he could hear the grief in the elf's broken voice. "This is a great loss for us all. Not only dwarfs but elves and humans, too. He was a proud dwarf in appearance but he possessed nothing of his species' typical stubbornness and pride. Dalnur was open-minded, diplomatic, and always behaved without prejudice. He was an ally to all."

James contemplated his words, and Dalnur's burned body after his bout with Stacey Brick flashed before his eyes. He tried to shake it off by asking another question. "How did the dwarfs arrive so fast?"

"Dwarfs are scattered all over the world just like elemental humans and elves. Every time a dwarf dies, it is, according to their custom, essential to be buried as soon as possible. It must hardly come as a surprise to you that dwarfs believe they come from the earth, so to the earth, they must return. Most of these dwarfs came from the nearby islands the minute I informed them of Dalnur's passing."

"For how long will they guard the tomb?" Mike whispered.

"They will guard the body for the next twelve hours. Then return to their homes."

Mary wiped her eyes. "This is the first time I've seen a dwarf funeral. No one gave a funeral speech or anything like that. Why?"

"No one is allowed to speak at the dwarf's funeral about the deceased. Everything there was to say would have been said during his lifetime."

James thought about asking Kymil about the funeral rituals of elves but bit the inside of his cheek to avoid doing so. It wasn't the time for his curiosity to get the better of him. It was a time to mourn their beloved friend.

Marcus raised an imaginary glass. "To Dalnur."

Kymil repeated the gesture, and with a smile on their lips, so did everyone else.

After that, Kymil rose to his feet. "I'm going away for a few days to visit Dalnur's family. Keep in mind what John said, James. Learn, practice, and get as much help as you need. Farewell."

After waving Kymil off, Marcus stood up next. "Your first class will be with me, James. We'll start first thing tomorrow. Arick is going to wait for us outside after breakfast."

CHAPTER 14

MANEUVERS

AFTER AN ALMOST SLEEPLESS night in which images of the man he'd killed haunted him, James and Marcus went for a walk around the island so James could clear his head. They passed Dalnur's tomb, where the dwarfs were still standing, and a little while later, came across Arick and Mary sitting on a bench that overlooked the ocean. Arick looked even older and more tired than usual, but that didn't stop him from getting up when James approached.

"Now, you have seen what sadness and devastation the elements can cause when they are used by people like Damyan. We thought we had more time for you to train, but I'm afraid we were wrong. Very, very wrong. I'm sorry your introduction to this world has been so rushed, James, but we need to speed up your training even more now."

"Starting right now," Marcus added, rubbing his palms together.

James fiddled with his mother's necklace that he had decided to wear. He didn't feel ready, but he said what he knew everyone wanted to hear: "Let's begin."

From the corner of his eye, James saw four figures approaching in the distance. As they got closer, he saw it was Tony and Alex, both of whom were wearing long white lab coats. Behind them, Mike and Venessa gave James soft, sad smiles.

"You will practice with us," Tony said as he got close enough for James to hear him. "It's time you learn to use your abilities alongside your friends and allies. Alone, an elemental is powerful, but they are limited by the elements they can master and their energy levels."

"Marcus will help you, and Arick will oversee everything," Alex added, "while Venessa and Mike will be our energy donors—elementals who willfully allow mediums to channel and manipulate their energy and power to use as they see fit."

Arick started to pace back and forth with his hands behind his back. "The most important thing you have to learn now is defense. Mary tells me you saw the barrier Tony and Alex created during the battle. This is something you can use your elements to do, too, and it is one of the most essential tools in your arsenal when it comes to defending yourself from attacks.

"The one good thing to come out of the attack on Leilani Reef is that we now know you are one of the few elementals on the planet who can control four elements. This means you have more you can draw upon not only to attack your enemies, but also to defend yourself. You can summon barriers of wind, earth, water, fire, or any combination of them. Thus, your only limitations are your...?" Arick waited for James to finish his sentence.

"Erm, my imagination, my concentration, and my energy reserves."

"Precisely," Arick said, resuming his pacing. "Now, give it a try."

James stepped back a few feet away to ensure he had enough space, then he closed his eyes to concentrate. While he had now manipulated every element at least once, he'd mostly practiced with water, so it was with the water in the air around him that he felt the strongest connection. Sure enough, as he imagined the water droplets emerging from the atmosphere around him and gathering in front of him, he opened his eyes to see a wall of mist. As the seconds passed, the mist became thicker and thicker, until James couldn't see anyone on the other side of it.

Suddenly, James saw the faint flash of blue light through the barrier he had conjured, then a sphere came shooting through the mist and hit James squarely in his chest, knocking him off his feet and leaving him drenched in water.

When James was finally able to catch his breath and get to his feet, he saw that his barrier of water had vanished, and Alex was standing before him with his hands raised in his direction.

"No, no," Arick said, coming closer to stand over him. "Get up."

Marcus gave James a hand and pulled him back to his feet. "Watch me first, then we'll try it together."

Also using water, Marcus quickly formed a barrier in front of Marcus, and once again, Alex raised his hands, a blue pointer flashed, and a sphere of water flew toward Marcus. Only this time, the sphere disintegrated the instant it touched the barrier.

Marcus put his hands on his hips before pointing his right index finger at the ground. "This barrier shall not be crossed!" he said in a deep, comical voice.

But then, Tony conjured a ball of fire and propelled it at the barrier, which was immediately followed by another water sphere from Alex. The ball of fire struck the barrier, causing it to disintegrate at once, and the water sphere hit Marcus flat in the chest. Just as it had done with James, the force of the strike sent Marcus flying a couple of feet and landing hard on his back.

"Never allow yourself to be distracted," Arick said, raising his finger at James. He then rotated until he was looking at Marcus. "And never become arrogant. You never know who you're going to run into and what that person can do. There is always someone who will be better, so always expect anything."

Marcus pushed himself onto his feet, then helped James up. "OK, this time, we work together," he whispered. "You focus on holding the barrier; I'll take care of the rest."

James closed his eyes and concentrated harder than ever. In an instant, the outline of the barrier appeared and quickly became denser and denser. Even before he opened his eyes, James could tell Marcus was joining in as the water somehow felt more powerful, more energized, and when James did finally feel confident enough to look, he saw the barrier resembled a wall of solid ice.

Alex took a shot at the barrier with a sphere of ice. When it crashed into the barrier, it broke into a million small shards that bounced back at him, and Alex had to duck to avoid being hit. James felt the vibrations from the impact against the barrier and his legs wobbled, which caused his concentration to drop a little. Before he could compose himself, Tony directed a fireball toward them. The barrier barely held in place, but Marcus parried the attack before summoning lightning bolts. They snapped and tore through the air, but Tony and Alex deflected them like they were swatting away flies.

"Very good," Arick said after the four had trained for what felt like an hour, "all of you." He turned to James. "Your progress is swift. You are a natural, just like your mother was."

"You...you trained my mother?" James said in between breaths.

"I did. She was—sorry, is—one of the most remarkable air elementals I have ever known. But let's not get distracted. We are not done for today. You saw that one of the most effective ways Alex, Tony, and Marcus distracted each other or deflected each other's attacks was with attacks of their own, yes? So, you, too, must learn to use offensive techniques for this purpose." He then stepped closer to James and grabbed his shoulders. "Have you ever heard the saying that offense is the best defense?"

"Of course," James said, thinking about some American Football movie he had watched at the orphanage.

"All right, then, show us what you can do. And remember the two most important pillars: concentration and imagination."

James turned away to avoid as many distractions as possible. He started small by summoning water and turning it into a shard of ice, then he strained as he used the air element to generate a powerful wind that sent the ice sphere flying into a nearby tree trunk at enormous speed.

"He could use a little help," James heard Arick say, and then a moment later, Marcus was standing next to James.

"That's a good start," Marcus said, "but we don't have time for child's play. It's time for you to do some real damage." Marcus pointed his finger at three objects: a large boulder the size of a truck, an old tree as tall as a building with antler-shaped branches and a huge trunk, and an abandoned car that must have been collecting moss and rust for decades.

"They are your enemy," Marcus said. "Destroy them."

James' first instinct was to protest because the objects were too big and tough, but he trusted the people around him who were guiding him, and more and more, he trusted his own ability to control and use his power. He focused on the boulder and started to imagine all the possible ways he might destroy it. He looked around and spotted another huge rock and decided to smash it into the boulder, but was interrupted instantly.

"Try another approach," Arick said.

"Why? James asked. "How do you know what I'm thinking?"

"It takes a lot of energy to lift such a heavy object, and conserving your energy and using it wisely is one of your most important concerns during a fight. You would pass out before getting it an inch off the ground."

Arick then turned to Tony, and in a split second, hundreds of small steel pellets rose from the ground and shot toward the boulder at extreme velocity, splitting it in half.

"That's what I am talking about," Arick said. "Minimum energy, maximum damage. Now, use your imagination."

James turned around again, and this time, his attention fell on the car. "OK, James," he whispered to himself. "Destroy it using only your elements. Which one? Fire? Sure, but what about something else? The car is made out of steel, which is made of the metals of the earth."

As he raised his hand, he concentrated on visualizing what he wanted to do. The sound of breaking glass, bending steel, and cracking plastic lasted for barely a second; almost as fast as James had been able to picture the outcome in his mind. He opened his eyes and saw the car was no more. Arick, Tony, Alex, and Marcus all stepped closer to the flattened pile of metal, which was now barely two feet tall, with open mouths and pale faces. The car looked like it had been flattened by an extraordinarily powerful hydraulic press.

"What did I say, eh?" Arick was smiling at James but directing his question at the others. "The boy's a natural."

Delighted with what he had achieved, James turned to the tree Marcus had said was another of his targets, and it began to sway. The earth rose around the tree, exposing its roots, and the wind started to blow harder until a small hurricane of air and soil engulfed the tree. A loud crack sounded along the coast as the hurricane grew wider, taller, stronger. When James relaxed his muscles, the tornado dissipated, and the tree was gone. All that was left was a torn stump and shredded bark, branches, and leaves all around it. He turned and saw that he was not the only one surprised by how quickly he had obliterated the tree. Everyone was on their feet; Arick smiled to show his approval, Marcus laughed, and Mike even started clapping.

By the time James, Mary, Marcus, Venessa, and Mike reached the dining hall, the feast John had announced had already begun. The tables were filled to the brim, and by each seat was a cold appetizer of freshly baked bread, homemade spreads, and cheeses, while freshly squeezed juices adorned the tables in various colored jugs. There was a buffet in the middle of the hall filled with everything from roast beef, lamb shanks, and marinated pork to grilled lobster tails with lemon and herb butter, oysters, prawns, and smoked salmon.

After his hard morning had sapped his strength and the smells wafting through the dining hall sent his saliva glands into overdrive, James felt overcome with starvation and he promptly filled a plate to the brim and sat in his usual spot. Mary was already there with a plate half as full as his own, and it was clear to James that her thoughts lingered on Dalnur as she pushed the carrots around her plate. But in place of sadness, James saw determination; the warmth she normally radiated was gone.

A little while later, after James was sitting back in his chair, trying to stretch out his overstuffed belly, and after all his friends had finished their meals as well, he heard the sound of metal clinking on glass.

"Yesterday, we lost a friend," John said. He was standing on one of the tables in the center of the hall. "We lost family. Dalnur gave his life to save so many of our loved ones. Were it not for his bravery, the attack on our home could have been even more devastating. Dalnur has given us a chance to live on, rebuild, and fight back. He showed us how important it is for us to be united and to watch out for each other. May the memory of him never fade.

"We also remember our dear, dear Jimmy. That young man faced more challenges every day than most of us will have to confront in our entire lives, but he always did everything with a smile on his face. He proved that our limitations must not hold us back but that they can be a source of strength and courage. Leilani Reef will be a sadder place for having lost him."

John then raised his glass, and everyone in the hall returned the gesture. "To Dalnur, to Jimmy, and to all we lost. We will remember you all and we will fight for a stronger, safer community."

After everyone had repeated his words and taken sips of their various drinks, John continued. "Speaking of safety, we are all too aware now that our home has been compromised. Now that our enemies know where we are, we need to be extra vigilant to keep them out. Guards will watch the coasts and the perimeter of the town day and night. If you see anything suspicious, report it immediately to me, Alex, Tony, or Arick."

CHAPTER 15

THE STAFF OF HELETREA

JAMES SAT UPRIGHT, PULLED the maps he had found in the Blue Cave from under his bed, and unrolled them, one by one. The biggest map detailed the topography of the entire island, from its dwellings and pathways to the most significant natural features. The more he dragged his finger over unusual features and obvious coastal caves, the more convinced he became that Leilani Reef bore more secrets besides Drago's lost diary and ring.

He hovered his finger over a structure unfamiliar to him. It looked like a small cottage and was located not far from the Castle but away from the other homes. There were tiny letters next to it, and as James moved his head closer, he read them aloud: *"Individual drafts number seven."* At first, he didn't understand what that meant, but on the edge of one of the maps, he saw it had been marked as *No.12*. He pulled it out and quickly recognized it was a map of Arick's home; blueprints that detailed every floor. James rummaged through the scrolls until he found the one with the inscription *No.7*. Sure enough, it was a blueprint of the cottage. The building was small, but the plans clearly detailed two large subterranean levels.

James couldn't help himself, and after rolling up all the other scrolls but the blueprints for the cottage, he exited his room, and minutes later, he was standing in front of an old, cozy-looking dwelling with two chimneys on each side. It was built of wood and the roof was covered with fine tile. The old wooden door creaked on its hinges as James turned the handle and pressed the door inward. The floorboards bent slightly with every step he took, and sunlight shone through the dirty windows and illuminated the dust in the air that James had disturbed as he entered. It was clear that nobody had resided in this place for a long time but there seemed no reason that should be the case; it looked warm and comfortable.

James took out the map he had taken with him and tried to orient himself. He went to the back door, and after he stepped outside again, he saw a set of steps on his left that led below ground. He walked slowly, one step at a time, listening for any sounds that might indicate someone's presence. He heard nothing. At the bottom, he found a metal door, but the heavy padlock was hanging loose, and James stepped through. He entered a dark corridor, poorly lit by oil lamps that hung on the wall. It looked as undisturbed as the cottage above, but when he closed the door behind him, he heard distant, barely audible sounds. James stepped through the gloom slowly and carefully, ready to turn around and run if he caught even the slightest glimpse of movement in the dark. Every time he had to choose a direction, he chose the way that made the sounds louder and clearer and marked the map with a pencil so he'd be able to find his way back.

The route took him to a lower level, darker than the one above, and he hoped the map he held was complete; he didn't want to be surprised by another subterranean descent. The sounds were changing faster, now, morphing into voices that told him that he wasn't alone in this underground labyrinth. Eventually, the voices became clear enough to make out some of the words, and James knew he ran the risk of being discovered. He opened his map under the nearest oil lamp, squinted to strain his eyes, and resolved that he was in the hallway outside a small room. The map didn't detail what was inside, but with the door closed, he couldn't decipher enough of what was being said inside. James felt around in the dark for a door handle where he thought it should be and, much to his relief, he found one. He took a deep breath and pushed the door ajar slightly, hoping it wouldn't make any sound. When it didn't, and the voices carried on as usual, James leaned closer to look through the crack in the door.

Immediately, it became apparent that the blueprints were not lacking any detail because the room was empty but for a single chair that was facing the doorway James was peering through. The man sitting in it had his hands tied behind him, while three men stood in a semi-circle in front of him. Tony and Alex were on the right, so James could see them both enough to recognize them, but the third man was too far to the left for James to see around the door. All James could see of the man was his right hand, which he held out in front of him. Clutched in his closed fist was a long wooden staff, a little taller than Tony.

"You are giving me nothing," the third man said. "I'm going to ask one more time, how did you find us?"

The man in the chair remained quiet, only letting out a deep shout of surprise and fear when his chair was suddenly pulled backward by a fourth figure that emerged from the shadows behind him. James closed the door a little more so the figure wouldn't spot him, but he kept it open just enough to see the man pulling the chair was John. The broad, bearded man held none of the friendliness in his face that James knew so well. Rather, he looked angry, impatient, and like he wanted to unleash all the stress in his neck and muscles on the defenseless creature tied to the chair. John turned the chair so it faced him, leaned forward, and looked straight into the eyes of the prisoner.

"I really don't want to hurt you, but if you continue not to cooperate, I will," John said.

James shuddered. This is Mike and Venessa's father, James thought. Surely, he wouldn't really torture someone, right?

"You can leave this place unharmed, never to come back, on the condition that you tell us what you know. One way or another, you'll give it to me, but I'd really rather not feed you to the sharks. It's all up to you."

Even James' hair stood on end; he could only imagine how the man in the chair felt, who flinched and started to shake as John got closer and closer.

"It was James Tanner," the man blurted out, his voice breaking as tears ran down his cheeks. "James Tanner brought us here."

James felt his breath catch in his throat. Who had he brought to the island? When? How? He had no idea what was going on, but looking at the angry expression building on John's face, James knew he had to defend himself before the lie went any further. He pushed himself forward when, all of a sudden, a cold hand wrapped itself over James' mouth and pulled him back, away from the door, and back into the dour hallway. His mysterious assailant was strong and pressed his hand over James' mouth was so firmly that James could taste the tobacco on the fingers.

"Quiet, James," the man hushed, and James recognized the voice before the man's face came into view beneath the low light of the oil lamp. With recognition in his eyes, the old man pulled his hand away.

"A-Arick?" James whispered. "What are you—?"

Arick put a bony finger over his lips to shush James, pushed him softly back toward the door, and then stepped up beside him.

"What was that?" John asked.

"Probably a mousetrap," Alex replied. "These tunnels are infested."

"Hm," John mumbled before turning back to the man in the chair. "What do you mean James brought you here?"

"His watch. His old boss gave it to him for his birthday. Inside is a GPS device. That's all I know. Please, believe me," the man pleaded.

Without looking away, James felt for his wrist in the dark until he could feel the cool steel of his watch. With tears in his eyes, he thought of Stanley. The man who had taken a chance on James when he'd had no experience; who had given him a job and a place to live at his lowest moment, against all odds. James had thought finding such a good man during his darkest hour was a miracle. Instead, it had all been a setup. Stanley was...one of them, or else he'd been a pawn. Had that been how Damyan's followers had found them at the palace? Was Stanley to blame for the deaths of Alan and Ted at the docks, and George Cavano, who had died defending James in the palace? Blinking back the tears, James wrenched the watch free and put it in his pocket.

"That's a start," John said. "But I'm sure you know more."

"Please believe me. I don't know anything else," the man begged.

"As you wish." John turned away and peered at Tony.

Tony moved alongside John, so he was now standing in full view of James and Arick. He reached over to the fourth man, who James still hadn't identified, and took the staff from him. Holding the staff in front of him with two hands around the shaft, James, at last, had a good look at it. Whether it was made of pine, oak, or a light mahogany, James couldn't be sure, but the staff looked rough to touch. At the head, the pole split into five or six curving strands that curled around one another, like roots at the base of a tree. Pointing the head of the staff at the man in the chair, Tony's eyes widened and turned completely white, then he held his hands up and made some gestures that James didn't understand. At once, the man screamed like he was enduring the worst pain imaginable. He convulsed and jerked, and his knuckles turned white as he gripped the armrest of the chair with all his might. A moment later, his body relaxed, his grip loosened, and his head slumped forward.

"Damn it, Tony. I didn't say to kill him," John said.

"He's not dead," Tony replied, almost sounding like he was enjoying himself. "He'll wake up again soon but he won't forget the pain he's just experienced."

Before James could hear what they said next, he felt himself being pulled sharply away from the door and down the hall the way he'd come.

"What are you doing?" James asked Arick as he tried to wrench his hand away. But Arick didn't reply. Instead, the old man, who was far stronger than James felt he had any right to be, continued to drag James through the maze of corridors and up the dark steps until they emerged behind the cottage. The orange sunlight fell on Arick's face, giving it a warmth and youthfulness James hadn't seen before.

"You don't need to see how they operate," Arick said.

"Why the hell not? Is this how those men run Leilani Reef? Does everyone else know? Do Mike and Venessa?"

"They know what they are doing. John, Tony, and Alex have protected us for a long time, and they have done so effectively. We wouldn't still be here otherwise."

"What? Surely, you don't approve?"

Arick shook his head. "I have never been for torture, but I also know that it is foolish to expect everyone to behave logically at all times. Remember, this community has just seen Jimmy and Dalnur, one of its own and one of its closest allies, murdered. That man in that chair down there was one of the attackers. If they can find out how Damyan found Leilani Reef and what he plans to do, perhaps they can save more lives in the future." Arick looked down at James' wrist. "And whatever you think of their methods, it worked, didn't it? We now know how Damyan found us."

James instinctively moved his hand to the pocket where he'd put the watch. "I…I didn't—"

"Calm down, James," Arick said. He held no smile on his face, but when he placed his hand on James' shoulder, James knew he was being sincere. "I know you didn't bring Damyan here. We have been watching you for longer than you might realize, and I know you have been honest with me since you arrived. But it seems not everyone was honest with you, and you were tricked into bringing something that told our enemies where to find us."

"I'm-I'm so sorry." James sniffed and brought his sleeve to his eye to dry it.

"Hand it over, kid."

James looked up at Arick but knew it wasn't the old medium that had spoken. As he reached into his pocket to pull out the watch slowly, James turned to see John standing behind him. He was halfway up the steps, squinting as his eyes adjusted to the light.

"John, I—"

"I know you didn't know, James," John said, but something in his tone and the way he didn't make eye contact told James that he still partly blamed him for the attack on Leilani Reef. "Just hand it over."

Without hesitating, James passed the watch to him. For a moment, he thought the massive lumberjack was going to crush the device in his massive hand. Instead, John threw the watch on the ground and stomped it with his heel until it shattered. He then closed his eyes, and James watched as the ground beneath the broken watch started to boil and roll like waves in a storm. The moving soil and stones folded over the watch, pulling it to pieces, ripping it apart, and eventually burying it out of sight.

John turned to descend the steps again.

"You're not going to—"

He stopped. "Going to what, James? Kill him?"

James was too afraid to even nod. He looked at the floor to avoid John's hard stare.

"Like he and his kind killed so many of us? Like they killed Dalnur?"

"But..." James' voice shook.

"But?"

"But aren't we...better than them?"

John frowned and turned his back on James. "Maybe once, kid," he whispered, then he walked down the steps, through the door, and back into the dim corridor.

After a few moments, Arick put his hand on James' shoulder again and urged him to turn around and face him. "War is an ugly mistress, James. Things are never as simple as right and wrong. And allies rarely always agree completely. There are too many emotions; too much history and damage. Doing these...things is awful for everyone involved, but it is so often necessary. But we do our best to protect the young ones from it."

Arick finally let go of James' shoulder and stood a little straighter. "Which reminds me, only the most senior leaders know about this place. It's not somewhere someone just stumbles across. How did you find it?"

James realized he'd dropped the map by the door while he had been listening to the interrogation. Even if he lied now, Arick would soon discover the truth.

"Mike and I were exploring the Blue Cave. We found some maps. I guess I got curious."

Arick stepped closer until his mouth was inches from James. "I understand your need for answers, James. I don't judge you. I have no doubt, I'd do the same in your situation. But you will come to my house later tonight with all of those maps, all right?"

James nodded.

"Did you find anything else with those maps?" James shook his head but kept his eyes pointing at the floor. "James?"

James raised his gaze to Arick. "There was...something. A secret passageway. Mike and I found a diary."

"Whose diary?"

"We think it is Drago Wolgor's."

"Did you read it?"

"A little. We didn't learn much though, and I haven't read it since. I was more interested in exploring the island."

"OK, James. I'll take that diary, as well, if you please. Off you go. I'll be expecting you before sunset."

Arick turned to walk around the cottage and back in the direction of his home, but James shuffled to catch his attention.

"Who was the other man in the room with them? The man with the stick," James asked. "I couldn't see him properly."

"That was Victor," Arick replied. "And that was no stick. That's the Staff of Heletrea. A very long time ago, two identical staffs were made by an elvish queen, Heletrea, and they were given as a gift to humans and dwarfs to honor the respect and friendship between the three species. Sadly, we don't know what happened to the other staff. Dalnur told us it was lost—destroyed—during the war."

"What...is it?" James asked.

Arick sighed. "The staff is intended for healing. It allows the caster to focus their energy far beyond an elemental or medium's normal limitations. As such, the caster can very accurately heal diseases and injuries without difficulty. That is why Victor has it. He is our best physician, so is best placed to use it." Arick went quiet for a moment, as though lost in thought.

James wasn't prepared to entertain one of Arick's episodes. "But that's not all, right?"

Arick blinked hard a few times. "The staff focuses all energy, whatever that energy may be. If the caster has ill intentions, it can be used for death and destruction as well."

"What do you mean?" James asked.

"The staff has the power to absorb and ricochet elements. Remember, I told you that if an elemental tries to use their power to inflict damage inside another person, the same will happen to the caster? Well, if the holder of the staff uses their power to kill someone directly in this way, the staff absorbs that rebounded element, so the caster suffers no repercussions."

James thought for a moment. "So…the magic they are using down there"—James indicated toward the steps behind him—"is magic that, without the staff, would harm them as well? It's forbidden magic?"

Arick's eyes looked heavy and sad. "As I said, James. War is complicated and cruel."

"This is wrong, Arick."

"Perhaps. But John's techniques revealed you unknowingly carried a tracking device to our island. And better we have the staff than our enemies. Were it to fall into their hands, there would be no end to their destruction."

James could sense the defensiveness and anger in Arick's voice, so he resumed looking at the ground again.

"Now," Arick said, his voice ever so slightly softer. "Go and get the maps and the diary and bring them to me at once."

CHAPTER 16

The Fifth Element

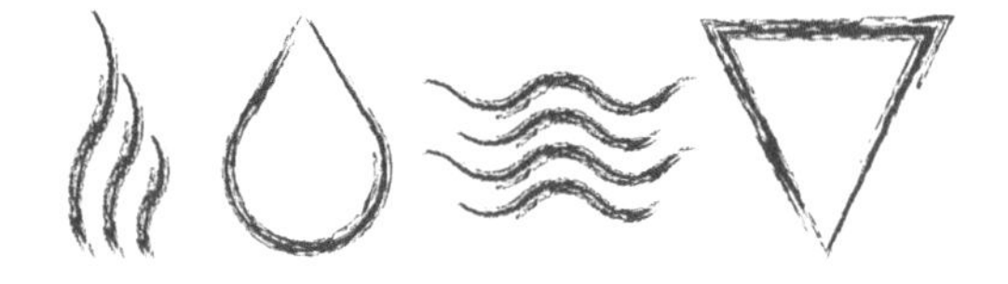

For the next couple of days, James threw himself into his training and studies. Without the maps to explore, and with the knowledge of how John, Tony, and Alex truly ran Leilani Reef, he didn't know how to feel, so thought it best to focus on expanding his knowledge of the elements. By day, he would receive practical training from Victor, Marcus, and others, and in the evenings, he studied theory and history in Arick's library. Arick repeatedly expressed how impressed he was at how quickly James grasped everything, and this sentiment was repeated by Kymil when he returned to the island. John, too, welcomed his progress and invited him to dinner at what the rest of the islanders had nicknamed "the leader's table." Despite its unofficial title, the leader's table was small and positioned at the back of the dining hall, meaning only a limited number of people could sit at it and overhear the conversations taking place at it at any one time. John, Alex, Tony, Arick, and Victor were regular attendants, as was Kymil when he was present. Dalnur, too, had been frequently seen dining with them before his death. While James had developed a relationship with every one of them, it was surprising to receive an invitation to such a prestigious table. He would need his energy to be at his best, so after so many days and nights of developing his skills, he decided to take a nap before attending dinner.

Loud shouts and continuous pounding awoke him from his sleep. He jumped out of bed, opened the door, and started running toward the source of the noise. He felt the cold on his skin and the smell of burned rubber entered his nostrils. His legs were so heavy that he felt as if he were running in place, never reaching the end of the hallway. The windows in the hallway were frozen over with the tendrils of creeping ice, while the sills outside were piled high with ash. When James eventually reached the top of the stairs, he looked down to see a fire blocking the Castle's main entrance. But it wasn't any kind of fire. The flames formed the shape of a woman, with flares that swayed from the top of the head, tying around one another to form thin braids. They looked like fiery whips that thrashed and flicked in every direction, destroying everything they touched. These skinny tentacles whipped at the handrails and pillars, cutting through them as if they were made of butter. The fire reached all the way to the ceiling and slowly creeped toward him, swallowing everything in the path of the slow-moving figure of flame. The eyes of the fiery women were so bright that he had to turn his gaze away, yet he also felt so cold that his lungs were starting to seize. He tried to step backward, again feeling like his body was moving through thick mud that made every movement slow and arduous. But the floor behind him had burned away, and James fell through the hole and landed hard in the reception below.

He got up and what he saw rendered him motionless. His whole body trembled, not from the cold but from fear, sorrow, and anger. The walls of the building burned away like paper. Beyond the limits of the Castle, the land was desolate and black. There were no forests, no greenery, no houses where people lived. All James could see were burned bodies—hundreds of them, in every direction—lying motionless on the ground and surrounded by hot ash.

He could not take it anymore. He turned back to the fiery woman. She was closer now, but while her spidery hair continued to lash at everything around her, James remained untouched. James tried to use his elements against this unknown plague but failed. Is it just that I cannot concentrate, he thought, or have I lost my abilities entirely? Suddenly aware of how truly helpless he was, James took a step back to get away from the approaching demon of fire, only to feel something grabbing his leg. He turned and saw a hand, burned to the bone, holding his shin. The body, too black and ruined for James to recognize, raised its head slightly and said, in a hoarse voice, "Help us."

James jumped out of bed, ran to the door, and pulled it open. The Castle hallway was still whole and standing. He realized that it had all been a terrible nightmare. The hallway was empty, the late afternoon sunlight came in through the windows, and beside the odd chatter coming from the other rooms, all was quiet. He closed the door while letting out a sigh of relief, then moved to sit on his bed to catch his breath. No sooner had he sat down and ran his fingers through his hair did he heard a knock on the door.

"Who is it?" James said, trying to hide his trembling voice.

"It's me," Mary replied. "I just wanted to make sure you had not fallen asleep. Dinner is about to begin."

"I'll be right there"

After taking a shower and getting ready, James went to the dining hall and took a seat at the main table, where John was already waiting. As he did so, he spied Mike and Venessa looking back at him with furrowed brows from their usual table. James was dreading the number of questions Mike would have for him the next time they spoke.

"How are you holding up?" John asked.

"I'm OK," James said, looking around the room to see other familiar faces.

"We need to talk."

"About?"

"Let's wait for the others first."

As he uttered this, Victor appeared at the entrance, holding a roll of old paper in his hand. Soon after, Alex and Tony showed up, with Arick behind them, limping slightly.

"What happened?" John asked as Arick sat down with a painful expression on his face.

"I twisted my ankle snowboarding. What do you think happened? I'm old," Arick replied, trying to find the best way to position himself comfortably in the chair.

Victor put his palms on the table. "OK. Let's begin."

"Shouldn't we wait for Kymil?" Arick asked.

"He already knows everything. We can start without him," John replied.

The hall began to fill with people and conversation and laughter echoed at every table.

"As you can see, I have invited James to join us," John said. "As the only one of us capable of controlling all four elements, I felt he would be a good asset. Plus, he has been making great progress these last few days."

"And this has nothing to do with the fact that he was nosing around in places he didn't belong, right?" Alex said. There was humor in his voice, but his expression was dry, and James gulped.

"What he saw us doing is regrettable," John said. In contrast to the terrifying man who had marched up toward him outside the cottage, the bearded giant seemed to have genuine regret in his eyes. "But were it not for James' snooping, we wouldn't have found Drago's diary."

John swiveled on his seat until his shoulders were squared with James. "I'm sorry for what you saw us do, James. There will be time for questions about our methods later, but you heard with your own ears how Damyan and his followers found us. Your watch was a decoy; it seems your boss at the docks, that Stanley fellow, is one of them. Or else, the watch he gave you had been tampered with. Either way, it wasn't your fault. We should have been more thorough about checking the belongings you brought with you." He reached across the table and put a hand on James' shoulder. "The attack wasn't your fault. The blame lies with Damyan alone."

James nodded but didn't say anything. Speaking would reveal the emotion that was bubbling at the surface.

"While your snooping unveiled our darker secrets, which we hope you'll keep to yourself for the time being," Tony said, "we must also thank you. We weren't able to get anything else out of our prisoner. But your discovery of Drago's diary, together with your mother's letter, has revealed something useful."

James sat forward in his seat, but Arick took over.

"The diary you brought me," he said, "revealed the name of a place where Drago used to take his wife and child. He also explicitly mentions how, if the war ever got too dangerous, he would use it as a refuge to keep his powerful daughter safe from any who would do her harm."

"You think that's where Wanda and her mother went after they found Drago dead?" James said.

"It is an island off the coast of Brazil, near Sao Paulo, called Ilha de Queimada Grande, but locals have nicknamed it Snake Island. I think this is our first ever real hope of finding Wanda. I have called this meeting because I would like to propose sending a team to see if she is there and, if so, to convince her to come back here."

"We disagree," Alex said, and Tony nodded beside him. "She is much too dangerous and too powerful."

"Erm," James said, unable to contain his questions despite how out of his depth he felt, "do we know for sure she is as dangerous as everyone fears? Other than the fact she is the daughter of a human and an elf, has anyone ever seen her use her powers to hurt anyone?"

Arick patted James' hand. "We don't know the full extent of her powers. But she didn't leave our community until she was thirteen. While her training had been basic until that moment, she showed...extraordinary potential. Like you, she could manipulate fire, air, earth, and water. And—"

"And she would be an asset to us, James," John said, cutting Arick off. "But more than being a powerful ally, she would be a truly terrible and devastating enemy. We need to find her and bring her here not so much because we need her on our side, but because we cannot let our enemies use her against us."

"But only we know where she might be, right?" James said. "If I hadn't found the diary, we wouldn't even know. What hope does Damyan have of finding her?"

John sighed, peered at Alex and Tony, who were shaking their heads, then looked back at James. "OK, truth time." As John lowered his voice, James leaned in to hear him better. "We think that Drago, Wanda's father, is still alive."

"Alive?" James said, a little too loud, and Victor shushed him. "Mary told me he was killed."

"That's what we thought," Arick said. "Wanda and her mother were under that impression; Wanda even swore revenge against your mother as a result. But we only know what happened because your mother told us. Drago's body was never recovered. When we went to see it, it was...missing."

"Missing? How does a dead body go missing?"

"We assumed Wanda and her mother took the body with them. But the ring you found alongside the diary has led us to believe that he is not dead, but that it was all carefully planned."

"The ring? How?"

"Those types of rings are used to administer poison or other such substances to their poor, unsuspecting victims," Arick said. "However—"

"However," Victor continued, "we suspect Drago may have used it on himself."

"W-Why?" James said.

"After you gave me the ring last night," Arick said, "I had Victor here examine it for traces of any unusual substances. While it has been many years, he found evidence of a paralytic agent."

"A what?"

"A poison...but one that doesn't kill. Rather, it only gives the appearance of death. The person's heart rate would slow to an imperceptible rate, and anyone looking at the body would think the person was dead. But several hours, days, who knows, later, the poison wears off and the afflicted person would be alive and well again."

"I think it's worth pointing out that the poison used was a very specific type. It is one of the few substances that is more damaging to elves and dwarfs than it is to humans. While it would only incapacitate a human for an undetermined amount of time, it would kill an elf or a dwarf."

James thought about the pages in the diary he had read; the remorse Drago had shown. "But why would he do that? I thought he wanted to protect his family. Why would he trick them?"

Again, Arick spoke. "We think the words he wrote in the diary were all part of the ruse. Drago was never a loving father. If anything, he was jealous of his elf wife's power and even more of her connection with their daughter. You see, Drago didn't fall in love and have a child that accidentally started a war; that's just the story people tell today. He had a child with the expressed purpose of starting a war, and using his child to win it."

"But...why? Why do such a thing?"

Arick shrugged. "Drago, like Damyan, believes elementals should rule the world, not hide from it. But to defeat the other elementals, he needed a weapon stronger than any other. He needed Wanda."

"So, he faked his death to drive his wife and child into exile and to start a war. But he's been in hiding ever since. Why do all that and then not act? Why hasn't he already tried to find her?"

"We don't know," John said. "My theory is that he needs Wanda to enact his plans, but he knows he risks upsetting her once she finds out he's alive. Therefore, he needs a tool to increase his own powers so that he has any chance of subduing her."

James thought for a moment, then he remembered what he had seen in the underground labyrinth. "The Staff of Heletrea."

"Precisely. I think Drago teamed up with Damyan, and Damyan got his people to give you the watch so they could follow you here. They then attacked to retrieve the staff. Fortunately for us, they failed, but they will try again. The staff is the only thing capable of giving Drago the power to match his daughter."

James sighed. It didn't make any sense. If Damyan had so many followers—so many elementals and mediums—capable of causing so much devastation, why risk so much for one person?

James clenched his jaw as he summoned the strength to say what he knew he had to. "There's something you're not all telling me. Damyan has an army at his disposal; he doesn't need Drago or Wanda, even if they are alive. He need not risk so many lives or his own position to secure one powerful elemental. What is it *really* about Wanda that makes her so important?"

John rubbed his hands together and bit the inside of his cheek. He looked up at Alex, then Tony, and then his gaze settled on Arick.

"James," Arick said softly, "what I'm about to tell you must not leave this table. Only a handful of others in this hall know the truth, and that is how we want to keep it. The knowledge is too dangerous."

"What is it, Arick?"

"You know the sigils we use to represent the four elements, yes? And you know that they often appear alongside a fifth; a kind of saw-like figure-of-eight on its side? That is the symbol of the fifth element, time."

James pulled his face back into a frown as he tried to process the full meaning of Arick's words. "Time? As in—?"

"As in," John continued, "throughout history, a handful of elementals have had the power to control time. Some could slow it down; others could speed it up. Legend has it that one elemental could even stop it temporarily."

"That's...incredible," James said.

"And dangerous. It is a power that has only ever been abused, James," Arick said. "Long ago, it was decided that only the elders and leaders of the various tribes and communities should know about the fifth element."

"It was believed that if we didn't teach about it, we would limit the number of elementals who would discover they possessed such a skill," John said. "In turn, this would make it easier to control them."

"Control?" James said.

John held a hand up. "Sorry, not control. I mean, it would make it easier to keep them isolated until we could help them to understand their power and use it responsibly. Fortunately, the ability to control time is rare among elements, and until Wanda, none of us had ever had to deal with it.

"But you must understand, James, that this ability makes Wanda the most dangerous person alive. With the ability to slow down time, she can act and react faster than any of us can even think. Combined with her ability to control the other four elements and her inhuman energy and concentration levels, she is a one-woman army."

A fifth element? James thought. How did I miss this? All the times I studied in Arick's library, yet I never once thought to ask about the symbol. I even saw it back in the palace in the Miami suburbs, yet I said nothing. Still, it made sense why everyone at the table was so tense about the idea of Drago possibly being alive.

"I know it's a lot to take in," John said, tapping his fingers on the table. "But for now, we must decide what to do about Wanda. If I'm right, we must act now."

"I don't know," James said, his voice trembling. "I mean, maybe. This all sounds like a lot of guesswork. Like, if they wanted to wait for me to lead them here, why did they attack us at the palace before we left Miami?"

"I don't know," John said with a sigh. "Perhaps a disagreement as to how to do things? Maybe they got tired of waiting and wanted to force Mary to move you sooner than she was going to?"

"I agree with James," Tony said, sitting forward. "There are too many dangers and too many unknowns. John, I'm sorry, but even if your theory has some truth to it, what if the diary is a trap and Damyan's warriors are waiting for us? Or what if it is designed to lure us away from here, so they can attack when our best warriors are occupied? What if it's not the staff they're after but something else? No, we should keep everyone here and prepare to defend against the next attack."

"And I say his warriors will be better prepared next time," John said. "They know the layout of Leilani Reef now, and they know our numbers. We will not survive another attack."

"Then we should move the staff," Alex said. "Let's lend it to another community to protect until we can guarantee its safety again."

"No!" John said, slamming his hand down on the table. For a moment, the tables around them went quiet. James looked up to see Mike and Venessa wore worried expressions. "The staff was entrusted to us. I will not pass it to another only to put them in danger. It is our responsibility."

"It seems your mind cannot be changed, John," Tony said, his shoulders slumping. "You know we will always support your decision. But we don't agree."

"I understand that," he said, "but my gut tells me this is the way. James, what do you think?"

James felt the sweat rolling down his neck and back. "I don't think I'm qualified to make this decision. I mean, you've only just told me about time being an element."

"James, as the elemental among us with the most potential, I would like you to go to Snake Island."

James laughed. "You mean, as the only other person who has grown up as an outsider, I might be able to sympathize with Wanda and win her over. I say it's more likely that she'll see the son of the woman who she thinks killed her father and attack on site."

John winked at Arick. "You're right. He's too smart for his own good." John turned back to James just as the doors to the dining hall swung open. As everyone turned to see what was happening, John leaned in close. "You're right, kid, I'm sorry for trying to mislead you. But you've more than proved your capabilities in the short time you've been here, and I think you can win Wanda over better than anyone else here. And look," he said, pointing at the doors, "you won't be alone."

John got up and asked for silence in the hall. "Thank you, everyone, for your dedicated work over the last few days. I know it hasn't been easy since the attack, which is why we decided to call upon some of our friends to make us all feel safer. They will help us rebuild our homes that were destroyed and prepare us for the battles to come." He then waved at someone through the doors that James couldn't see.

A moment later, Kymil entered the hall. Mary and Marcus followed, leading a procession of a dozen young men and women. They bowed politely to no one in particular, then Mary and Marcus led them to a nearby table that had been kept free for them. After them, two male elves entered, followed by two female elves. All four wore identical silver clothing that James assumed must be some sort of military uniform. Their silver hair was tied into ponytails and pinned behind their pointed ears. Each of them carried a staff in their left hand while hiding their right hand behind their back like a waiter when pouring wine for a patron. They also bowed, uttered a few words that James did not understand, and sat down at a table beside the young men and women before them. Finally, four dwarfs strolled in with axes on their backs and daggers in their belts. They wore shabby black denim pants with boots and a leather jacket with t-shirts of varying colors underneath. Unlike the humans and elves before them, the dwarfs did not bow. Instead, they stopped in the middle of the hall.

"Greetings!" one of them said. "We are here to help our allies of Leilani Reef. Just ask for whatever you need; we dwarfs shall provide."

John thanked them and pointed to the empty table reserved for them. As they sat down, John announced for the feast to begin, and carts full of food and drink were wheeled out of the kitchen. When he sat back down, he took his time looking at everyone at the table, one by one.

"I know I do not have everyone's support. It is a bold plan based on little more than theory and gut feeling. But I am convinced that we cannot wait for the staff to be taken from us or for Drago, Damyan, or whoever else to find Wanda. James, no one here will force you, but if you go to find Wanda, you will not be alone. People you know and trust will go with you while the rest of us, including these new warriors, will help to keep Leilani Reef safe. What do you say?"

This is absurd, James thought. How can I possibly be the one to go on such an important mission? I've barely begun to understand my powers. If this Wanda is alive, and that's a big if, I will be no match for her, especially if she can manipulate time for goodness' sake. How can John be so sure she is alive after all this time? How can he be sure Drago is alive? Then again, if Drago is alive...

James turned to Arick next to him. "What do you think, Arick? Do you think Drago is alive?"

Arick frowned in sympathy. “I think John is right about one thing. I think we are doomed to be overwhelmed if we don’t do something, and this plan is the best we have.”

“Do you...?” James swallowed down the rising emotion in his throat. “Do you think, if Drago is alive, that he might know where my mother is?”

“I don’t know, lad. But if Drago is working with Damyan, then it’s likely.”

James closed his eyes, took a deep breath, and pressed his hands into his legs to stop them from shaking more than they already were. After a few moments, he looked up at John.

“OK,” he said, at last. “I’ll do it.”

James had underestimated how determined John was to make the mission go ahead, and just two days later, the team to travel to Snake Island had been decided and the boat prepped and packed. Despite his objection to the mission, Tony had been designated its leader, supported by Mary and Marcus. Alex and Victor would remain on Leilani Reef as the only remaining mediums. Of the newcomers, the humans Patrick, Kyle, Amy, and Nicky had been selected to accompany them for their abilities. None of the four looked older than twenty, although Patrick and Kyle had impressive builds that were only exaggerated by their tight t-shirts. Tall and black-haired, they contrasted with Amy and Nicky, who were both beautiful and lean, with long brown hair and pale skin. All the elves had been assigned to stay on the island, while the only dwarf to join them on the mission was one named Galman.

"Do we really need all of these people with us?" James asked as he finished his breakfast and prepared to leave the hall to walk to the Blue Cave. "If we come in such large numbers, Wanda may feel threatened."

"Normally, I would agree, but to reach her island as fast as possible, you need to use elements, and that requires energy," John replied. "You'll all have to take it in turns on the journey to get there and back again in good time. Besides, if something goes sideways, you will be in a better position to escape if you have seasoned warriors with you."

"Let's not waste time," Tony said. "The sooner we arrive and discover she's not there, the sooner we can get back and come up with a better plan."

One by one, the selected crew got up from their tables, hauled their bags onto their shoulders, and headed for the exit. James paused briefly when he passed Mike and Venessa.

"Don't get into trouble while I'm gone," James said with a smile.

"With you away, I might actually go a week without having to do kitchen duty," Mike said, laughing.

Venessa wiped a tear away. "Make sure you come back in one piece,"

"I wish you guys were coming with me," James whispered.

"Us, too."

As James left the hall, he passed a small group of children in the hallway. One of them was Tanya, Mike and Venessa's little sister, whom he had seen the day he'd met John. He noticed her beautiful golden hair and big green eyes, and she saw him, she greeted him with a shy smile. She couldn't have been more than seven or eight years old and looked as happy as any girl her age should. He smiled back but realized too late that his own was sad. There was something about the girl that made him think of two women he had never met but had a sudden urge to protect. Wanda would have been like this girl once, more interested in playing with her friends than wanting to commit violence. And his mother would have looked at him with the same admiration once upon a time; a woman who was apparently still alive and suffering. As James and the little girl passed each other in the hall, he felt something inside him that he could not describe; some sort of energy. He could sense his heart slowing down, while at the same time, pounding harder, as if he were listening to drums in slow motion. Buuuummmmm-Buuuuummmm-Buuuummmmm. Everything became sluggish; even inhaling and exhaling felt awkward. He could hear the air gently coming in and out of his lungs. The feeling lasted only for a few seconds before it was gone again, but James knew at that moment that he was on the right course. He had to find Wanda so he could find his mother. He had to convince Wanda of the truth to save the families of Leilani Reef. And he had to help Wanda redeem herself, so she could be the happy little girl she once was. James managed to soften his features and warm his smile at the golden-haired girl as she entered the dining hall behind him, where James lost sight of her.

When James reached the Blue Cave, he saw the ship he was about to board was much larger than the one he had arrived on. Arick was standing on the walkway beside the ship.

"Are you joining us?" James asked.

Arick shook his head. "I am too old for this. It would do you more harm than good if I came along."

"I don't think you really mean that."

"Sadly, I do. Be careful. If Wanda is anything like the children of inter-species parents of the past, she may be sensitive and quick to anger. Under no circumstances should she feel threatened or endangered. And remember, you may face your own temptations on this journey. Your choices determine who you are."

Even though he didn't know what Arick meant exactly, James smiled, shook his hand, and clambered aboard. He went under the deck, found an unoccupied cabin, and put his things away. Sitting on a small bed, James ran his fingers through his hair as he thought about what awaited him on this journey and how foolish he'd been to agree to John's plan.

It wasn't long before James heard a low rumble of the engine as it kicked into life and he could feel the boat moving slowly out of the harbor. He looked through the window at the shore where Mike and Venessa were standing beside Arick. James had planned to stay in his cabin for as long as possible; knowing what he now knew about the existence of a fifth element and the true danger they were sailing toward, he didn't trust himself not to warn the others—something he was sure Tony would object to.

"Doing OK?" Mary asked, coming to his cabin door. "You seem a bit off."

"I'm fine. None of it seems real, still."

"I know how you feel."

"Do you?" James said, looking straight into her eyes. Mary was taken aback at the question, and James saw it right away. "I'm sorry. I didn't mean to say it that way."

She put her arm around him and kissed him on the cheek. "It's OK. Cheer up, will you? And we could use your help outside."

James felt somewhat relieved and nodded while the engines rumbled louder. "Let me just unpack, and I'll be right there."

"You can do that later. Come and join us."

"In a minute. How long is the journey?"

"Why?" she asked.

"Just curious."

"It depends?" Mary said.

"On what?"

"On if you're going to help us." A small smile appeared on her face as she exited the cabin.

Intrigued, James took his bag, shoved it under the bed, and followed her. Outside, they were already quite a distance from the shore. Looking forward, he admired the blue sky without a cloud in sight. A light breeze and the smell of seawater filled his senses. Instantly, he felt relaxed and fulfilled, as if someone had lifted a huge load off his shoulders. James turned to see Patrick and Kyle pulling the ropes and raising the sails, while Mary stood behind the helm. Marcus was at the edge of the ship, talking to the girls. When he saw James, he jumped down and came up to him and grabbed his shoulder.

"And?"

"And what?"

"And which one do you like?" Marcus said, glancing at the girls.

James looked at Amy and Nicky leaning on the rail, who seemed to be enjoying the view. He felt his stomach clench and an unexpected warmth inside him. His cheeks started to heat up, and feeling a little lightheaded, he turned away. "Now is not the time."

"Come on," Marcus said, his voice full of confidence. "Aren't they gorgeous?"

"They are both nice." James felt his stomach clench even more.

"Both nice? They are hot as hell!"

James took another glance at the girls and saw Mary coming over.

"Guys, are we ready to go?" Mary asked.

"Yes, Captain. Aye-aye, Captain. We are born ready!" Marcus said loudly, using a raspy pirate voice.

"What do you mean ready to go?" James asked. "We're already going."

"I keep forgetting how much you still have to learn," Mary whispered so no one would hear her. "And you keep forgetting about the elements."

Mary took his hand and led him to the front of the boat, and Marcus followed. There, Marcus spread his arms wide, and moments later, a canal appeared in the sea that looked like a slide so the boat sailed right through the middle. At once, the bouncing stopped as the boat no longer collided with any waves. At the same time, James felt the wind pick up. He looked toward the sails, which were taut as if a strong wind was blowing. The boat began to accelerate at high speed. When it reached full speed, the boat glided effortlessly through the ocean's surface like a speeding car on a highway.

"Did you think we would take the slow route to Snake Island?" Mary asked. "That'd take ten days at least, assuming we had good weather the whole way."

James smiled slightly. "Probably a silly question, but why is it called Snake Island?"

Mary's eyes lit up. "Well, it's full of venomous snakes. By some estimates, there is one for every ten square feet. That's a lot. The Brazilian Navy closed the island to the public years ago. Probably another reason why Wanda feels safe there."

"If it's closed, wouldn't the government notice someone living there?"

"Not necessarily," Mary said. "Think about our own home. We've used the elements to keep it secret for hundreds of years. She could be doing the same to hide herself."

"Why not hide the whole island like we do at Leilani Reef?"

"Too late," Mary replied. "Our people occupied our island before the Bahamas was mapped in the fifteenth century and long before there were satellites and planes. So, it isn't recorded anywhere; it's not on any map. But Wanda only went into hiding a little under two decades ago. All the spare islands without elementals living on them are already known. If an island suddenly disappeared, it might prompt people to investigate. The next best thing these days is to choose an island no one is allowed to go to, extend it using earth magic, and then hide the changes to everyone else."

"Wait! You lost me," James said, almost laughing. "You're saying she extended an island?"

"Maybe. It's not easy, I admit, but a powerful enough elemental could pull land up from the seabed. And Wanda is no ordinary elemental."

Despite their powers, it still took a day to travel the distance. The various wind and air elementals aboard took it in turns to keep the channel open for the boat and the winds strong and southerly. Those resting enjoyed the view of their blue surroundings, and everyone was in good spirits, especially Marcus, who took the opportunity to show off his elemental skills to impress the girls at every opportunity. Naturally, he was also the first to use up all his energy reserves, and he ended up sleeping more than half the journey.

"There it is," Mary said eventually, pointing ahead.

They all moved to the bow to get a better view, and as they approached, the dot on the horizon started to take shape. At the same time, the blue sky that had accompanied them the whole way began to darken and it became clear that a storm encircled their destination.

"That's not good," Tony said.

"You don't think we'll make it to shore?" James said.

Tony shook his head. “No. The storm is only over the island and nowhere else. It means there is an elemental there who doesn’t want to be found.” He put a hand on James’ shoulder and gave him a gentle squeeze. “It means Wanda is alive.”

CHAPTER 17

Snake Island

APPROACHING THE NORTH SIDE of the island, Tony pointed to an old wooden dock that had definitely seen better days. The pillars were tilted to one side, many planks were missing, and those still there were in very poor condition. Mary steered the boat and brought it slowly to a stop while Marcus waited with a rope in his hands to moor them to a post. Beneath the dark gray clouds, the place looked deserted, lifeless even. At the end of the dock, there was a pathway of bare, broken flagstones, pulled apart and lifted up at all angles by overgrown grass and wild weeds. Beyond, a dense rainforest loomed.

One by one, the crew disembarked and carefully navigated the loose planks. James felt them bending slightly under his weight, and he prayed he wouldn't fall through any. Halfway along the dock, James had to jump over four missing boards.

He landed on the other side and almost slipped back into the gap behind him but managed to cling to the guard rail. Before reaching Tony at the start of the stone path, James looked back and offered an uneasy wave to the dwarf, Galman, who Tony had asked to stay with the boat in case they needed to make a quick getaway. James hadn't had a chance to speak to the dwarf on their journey, but he had learned from Mary that he was one of Dalnur's brothers, and he'd volunteered for the mission.

"This is Snake Island," Tony said, once the last of the team had reached him. They had to huddle close to hear him over the wind and the thunder. "It lives up to its name. There are a lot of snakes here, but no one has to be afraid of them. Just follow my lead and everything will be fine. Two by two please."

"What if we get bitten?" Amy asked with a quivering lip.

"You won't get bitten. I'll stand in the middle of the group and use the energy of those of you with fire magic to make sure no snakes reach us. Let's get going."

"How can Tony stop the snakes from taking a crack at us?" James whispered.

"I don't know exactly, but smoke should do the trick," Mary replied.

And so it was. They walked a stone path that had not been used for years, with smoke rising from the ground ten feet from them on every side. Amy was especially careful with every step. Although they were already far into the island, they did not see a single snake or hear any sign of one. It wasn't until they reached the other side that they detected the first signs of life when birds in the thickening canopy overhead swooped from one tree top to the next. As the jungle around them became denser and they lost all sight of any sort of recognizable path, Marcus used a machete to cut a way through for them while Tony continued to focus on keeping the snakes away. But as the trees became more tightly packed together and it became harder to clamber over exposed roots in the damp dark, Tony started to lose his focus. A few dozen yards further, Marcus suddenly stopped. James looked over his shoulder to see a pile of several snakes, one entwined with the next, while the biggest of them all had raised its head and was staring back at them. Behind them, James spied a nest of small snakes, possibly dozens of them, all entangled with each other, and as though it had caught him staring, the big snake started to hiss so loudly that James could hear it over the rolling thunder.

"Back up, everyone," Tony said quietly. "We'll find another way through."

James didn't breathe properly again until the snakes were well out of sight and he was sure the sweat he could see on Marcus' neck was not only from the intense humidity. They walked around the nest while the others followed in near total silence.

It took them about two hours to walk through the entire rainforest, where everyone had to use their elemental powers at one point or another to drive away the huge number of snakes, large insects, and spiders they encountered.

When they came out on the other side, there was no sunlight or light breeze to greet them. The storm raged, dark clouds covered the sky, and lightning flashed all around them. The wind was blowing relentlessly, pushing them back the way they'd come, and heavy raindrops started falling on them.

"Why didn't we bring the boat here instead of trekking across the island?" James asked, trying to make himself heard over the howling wind.

"Because of this!" Tony replied, pointing to the sky. "If Wanda had seen us coming and decided to sink our ship, I don't think we could have done much to stop her. Keeping the ship further back should help keep it safe, meaning we still have a fighting chance of getting away."

Soon after, they reached the southern tip of the island where, apart from the persistent black clouds, the wind and rain started to ease. Before them, a thick white mist hovered over the sea, limiting the view.

"Can someone explain this," Kyle said bitterly.

"We came all this way for nothing?" Patrick added.

But no one answered, and James watched Tony stare into the mist. After a minute or two, Tony stepped into the water. He moved forward slowly, but the thigh-deep water didn't seem to rise any higher as he fought his way through, and the fog ended up swallowing him before the seawater could. Amy gasped while the others waited. James could only hope his wasn't the only heart that was pounding so hard he thought he might suffer a heart attack.

A little while later, which felt like an eternity, Tony emerged out of the mist. "Come on," he said calmly. "There's a way through."

At first, nobody moved, but after James summoned the courage to follow Tony, careful to step only where he'd seen Tony had done, the others did the same.

The route through the water was short, and when James climbed the slippery rocks on the other side, he saw a high rock rising in front of him with a passage through the middle that was barely wide enough for one person. Tony invited everyone to gather at the entrance to the passage before he led the way through. He promised that if he could get through, everyone else could; only Patrick and Kyle looked doubtful.

As they edged their way through, feeling their way along the steep, slimy rock on either side and trying to place their feet on stones that weren't likely to roll away and crush their feet in the process, James heard a gentle female voice, and everyone stopped in their tracks.

"It is only for my curiosity that you are still alive."

Everyone turned their head sharply as they sought the source of the voice, but it seemed to come from every direction. James felt an icy chill pass through his veins.

We were stupid to come through this gorge, James thought. If she's as powerful as everyone says, she could fold the rock closed around us without breaking into a sweat.

With his mind racing, James urged Tony to walk faster as he began to feel claustrophobic and scared.

"I feel your fear," the female voice said.

This time no one stopped; instead, everyone started pushing to get out as soon as possible. Had the passage been slightly wider, people probably would have fallen and hurt themselves in the growing panic. As it was, the gorge was too tight for anyone to fall anywhere but into the person in front or behind them, and after a few bends, they all managed to get through to the small clearing on the other side. Still, the mood among the group was notably tenser than it had been, James realized. For the first time, everyone understood the true gravity of the danger of the situation in which they had volunteered themselves.

Ironically, they had probably reached the most beautiful part of the island so far. In front of them, a winding pathway led up the side of a high cliff with a wide waterfall that splashed onto the rocky riverbed a few hundred yards away. The path disappeared behind the curtain of water and into a cave. Without thinking, Tony headed for the waterfall when Mary stopped him.

"You think it's safe?"

"If she wanted to kill us, she would have already done so," Tony said with a determined look on his face. "You think she made this passage by accident? This whole route was designed so she could drown or crush any intruders. We've made it this far because she has let us, and I believe we will pass this waterfall without any problems. I think she wants to talk. I'm more worried about how we get out of here if the conversation doesn't go well."

"It's glad he is so confident, but what if he's wrong?" James asked, leaning into Mary's ear. But she moved on without giving him an answer.

Tony led the way up the cliff, but the loose stones were so drenched with water from the waterfall that James and

Marcus positioned themselves at the more difficult points to help the others make the climb. By the time James passed behind the water and entered the cave, he was the last in line.

The moment he stepped into the refreshingly cool air of the cave, the waterfall went silent. James turned to look back at it, but the water had stopped in midair. He reached out to touch it; it still felt cold, but it was more like touching beads than liquid, and the water moved only as much as his fingers displaced it. It was as though someone had hit the pause button, and the droplets of water that James had separated from the waterfall hung in the air. Still mesmerized, James felt a presence behind him and, in a swift motion, he turned on his heel to face it.

"Hello, James."

The woman in front of him had a pale face, blue eyes, and thick black eyelashes. Her silvery golden hair was so long that it reached to her knees, and she wore a silky, loose-fitting dress that reached only slightly further. The dress left her shoulders bare and her skin gleamed in the rays of sunshine that entered the cave from around the waterfall. Over her thin shoulder, James could see the back of Marcus, and the rest of the group beyond. Like the water behind him, they were as still as statues, frozen in mid-step as they made their way through the cave.

James took a few steps back. He remembered the fiery woman in his dream. Although he'd not seen any details beyond her thin frame and long hair, he was sure she was this beautiful and deadly woman before him now.

"Wanda?"

"You are the most powerful among them," Wanda said with a soft smile. "I can sense it in you, your ability to control the elements." She looked James up and down. James couldn't tell if she admired him or was offended by his presence. "Are you afraid? You should be."

It took him a while, but eventually, James found enough strength to speak. "So, this is what manipulating time looks like. What have you done with my friends?"

"Friends?" Wanda asked, still smiling slightly. "You consider them friends? They betrayed me along with your mother."

"You know who I am?"

Wanda's eyes softened for a moment, but as soon as James allowed himself to admire them, he was frightened by their intensity again.

"I looked after you as a baby for a short time. You may be all grown up now, but I can see that innocent child in you still." She blinked back a tear. "Why are you here? Did your mother send you to beg for forgiveness for what she did to my father?"

"Wanda, you aren't the only one who suffered that day. I was left to grow up in an orphanage. Until very recently, I thought my mother was dead."

"Victoria Tanner isn't dead yet? Well, that's some good news. I was beginning to worry I was wasting my time trying to find her."

James wanted to tell her that she was wrong, but he didn't know how much to say in case he risked angering her. He glanced over her shoulder at his companions. They were totally at her mercy if she decided to hurt them.

"You shouldn't be worried about them," Wanda said. "You should be worried about yourself. You came to my home uninvited, disrupting my peace." Wanda took a few steps toward James. She looked absolutely stunning, but at the same time, utterly frightening. She stared at James, waiting for a response, still wearing her uneasy smile.

"We are here because we need your help," James said with a tremble in his voice. "*I* need your help."

Wanda's face darkened, her smile was gone, and her demeanor changed from pleasant to one of rage. James could see her veins pulsating in her neck. The pace of her breathing increased, and he expected to be struck down at any moment. But it didn't happen. Wanda calmed herself down with a few deep breaths.

"None of you are capable of harming me. It was foolish of you to come, but I will hear what you have to say."

With a blink of his eyes, Wanda was gone. He could hear the waterfall flowing again behind him, and just ahead, Marcus and the others were walking deeper into the cave as if the last few moments he had spent with Wanda had not happened. He thought about stopping the others and warning them.

No, he decided, everyone was already on edge; they didn't need him to worry them more by describing Wanda's ability to slow down time to a crawl.

"James!" Marcus shouted, snapping James out of his thoughts. He realized it must not have been the first time Marcus had shouted his name. "Are you coming?"

Without a word, in case he said something he'd regret, James followed Marcus along the short path through the cave. They stepped out the other side where they found themselves underneath an enormous tree whose canopy of leaves obscured most of the sunlight. The grass on the ground was like carpet, neatly trimmed to perfection. Although the sunlight hardly reached the jungle floor, the flowers between the trees were beautiful and of various colors and shapes. Their divine scent mixed together, and James inhaled deeply. Tony led them along the only path until, over the brow of the low hill, they spied a cottage below.

James decided he should share what had happened to him before they entered the cottage. But before he could say anything, they heard a rumble behind them as the rock in the cave folded over itself and the entrance disappeared. When they turned to face forward again, Wanda was waiting on the road leading to the cottage.

"Welcome," Wanda said with yet another smile, as if she was glad to see them.

Everyone winced. Tony, who was closest to her, widened his stance.

"No need for that...yet," Wanda said, and James came to the front.

Tony grabbed his hand and tried to pull him back, but James shook him off. Wanda gestured for them to follow her as she walked, barefoot, across the soft grass to the cottage.

She invited them inside and to sit down in a big, spacious, circular room. The floor inside, as it was outside, was covered in soft grass that helped James to feel more relaxed than he knew he should. The glass roof above gave a clear view of the sky; it seemed Wanda had left a hole in the storm that hid her side of the island so the sun could warm her cottage during the day, and so she could gaze at the stars at night.

Wanda sat down in the circle, though her seat was slightly raised. She crossed her legs and looked at everyone present without saying anything. That awkward silence lasted for a long minute before she spoke. "So, you need my help. The person you rejected, whose life you ruined, whose parents you have killed."

Tony wanted to say something, but Wanda raised her hand. She wasn't done. "You need help from a person who was *helpless*. And you dare to come here, accompanied by the children of the person who killed my parents. Now, tell me, why should such a person help you?"

James looked taken aback by the statement, and Wanda noticed at once.

"Well, well," Wanda said, "it seems there is a lot you don't know, James Tanner."

"Nobody killed your father!" Tony exclaimed. "And your mother was alive when she left Leilani Reef with you."

"Silence!" Wanda shrieked. "Liar! My mother left to protect me. And Victoria, his mother"—she pointed an accusing finger at James—"poisoned her. Did you know that she struggled with the pain for almost a year before she eventually died?"

"Wanda, please, listen to me," Tony said, the veins pulsating in his neck and face, "your father is still alive."

Then the smile vanished from Wanda's face. James could feel the air getting colder and he remembered what Mary had once told him about the conflict between Wanda's human and elf sides. He had to prevent that from happening before she unleashed her power on them.

"Please, Wanda. Just hear us out. Please. After that, you can do whatever you want," James pleaded. "You have nothing to lose here. We know we are no match for you. Today, you either accept what we have to say and learn something about your father, or you reject it and you have your revenge."

Wanda turned to James, and he felt the air warm up again. She let out a soft growl, though her features softened a little. "Of course, you are no match for me, and I know I have nothing to lose; I've already lost everything. What have you lost? Your childhood, perhaps, but your mother is still alive and you still have your sister."

James' eyes widened and he felt a lump in his throat. "Sister?"

Wanda bit her lip to keep herself from laughing. "Don't tell me you don't know about your sister? You ask me to trust these so-called friends of yours when they have hidden so much from you? When *she* has hidden so much." And with that, Wanda slowly turned her head.

James followed her gaze and saw Mary and Tony exchanging looks. On instinct, he grabbed his mother's necklace around his neck and read the inscription again; the letters M and J, separated by a heart. Mary and James.

Then he understood. He understood why Mary was so protective of him, why she was always there when he needed her, and why she had insisted on having such an important role in his training. But why had she kept the truth from him? Was she ashamed of him? Had she blamed him for their mother's disappearance? The questions flooded his mind so that he felt no relief, no happiness; only disappointment and resentment.

Mary leaned forward and reached out, even though she was on the other side of the circle. "James, please—"

"Well, now, this is getting better and better. Obviously, you don't know much about anything," Wanda said.

"Obviously," James replied, forgetting why they had come to Wanda in the first place.

After that, silence reigned for a few moments until Wanda spoke. "Well, I'm pleased to see your reunion isn't a happy one, at least. But if you don't mind, I'd like to hear whatever creative story you have come up with to change my mind about killing you all."

"Your father is alive. He did not die that day," Tony said.

"I saw his body. If you're trying to fool me, you are doing a terrible job."

"Nobody's trying to fool anyone, except maybe your father. He is alive. We think he staged his own death to fool us all."

"Be very careful." Wanda raised a finger. "Don't say something you'll later regret."

"I am not afraid to tell the truth," Tony said with determination on his face. Slowly, carefully, he moved his hand to his pocket.

Wanda watched his every movement closely, and James feared Tony was one wrong word away from being incinerated on the spot.

Tony pulled out a small object and threw it into the center of the circle, and James instantly recognized it as the ring he had found alongside Drago's diary. "We found this ring among your father's effects in a hidden room. It held traces of a poison; the same poison we think that was used to kill your mother."

Wanda snapped her gaze to James. "Yes, which his foul mother administered to her."

Terry shook his head. "No! The poison, which is deadly to elves, only paralyzes humans temporarily but makes them appear dead. It would explain why you thought your father had been killed. He scratched your mother, then scratched himself. You saw the effects in him first, after you saw Victoria Tanner standing over him when she found him, and your mother had just enough time to get away with you before she started to suffer the poison in her system."

Wanda's eyes were bloodshot and tears were welling in the corners. "Why? Why would he do such a thing?"

"Your father wants to use you to assert his power over others, but he was inferior to your mother. He has a lifespan of eighty, maybe ninety years, while your mother had a lifespan of hundreds of years. In addition, she was more powerful as an elf than he was as a human. His plan, as we understand it, was to get you away from your mother so he could control you. But the only way to do that was to kill her. And to do that and still have you trust him, he had to make it look like someone else—someone who was trusted more than any other by the community you grew up in—was framed."

Wanda listened intently, her expression never changing.

"Why do you think my mother killed your father?" James asked.

"And my mother," Wanda added. "We found her standing next to my father's body when my mother and I returned home. My mother attacked her. I don't remember what happened exactly, only that my mother got sick shortly after. Instead of staying and fighting, Mother decided the only way she could protect me in her weakened state was for us to flee. She would tell me afterward how it must have been during her scuffle with Victoria that she poisoned her. The wound expanded and never healed, and eventually, the poison killed her."

"Please," James said, as softly as he could, "I know I'm the last person you want to hear from, but I know something about what you're feeling." Wanda scoffed, but James continued. "You cared for me once. You cared for my mother. That's what made the betrayal all the greater, right? If it had been anyone else, it would have been easier to bear. But it was my mother, Victoria, the woman who represented your closest connection with the people of Leilani Reef. How could you ever forgive anyone if she, of all people, was capable of doing something so terrible to you?

"But ask yourself this? Did she ever give any indication of wanting to harm you or your parents beforehand? Was she ever anything but kind and caring?"

Wanda spat at the floor. "What do you know, James? You were an infant."

James held up his hands in surrender. "You're right, Wanda, I don't know. I never knew my mother because she feared so much for my life that she left me on the doorstep of an orphanage. She gave me up, so I'd be far away from her in case you ever came looking for revenge, or in case your father ever came back to start another war.

"You see, Wanda? Both you and I had the love of my mother, and we both lost it the day your father betrayed your mother and mine. He deliberately used my mother in his scheme because he knew it would isolate you the most."

"Enough!" Wanda exclaimed, standing up. "After nearly twenty years, you think you can just waltz into my home and insult my intelligence with some made-up story? Proof! Give me some proof!"

"I'm sorry, Wanda," James said. "The ring is all we have, and I know it's not much. But come with us, help us, and I promise you that we'll find the truth together. I want—no—I need to know it just as much as you do."

"I don't need to prove myself to you! I know what I saw and that is proof enough for me!"

"You don't know anything!" Tony blared, and James saw Wanda's eyes flicker. "You were just a kid. An ignorant thirteen-year-old girl who knew nothing about anything! You wasted twenty years of your life sulking in this godforsaken place about something you're not even sure about!"

"I am sure!" Wanda growled.

"And what if you're wrong?" Tony shouted even louder, who was ignoring James' gestures for him to calm him down. "Did you forget about the day before it all happened? You were present when your father returned after a few days of absence. Most of us were sitting outside by the fire when he came back wearing a ring on his hand that no one had seen before? A gold ring with a pointed top. That ring!" He pointed to the ring in the center of the room. "Do you remember when your father sat next to your mother, put his arm around her, and she winced and told him to be careful with that ring?"

James had no idea if what Tony was saying was true. It sounded plausible, but Tony hadn't mentioned anything before. Could he really be risking all their lives right now by telling a lie?

It didn't matter anymore. Everyone could see the rage in Wanda's eyes and they had risen to their feet. James searched his mind for anything to say that might ease her, but it was too late. She took a staff leaning against her armchair, lifted it high into the air, and drove it onto the ground with great force. The wave of vibration it caused was massive; the ground shook and lanterns hanging from the ceiling shattered and spilled their flaming oil, causing a huge fire to erupt around them. Even the glass roof cracked in several places. Wanda then put her hands together and sucked the fire from the shattered lanterns into her palms. With her hands consumed by flames, James saw the image of the woman on fire from his dream again, and a moment later, a stream of fire erupted from her hands toward everyone present. Had Tony been a second too late to raise the barrier around her, James was sure he and everyone else would have been engulfed in fire. Instead, her attack crashed into the barrier. Before she knew what had happened, Tony pushed the barrier toward Wanda, slamming it into her and pinning her to the ground. She shrieked and shook violently.

"This is going to keep her in place but not for long," Tony said, turning and rushing outside. "Run!"

He ran down the path as the rest of the team followed. As they approached where the cave had been, James used his earth power to fold back the rock blocking the cave entrance, and they ran through and out the other side. By luck or by design, he didn't know, but they all somehow made it through the tight passageway without Wanda catching up to them, and when they reached the small patch of water that divided Wanda's haven from the rest of Snake Island, James was relieved to see their boat sailing a few hundred yards out to sea. Mary used her powers to freeze the water so they could run the short distance to climb aboard. A loud shriek, followed by a heavy bang, was heard in the distance while they clambered up the ladder.

"She's up!" Tony exclaimed. "Let's go!"

Everyone on board worked together to use their powers to turn the boat around and make it travel as fast as possible back north. Back to Leilani Reef.

CHAPTER 18

The Drums of War

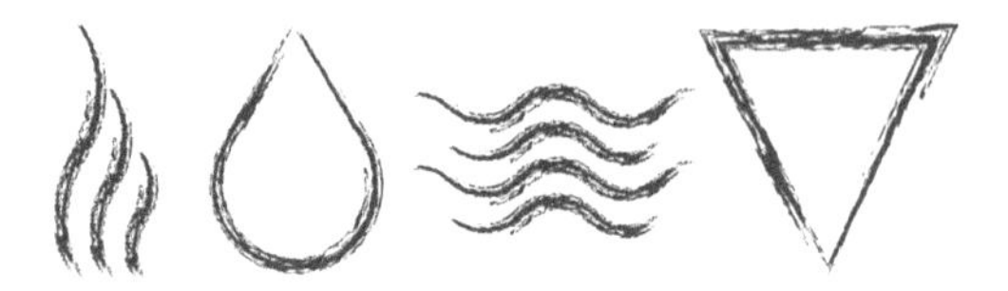

James was sitting on the edge of the boat, looking into the black void above and listening to the *woosh* of the water encircling the boat as they traveled through the channel. Mary kneeled beside him, taking his hand in her own.

"Why?"

"There is no real answer," Mary said, after taking some time to think. "Before we went looking for you, I spoke with John, and we decided it was best not to tell you until later."

"But that later never came." James pulled his hand free. "And you decided. You and John. Nobody asked me."

"I was wrong, I admit. We were wrong. We thought all this would be too much for you. Finding out about your mother, about the powers you possess... It was hard for me, too, not being able to tell you. I just wanted to—"

"You just wanted what exactly? To protect me? Is that it? You sound like some actress in a bad movie." He saw tears welling up in her eyes. "Do my words hurt? Well, you not telling me that I had a sister all this time hurts even more."

Mary nodded and stood up, and James turned his head away. She slowly leaned over, kissed him on the top of his head, and walked away. James felt bad about what he'd said but he was determined not to give in.

Moments later, he heard footsteps behind him. "Stop sulking," somebody said, and James recognized Tony's voice.

He tried to ignore him, but Tony sat next to him and tapped him on his shoulder. "You should be thankful you have a sister at all. Especially a sister like Mary. I remember how she cried the day your mother left you at the orphanage. And I've seen what it's done to her all these years. Not a day went by that she didn't want to get you out of that place to bring you home. Having you back with us has transformed her. After seventeen years, she's finally like the Mary we all used to know."

James felt his cheeks growing warm but he couldn't ignore that everyone had kept quiet all this time. Instead, he just continued to look out to sea, when a thought crossed his mind. "Tony, why did you make Wanda angry that way? You know she can control time, and she could have destroyed us just like that. It felt like we were getting somewhere with the soft approach. Maybe it would have turned out differently."

"Her most dangerous power is her ability to manipulate time. As you can imagine, it also requires the highest levels of focus and concentration. She can't use that against us when she's emotional, so getting her riled up was our best chance of escape."

"But why escape like that at all? Couldn't we have brought her with us?"

Tony shook his head. "We had said all we could but we were never going to convince her with one conversation. Our evidence is too weak, our theory is incomplete, and she has been convinced of her story for almost twenty years. But we succeeded in planting another version of events in her head. Now, she has time to calm down and consider our words."

James released a small grunt from the back of his throat. "You took a big risk, Tony. You jeopardized all our lives without telling us the plan first. You couldn't know how she would react; you had no idea if she was the kind of person to respond emotionally or not."

"True," Tony replied, "but it was a calculated gamble. Someone who has lived in solitude for twenty years, separated from civilization and full of hatred, is hardly the type of person to remain calm when confronted by the people they think are responsible for everything that happened to them."

James was quiet after that. Tony's gamble had paid off, true; but it had been a gamble nonetheless. He had bet their lives on the outcome without warning any of them first. There was no changing the minds of people like Tony, Alex, and John, James realized.

And so, James excused himself and went down to his cabin to rest the remainder of the journey home. He fell asleep quickly, such was his exhaustion after having trekked through a snake-infested jungle, survived an encounter with the most dangerous elemental alive, and discovered he had a sister.

Whether he had slept for hours or minutes, he didn't know, but he woke up abruptly when he heard the sound of a deep rumble. He realized almost immediately that it wasn't the sound of thunder; the rumble had a repeating rhythm, like the sound of drums being beaten fiercely in the distance. James made his way on deck and looked around, curious to know if anybody else knew more than he did. By the gaunt looks on their faces, James decided they didn't, but assumed it was bad news. He turned to Mary, his sister, and reached out to hold her hand. "What's going on?"

"They need our help?" Mary replied, signaling something to Marcus with her hand.

"Who does?" James asked while the boat started to gain momentum.

"Back home. Something is happening. Something is wrong. Those are war drums you can hear."

"We're still miles away, aren't we? How can we hear them already?"

Marcus looked over at James. "I don't know who is banging the drums, us or them, but someone on our side, an air elemental, is pushing the sound toward us. They're warning us."

"Home is under attack..." Mary squeezed James' hand with both of her own.

"We need to prepare," Tony said. "When we get back to Leilani Reef—"

"Damyan will be waiting for us," James said.

A couple of hours later, Marcus pointed at the light in the distance. The barely visible red dot glowed in the darkness and was getting bigger and brighter as they sailed toward it.

"Is it a fire?" Amy asked, but nobody responded.

Loud footsteps and even louder commands echoed across the boat as James stared in the direction of the light. He knew the answer to Amy's question as well as everyone else on board.

Once they were within sight of the Blue Cave, James stood on the bow and watched the magnificent and terrifying sight. A fire, so tall that its sparks reached far into the sky, well above the tallest trees, and so grand that its fierce glow completely surrounded the island. James heard the engine cut out while they were still some distance from the harbor when Tony pointed out that there were two boats anchored outside of it.

"Patrick, Kyle, Amy, and Nicky. We'll use the wind to push us quietly to shore. When we reach it, head to the Blue Cave to pay anyone waiting there a visit!" Tony exclaimed, pointing at the two unfamiliar boats. "Eliminate any threats and secure the boats; we might need them if we have to escape. As for the rest of you, we'll head to the Castle."

As the boat pulled up alongside the coastal rocks, James felt the heat emanating from the fire. Even this far down from the steep cliff, he could hear the cracking and snapping of burning wood. The light from the fire itself was painful to his eyes until Mary stood in front of everyone and raised her hands to absorb the heat and make it safe for everyone to disembark the ship. They needed no words when the group separated. James, Mary, Tony, Marcus, and Galman looked into the eyes of Amy, Nicky, Patrick, and Kyle, and they looked back. A heartbeat later, the latter started to clamber over the wet, jagged rocks as they made their way toward the Blue Cave, while Tony indicated to everyone else to follow him up the cliff.

James used his earth and air powers to raise them up the cliff as quickly as possible, while Mary concentrated on keeping the fires from burning them. They reached the top in a matter of seconds, barely out of breath, and they began to find their way through the burning forest.

Predictably, the wooden bridge that connected the outer island to the inner plateau had been destroyed; most of it was missing but James could see the ropes and planks dangling from the side were still smoking from having been set aflame. Without any warning, James felt his energy being drained as Tony channeled his power to dislodge the rock they were standing on and float it across the gap. After Tony had settled them down on the other side, James bent forward to catch his breath. Tony put a reassuring hand on his back as if to apologize, but he didn't say anything. He then set off toward the rows of burning homes just ahead, followed by Marcus and Galman, while Mary waited until James could move again.

When they had all regrouped again behind a burning building, just a few hundred meters shy of the Castle, Tony gathered everyone in close. “Now, listen carefully,” he whispered. “I will go first; you follow. Understood? But I’m counting on your support. I’m just a medium and without your powers...”

Tony stopped talking, and James felt something moving beneath his feet. At the same time, several lightning bolts struck in the direction of the main building, followed by thunder so loud that they instinctively covered their ears. Tony rounded the wall immediately but halted when he saw a man standing with his arms outstretched. The man had his back to them and seemed so focused on what he was doing that James assumed he was a medium. Tony grabbed him by the neck while Marcus kicked him in the stomach. As the man tried to inhale, Tony squeezed his throat and the man lost consciousness and fell limply to the ground.

“Get ready, everyone,” Tony said. “They’re waiting for us.”

CHAPTER 19

Out of Time

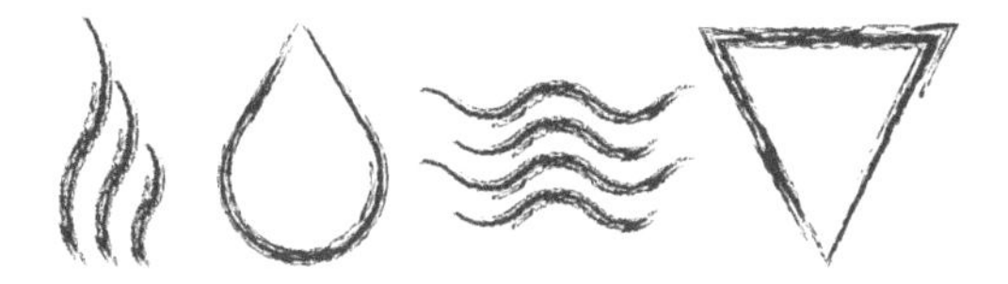

As James and his companions ran toward the Castle, numerous flashes appeared in the sky accompanied by loud bangs. The ground shook beneath their feet, and at the same time, an explosion echoed from behind them. When James turned to see the cause, he could only see a thick cloud of smoke rising up from behind the illuminated forest they had run through not long ago and he assumed it must have come from the Blue Cave. But before he could worry about Amy, Nicky, Patrick, and Kyle, people started running out of the Castle and its surrounding buildings. They screamed as two dozen dark figures strolled behind them slowly. James recognized Damyan as one of the people leading the pursuers. He walked beside a tall elf with long black hair tucked behind his pointed ears. As they got closer, several people emerged from the forest on either side and lined up to face the approaching enemy while forming a protective wall for those trying to flee. Among them, James recognized his comrades, friends...family—Mike and Venessa, Kymil and Arick, even John, Alex, and Victor—and he ran to stand alongside them.

Before James could reach them, he saw a flash, and a moment later, he flew backward and found himself sprawled on the ground, looking at the sky. He felt like he had been hit by a cannonball. Before he managed to come to his senses, Tony was standing over him and deflecting another attack from one of the black figures while Galman helped him to his feet. The dwarf's grip was like a vice and his skin was as rough as sandpaper; James couldn't have stayed on the floor even if he'd wanted to.

James touched the blood coming from his nose and found himself overcome with burning anger. Mary came beside him, and James could see she carried an equal amount of fury in her eyes. Moments later, Marcus was with them, and together, they moved up and toward their friends and allies.

"Besola," Kymil called out to the tall elf standing beside Damyan, "I knew you had turned your back on our way, but I never imagined you'd throw in with the likes of this rat."

James tried to recall what Kymil had told him about Besola, the elf who lost so much in the war and wanted to put elves first. Why, then, had he allied with human elementals like Damyan?

"He did not betray anyone," Damyan said. "We are all here because we want what is best for our people. It is you lot—this community and others like it—that insist on clinging to the past, denying our progress, our right to rule a world of powerless weaklings who are good for nothing but to serve us. You would have us be ashamed of who we are, *what* we are, whereas we would embrace our power and glory."

"You can be quiet," Victor snapped. "Vermin have no right to speak here."

Damyan looked furious and ready to fight when Besola stopped him by stepping forward. "If anyone has betrayed their people, then it is you, Kymil. You insist on helping humans and dwarfs, while elves are left to hide in the ever-smaller forests, woods, and jungles of this poisoned world."

"It was never that simple, Besola. If we only ever treat each other as an enemy, our planet is doomed to be a battleground forever. We have to work together." It was the most emotion James had ever heard in Kymil's voice, and he wondered if Besola had been closer to Kymil than he had let on.

"In case you haven't noticed, we outnumber you," Damyan added, spreading his arms and turning toward the forest, where yet more dark figures were emerging. "If you're so determined to avoid war and death, I suggest you surren—"

Victor hit the ground with the Staff of Heletrea, causing vibrations to pass through everyone's bodies. James felt a wave of nausea and he had to hold on to Mary to compose himself. When he looked up at the dark figures, he saw many of them doing something similar.

"Your numbers are nothing," John cried. "I'm giving you only this one final chance to leave and never come back!"

Damyan smirked. Even at this distance, James could see his rotting teeth. "I don't think so."

"As you wish," Victor replied, and again, he lifted his staff high into the air. Flashes of light emerged from Damyan, Besola, and the men and women around them, but Tony and Alex, protected by everyone else, had already raised a barrier to deflect the attacks away from Victor. When he struck the ground with the staff for the second time, nothing happened at first. But moments later, some of the elementals beside Damyan fell to their knees, clutching at their throats as they struggled to breathe before they passed out.

Wide-eyed, Damyan stamped his feet and ordered his people to raise their own barrier. "Hypocrites! You keep the staff hidden because you forbid people from using it to harm others, then you use it for that very same purpose!"

"I think our numbers are slowly aligning," John said.

When another six followers started to claw for air, as well, Damyan motioned to attack, and his unafflicted followers unleashed the elements. James tried to cast his own spells to defend his friends when he felt the same breathlessness he had felt when Tony had sapped his energy to cross the chasm. As he struggled to keep himself from passing out, he watched the scene unfold out of the corner of his eye. Tony and Alex were using all manner of fire, air, water, and earth magic, and James realized they were both drawing on his energy. Mary, too, was on her knees beside him, breathing heavily, so he assumed they were using her energy, as well. Before long, James caught Arick peering at them before the old man said something to break Tony and Alex's concentration. A moment later, James felt his energy return. After helping Mary to her feet, he saw Mike and Venessa crumble to the floor as their energy was then channeled through Alex and Tony.

But there was no time for James to question the ethics of their approach. The battle was now in full swing as flashes appeared in every direction, lighting up the clearing more brightly than the fires just beyond. James saw Besola outstretch his hand and a blazing ball of fire erupted from his palm. It hit the ground at the feet of one of the men standing beside Victor, and he was quickly engulfed in the flames. His screams were loud but short-lived, and the man fell to the ground. Others among them failed to deflect a wall of tiny stones that hit them as fast as speeding bullets, and James watched as blood started to seep out of the holes they left behind before the men and women collapsed, as well. James had never seen such destruction and he stood still in shock until, out of the corner of his eye, he saw Mike get hit by a boulder as big as a basketball that spun him around and made him hit the floor hard. James jumped over a dead body and, in a few steps, reached his friend. To his relief, Mike had been hit in the shoulder and was all right. James didn't have time to check if any bones had been broken, but when he pulled him to his feet, Mike didn't wince.

With renewed energy in his veins, James turned to Damyan's group and concentrated hard on what he wanted to do. Lightning flashed and hit two elementals in the back, ice shards pierced the chest of another two, and all four crumbled to the floor. As soon as he did it, he knew his actions would haunt him, and he had to swallow the rising sickness in his chest and throat. As more and more dark figures approached, James tried to summon his powers again, but nothing happened, and he knew at once that his mind couldn't concentrate. He fell to the floor and tried to blink away the tears, but the more he fought to suppress his sadness and guilt, the more his thoughts got away from him.

Damyan sent another ball of fire at Marcus, who moved sideways to try and dodge it, but the fire grazed his shoulder, leaving a heavy burn on his arm. The sight of his friend in pain helped James to focus again, and he splashed Marcus' arm with water.

Victor fell to his knees, and James feared the worse but quickly saw the doctor wasn't hurt. Rather, with one hand still gripping the staff, he placed the palm of the other on the ground and focused. The earth in front of him rose and fell as though a wave made of soil and rock was powering through the clearing toward Damyan. The wave moved so fast that Damyan barely managed to avoid it while those behind him were swallowed by it.

But no matter how hard they tried, more and more dark elves and rogue elementals kept appearing from the forest. James saw Mike and Venessa exchange heavy frowns as they continued to counter the attacks aimed at Victor. Kymil was losing his fight against Besola and his dark elves, but even with John's help, the two were slowly succumbing to the relentless barrage of fireballs, ice shards, and fast-moving boulders. Galman had pulled Marcus back to try and treat his burned arm, while their other allies, the men and women that James didn't know so well, also began to collapse in exhaustion, injury, or death under the constant wave of attacks. James looked at Mary, who looked back at him. Both had tears in their eyes as they realized it was only a matter of time.

A sudden rush of wind heralded a change. The almighty gust drove away the clouds and a clear sky appeared above the battlefield; one full of a multitude of twinkling stars. The fires faded, so the orange haze and heavy smoke that had obscured everything started to lift.

A light appeared in the distance that shone brighter with every passing moment. Heads on both sides turned in the direction of the light and the fighting stopped as everyone, James included, tried to figure out what was happening and if this light was a threat or not. The strong wind rushed by them again, this time across the ground and between their legs. Dust rose high in every direction, and everyone closed their eyes and shielded their faces.

When James could no longer taste the soil in the air, he opened his eyes, and for the second time in two days, he saw the most beautiful woman standing before him. She was in the very middle of the battlefield, dividing the two sets of combatants, with her hands spread out and her long hair fluttering gently in the wind. Wanda opened her eyes, and her small but very visible smile lit up as she registered the shock in everyone's expressions.

"Is this a bad time?" Wanda asked. "I thought you'd been expecting me." After briefly looking at James, she turned to face Damyan. Somehow, he was even paler than usual. "I recognize some of the faces behind me, which means you must be the ones working with my father. Is that right?" Wanda jutted her head forward, waiting for an answer and some clue as to who was the leader among them. "Is that right? Is Drago Wolgor still alive?"

James held his breath. While the evidence supporting John's theory had been tenuous, it had added up. How Damyan reacted now could determine if Wanda would use her powers to help Leilani Reef or destroy it.

Damyan practically skipped forward. "Yes, your father. Your father has been looking for you all these years. He has never stopped hoping to find you. And here you are. Wanda, I know who you are. I can take you to him." Damyan's attempt at a sincere smile made James' skin crawl, but he also felt a pang of pity among his relief. Damyan had confirmed Drago was alive, which meant John's gamble to send them to find Wanda had been the correct call. It confirmed that Wanda had been lied to. And by stepping forward as he had done, Damyan had placed himself firmly in Wanda's sights.

"Can you really?" Wanda asked. "Is he not here, fighting alongside you? Or is he still recovering from his death all those years ago?"

Damyan swallowed hard before answering. "These are questions only he can answer. I am not worthy of speaking on his behalf."

"Worthy?" Wanda said with a laugh. "Does he consider himself to be some kind of deity that you must worship? It seems to me he has fooled you and sent you to fight his battles for him."

Damyan turned red with rage. "How dare you? I am the governor of these people! They follow my orders, not those of some old man who couldn't even keep hold of his troublesome daughter!" Damyan raised a hand in front of his chest and a red pointer flashed.

But before he could summon whatever element he had intended to attack with, Damyan fell face first to the ground. James' eyes flickered between Wanda, who looked distinctly unimpressed, and Damyan, who struggled as though he was being crushed by some invisible force on his back that was holding him down. He was shivering and breathing hard. Besola ordered several of his dark elves to lift him up, but they failed to shift him. The harder they pulled, the stronger the force became, and the more desperate Damyan's screams sounded. Eventually, they stopped trying and the pressure seemed to diminish. Damyan, who was barely breathing, somehow managed to croak, "Kill her! Kill them all!"

James saw Besola and the others pause for a moment, look at Wanda, and motion to attack. At almost the same moment, a dozen flashes occurred, but instead of a flurry of explosions and collisions, a deafening silence arose. Nothing moved. At least, it seemed that way at first. James turned around to examine those closest to him. Mary was beside him, wincing as he had done at the bright flashes of the pointers. Tony was standing as still as a statue with his mouth wide open and one hand outstretched. Mike was holding Venessa's hand tightly and they had closed their eyes and averted their faces from the flashes. Victor and John were standing next to each other, both holding the Staff of Heletrea with a look of defiance in their eyes. Just beyond them, several fireflies hovered in midair, and James moved closer to them until he was just inches away. Like everyone around him, the fireflies hovered almost motionless in the air; their outstretched wings moved at such a low speed that James barely noticed.

He then turned to look across the battlefield once more. Damyan was still lying on the floor, saliva and blood spilling through his gritted, yellow teeth. A few feet away from him, Besola had his hands pressed together like he'd clapped, the tips of his fingers pointing toward Wanda, and out of them, tiny iron spikes protruded, some of which were already floating through the air, in her direction. His face was expressionless. Next to him was a hooded figure holding his arms out toward Wanda.

James wanted to touch Besola, to push him over and tie him up while he had the advantage, when he heard something to his right. He turned swiftly to see Wanda looking directly at him. Startled, he jumped backward, hitting one of the dark figures in his stomach with his elbow, and fell onto his behind. The figure didn't even flinch.

"Scary, isn't it?"

Baffled, James jumped up and took another step back. "Scary?"

"Time." Her voice was soft. "Time is a scary thing, don't you think? I remember the first time I realized I could slow things down." She took a step closer to the fireflies James had just been looking at and, ever so carefully, picked one up by pinching it between her thumb and forefinger. "I was playing on the shore down by the Blue Cave. I saw a lot of fish of different colors but I could never catch one. I remember wishing I could stop them from swimming away from me, just for long enough so I could examine them closely. And as though some higher being had listened, they began to move slower and slower until they were almost at a standstill.

"I always knew I was different. But I used to be proud of my abilities. But as I grew up and realized that everyone was afraid of me, I became afraid of them at the same time."

James swallowed hard and took a step closer to Wanda. When she looked at him with soft eyes, he couldn't help but smile a little. "Why did you come?"

"Curiosity," Wanda replied, looking back at the firefly. "Curiosity in the truth." Her eyes flicked up to James. "Curiosity in you."

"Thank you," James said. "Without you, we would be dead."

"I'm sure you would be. But don't thank me yet. I didn't come here to save you. I came here for answers." Wanda briefly looked down at the struggling Damyan on the ground. "This fool could have lied better, and I'd have not known who to believe, so I'd have probably killed you all. But it seems you and your friends were telling the truth, at least about my father being alive."

"I understand," James said swiftly. "I know there are still unanswered questions, Wanda. I know you have no reason to trust me, but I want to help you find them. You cared for me as a baby; you cared for my mother once, a woman I don't even know. We have a shared history, and I'd like to find the answers with you."

She dropped the firefly, which continued to hover where she left it, and studied James for a moment. "That is the reason you and your friends are still alive. I don't know if I can trust those of your kin who were there when everything happened between my parents and Victoria, but I sense you are innocent in all this."

"And what does that mean for me? For us?"

"It means you get to live another day," Wanda said with a big smile on her face; it quickly vanished when she looked at Damyan again. "He, however, will not."

"What do you mean?"

"I need somebody to die today. I was robbed of my childhood, robbed of my parents, and somebody is going to pay for this. My father isn't here to give me the answers I need, so this disgusting being will bear the brunt of my anger until I am satisfied."

"Killing him won't change things." James didn't know why he was arguing for her to spare Damyan; the man had led the attack that had killed Dalnur. His followers had killed Alan and Ted at the docks, George at the palace, and many more tonight.

"I'm sure it won't, but it will stop him from hurting someone else. Plus, it will make me feel better," Wanda said while walking to Besola.

She placed two gentle hands on the dark elf's shoulders as if touching a loved one, then turned his whole body and repositioned Besola's hands until the attack he had already begun was focused on Damyan. She did the same to two elementals on either side of Damyan so that when she was done, three people pointed their attacks at their leader.

James watched with tears in his eyes; not for Damyan, but for the innocent girl that Wanda had once been. "Please, don't do this, Wanda. We should capture him instead. He can tell us where to find your father. And where he's been keeping my mother."

She took James' hand in hers and walked them to the side of the battlefield. "There are plenty of others here we can interrogate, James. I'm not going to stop. Now, pay close attention."

James gasped as time returned to normal. The deathly silence was filled with loud bangs and cracks and shouts, and the attacks, which had been intended for Wanda, struck Damyan in an instant. Tiny iron spikes from Besola hit him in the back, then a spear-like shard of ice from another dark hooded figure pierced him through the neck. An attack from the third person never materialized because Tony had managed to stop it with his counterattack, and the perpetrator collapsed in a heap. James hoped Wanda had noticed what Tony had done to try and protect her, and sure enough, her gaze was on Tony. Everyone else, though, was looking at Damyan, dumbfounded at what had happened, not least of all Besola. For a few seconds, Damyan struggled to breathe, reaching as though he was trying to claw himself away from the ground, when he fell silent and stopped moving entirely.

Wanda released James' hand and stepped forward. "Now, before you try that again, you should ask yourself, am I ready to die? Am I ready to leave this place and go to the unknown?" Nobody spoke, and Wanda took her time to look into the eyes of each of the island's invaders in turn. "No? Then turn around and go back to where you came from. And never come back." She stopped in front of Besola. "You can tell my father that he doesn't have to look for me anymore. I will find him soon enough. And take this scum with you." She pointed at Damyan's body.

But Wanda had overestimated her ability to intimidate others, and James saw the fire and rage in Besola's eyes. Without the briefest of pauses after Wanda's words, Besola lifted his hand high above his head and screamed, "Now!"

Wanda slowed down time almost to a standstill again, but James could sense something was different this time. The whole enemy party in front of them was standing as still as before, but James could hear the shifting of feet and the confused words coming from those he cared about behind him. As he turned to reassure them what was happening, he caught sight of Wanda's expression; it was full of fear and regret. When James opened his mouth to ask what was going on, Wanda reached out and pointed toward the tree line of the forest.

"They're using kamikazes!" Tony said, coming forward to stand by Wanda's side. "How bad?"

At the mention of kamikazes, James recalled his lesson with Arick. Somewhere in the distance, a rogue elemental or dark elf had used their elemental powers to summon magic inside Wanda to kill her. The caster would die the same death, but as far as James knew, there was no way to block such a spell once it had been conjured.

Wanda answered Tony, but she looked at James. "I can already feel it inside me. Twisting, ripping, burning. There is nothing I can do." She reached out to cup James' cheek in her hand. "I still see the little baby I loved so much. Remember this, James, you own your life and no one else. Don't let anyone control you or your decisions, friend or foe. And say hello to your mother when you see her. Tell her... Tell her, I'm sorry. Now leave and—"

"Wait, what? Leave? No! Tell us how to fix this. Arick, how can we counter the element inside her?"

But Arick's head was tipped toward the ground, his eyes shut tight and his frown heavy.

"My life is over," Wanda said. "But I can still give you time to get out of here."

"But this is our sanctuary. It has been for hundreds of years," Victor said. "We can't abandon it."

Arick lifted his head and opened his eyes. "We have no choice. It has been compromised. It is no longer safe."

"But where can we go?" John said. "Where is safe?"

"I know a place."

Everyone turned to face James, but his eyes were on Wanda.

She smiled. "Yes! Now, go!"

James didn't know what to say, so instead, he leaned in and hugged her. She felt tense at first, but James wouldn't relent, and her muscles eventually relaxed as she fell into his embrace. When James finally pulled away from her, he saw her eyes were red and her cheeks were wet.

"Thank you for finding me, James. Thank you for telling me the truth." She squeezed his hand one more time before releasing him, and James felt his stomach tighten.

He then turned to the others. "Let's go."

"But where to?" Venessa asked, still holding Mike's hand.

"The Blue Cave," James replied. "The ship we arrived on is just outside, and assuming everything went to plan, we should have at least two more secured, plus whatever is in the cave."

Victor ran toward James and handed him the Staff of Heletrea. "Here, take this and escort Arick and the others. Tony, Alex, John, and I will spread out and gather whatever survivors we can find and bring them to you. If you can make sure the boats are fueled and ready to go, great. If not, we'll use the elements to make our escape."

The four leaders of Leilani Reef muttered among themselves before running off in different directions, then James ushered everyone to head through the burned-down houses that had once been the happy homes of so many of the island's residents.

"The bridge is out!" James called to Mike and Venessa, who were leading the way. "Use your powers to get everyone across the chasm safely."

When it was just James and Arick left, he handed the old man the staff to use as a walking stick, then allowed him to lean the rest of his weight onto him.

"Thank you, Wanda," James said one more time. She returned his words with a smile, then turned her back on him.

Alex was the last to arrive on the walkway that served as the dock inside the Blue Cave. Once he was under the shelter of the cave, he ushered the dozen or so women and children he had brought with him toward the boat, where Arick offered them words of encouragement as they boarded. James watched from the deck as Alex handed the old man a set of books and scrolls, presumably from Arick's library, and the old man put his hands on Alex's cheeks as if he was about to kiss him. Mary was quiet and solemn but kind as she welcomed the new arrivals and offered to take them below deck to find cabins for them, all the while assuring them everything was going to be fine.

James looked out to sea at the handful of ships that had already set off, two of which Patrick, Kyle, Amy, and Nicky had successfully captured from Damyan's elementals and Besola's dark elves. Once they were out of sight of the island, their respective captains would wait to hear from John, who would share a destination with them.

As Alex helped Arick to climb aboard, the ship's engine rumbled into life, and they slowly started to reverse out of the cave. They were barely under the light of the moon when screams and shouts echoed from behind them. A loud rumble and a few bangs also reached them, all of which culminated with one big explosion and an enormous blue flash that illuminated the sky for miles in every direction. The force of the explosion pounded against the ocean, creating waves that pushed their ship out to sea faster than anyone on board had anticipated. Afterward, there was nothing but the low grumble of the boat engine and the gentle lapping of sea against the hull.

But the peace did not last long. A glowing fireball flew into the sky, illuminating the entire surroundings. James glanced behind him to see a long, thin figure, presumably Besola, already standing on the shore, his supporters close behind him.

A wave of white and blue started at the shore and began to project toward the ship at a lightning pace. At first, James thought Besola was summoning a tidal wave, but as it got closer, he realized it was ice. As the ocean around them froze, Besola and his surviving army started running across the ice toward the ship, firing off all manner of projectiles to try and disable the ship. "Destroy the boats! Sink them!"

Most of the ice was forming on the hull of the ship itself, severely hampering their progress whenever Patrick and Kyle tried to move the vehicle forward. Tony and Alex were doing a good job of deflecting more projectiles than James could count from harming the people on board, but they couldn't attack the streams of enemies running across the frozen sea toward them. James used fire and water magic to send numerous men and women tumbling into the ocean by breaking the ice beneath their feet. But they were too many of them, and in the blink of an eye, dark elves were clambering up the side of the ship while Damyan's elementals were using the air to lift themselves aboard, and when James turned to fire off an air spell, he found himself face to face with a dark-eyed elf.

But the elf didn't move. James scanned the deck and the ice around the ship, where he saw none of the other attackers were moving, either. But while everyone else on board was looking at the vicious faces of their enemies, frozen in time, James was looking for something, someone, else.

He found her hiding under the stairs that led up to the wheelhouse. Even though she had her head buried into her knees, James recognized her golden hair at once. Gently, he put his hand on Tanya's shoulder, and she flinched as she raised her tear-stained cheeks and looked up. When she saw it was James crouching beside her, she immediately jumped up and hugged him like she'd never let go. James stood up, still holding Tanya in her arms, feeling both grateful and sad.

"Mike! Venessa! Anyone!" James called, and he waited for an acknowledgment from either of them. "Create a channel for the boat and pick up the winds. Everyone else, push anyone off the boat who we don't want to bring with us."

As the boat moved away at high speed and the last of the dark elves and elementals were pushed into the sea, James stroked Tanya's hair. "You saved us," he whispered. "Thank you."

Moments later, John hurried over in their direction, pushing aside anyone in his way. He grabbed his daughter and embraced her tightly. James could see the tears welling up in his eyes as he held her like there was no tomorrow.

Half an hour later, James and his ship had caught up with the other boats that were waiting at the agreed spot. John and Victor had climbed aboard the main ship and invited all the usual people to the main deck to come up with a plan, but for the first time since he'd met any of them, none of them seemed sure about what to do next.

"Doesn't anyone have anything to say?" James said. "What happened up there? Was there really nothing we could have done to save Wanda?"

Tony shook his head. "She was already dead the moment she felt the element inside her."

"But she stopped time. You all saw."

Arick was still using the Staff of Heletrea as his personal walking stick, and he leaned on it before beginning his explanation. "By the time she'd frozen time, the spell had already been cast. There was no way to undo it. Any magic we may have cast would have only hurt her more. All she could do was use the last of her energy to keep time still for as long as possible for us to escape."

"I'm sorry, James," John said. "If it's any consolation, I think you saved her."

"What?"

"Not her life, but perhaps her soul. She wasn't the dangerous woman we had all come to fear in her final moments.

She was the young girl some of us remember from all those years ago. You did that."

James felt a pat on the shoulder. He turned to see Mike and Venessa smiling at him. Then he felt his fingers being squeezed and turned to see Mary looking back at him with tears in her eyes.

"And after all that, it seems we had another time elemental among us all this time," John said. He paused for a moment. "My own daughter... All this time..."

"She is a young girl, like Wanda was," James said. "We mustn't repeat history. Besola will have seen what happened from the shore and know we have someone who can control time. He'll tell Drago, who will come looking. It's our job to protect her, right?"

Mary, Mike, Venessa, and Arick all nodded. Eventually, Victor, Alex, and Tony did, as well.

When James turned his gaze toward John, who was still holding his daughter, John said, "Nothing in the world will keep me from protecting my children, James."

"And what about right now? What's our destination? Where are we going?" Mary asked, looking at all the faces around the table.

"Our new home," James said, raising his head up high. "The only other place we know people stay away from, where most aren't even aware just how big the place really is, and somewhere that is already set up to keep unwanted guests out."

"Are you talking about Snake Island?" Tony asked.

James smiled. "Sure, although I don't think the snakes were ever the real owners of that island. How about we give it a new name?"

Mary looked up at him. "Have you got something in mind?"

"What about Wanda's Island?"

John, Alex, Tony, and Victor all looked at each other with stony expressions, but smiles soon emerged on their lips.

"I think Wanda would have liked that," John said. "Set a course for Wanda's Island."

Mary pulled James' arm into her so she could hug it tightly. "I really don't care where we go. I'm just grateful that it's finally over."

"Over? I'm afraid not, Mary," Arick said. "It has just begun."

James leaned his head onto Mary's while he pinched the gold necklace around his neck between his thumb and forefinger. "Let's go and find our mother."

THE END

Acknowledgments

I'd like to thank everyone who supported me, but also everyone who doubted me. You drove me on when I needed motivation!

To my editor, Dan Cross (openbookeditor.com). Without his continuous support and vision, this book would not be what it is today, and for that, I sincerely thank him.

And to my designer, Leon Končić, who used his exceptional artistry to create the book's cover design and chapter headers.

Most of all, I owe thanks to my children. To my daughter, Vanesa, and my son, Majk, who constantly pushed me to finish the book. And to my youngest daughter, Tania, who taught me the importance of imagination.

Lightning Source UK Ltd.
Milton Keynes UK
UKHW040847021222
413231UK00002B/18